Vice President Bill Oxenhauer and his wife, Joline, stood with six other people at the railing surrounding the pendulum. The Vice President looked at Joline, who was staring at the ceiling. "What's the matter?" he asked.

A drop of bright red oxygenated blood hit the floor in front of him.

"My god, *look*," a woman said, pointing upward.

Now a series of red drops splattered the edge of the compass rose. The pendulum reached the side where the group stood, then swung back in the other direction, catching the marker and toppling it.

"Lewis...?" Joline said.

Slowly, as though having been photographed in slow motion, Lewis Tunney's body slipped over the second floor railing and fell to the compass rose. Protruding from his back was a sword that had once belonged to Thomas Jefferson.

The pendulum reached its apex on the other side, then headed back toward the Vice President, stopping for the first time in years as it thudded into the lifeless body of the night's keynote speaker, the late Dr. Lewis Tunney.

Another Fawcett Crest Book
by Margaret Truman:

MURDER IN THE SUPREME COURT

MURDER IN THE SMITHSONIAN

Margaret Truman

FAWCETT CREST • NEW YORK

A Fawcett Crest Book
Published by Ballantine Books
Copyright © 1983 by Margaret Truman

Library of Congress Catalog Card Number: 83-70479

ISBN 0-449-20502-9

This edition published by arrangement with Arbor House

From *Everyone but Thee and Me* by Ogden Nash. © 1959 by Ogden Nash. First appeared in Holiday. Reprinted by permission of Little, Brown and Company.

Manufactured in the United States of America

First Ballantine Books Edition: July 1984

*To all the dedicated people who make the Smithsonian
the wonderful place it is*

MURDER
IN THE
SMITHSONIAN

CHAPTER 1

LEWIS TUNNEY STOPPED IN FRONT OF A SMALL SHOP on Davies Street, in London's fashionable Mayfair district. A brass plate set into the door read: *Antiques. Peter S. Peckham, Prop. By Appointment Only.* An elaborate coat of arms over the door assured potential customers that the shop had provided goods to at least one royal household.

Tunney tried to peer through the window but saw only a reflection of himself and of vehicles passing behind him. The shop was dark. Big Ben's leaden chimes sounded noon from 320 feet atop Westminster Palace's clock tower.

He pushed a button and heard a musical triplet, tuned in thirds, from inside. A shaft of light cut through the interior darkness as a door at the rear of the shop opened, a man stepped through it, glanced at his watch, then came to the front door, unlocked it and said pleasantly, "Lewis, how are you, besides being your usual punctual self?"

"Fine, Peter."

They could have been brothers, both tall and slender, and with soft, brown wavy hair. Peter Peckham was dressed in gray flannel slacks, a turtleneck the color of port wine, a camel's-hair sport jacket and brown loafers. Tunney wore a three-piece blue suit, blue-and-white striped shirt with a solid white collar, narrow dark blue tie and highly polished black wing-tip shoes. Tunney was forty-three years old, Peckham forty-one. Both had brown eyes, with Peckham's just a shade darker. Tunney was American, Peckham British.

They proceeded through the shop to Peckham's office at the rear. The office, like the shop, was cluttered with artifacts of antique value.

"Tea? Gin?" Peckham asked.

"Tea. Do you have time for lunch, Peter?"

"Afraid not, but let's plan for it straightaway. It's been a while."

"Yes, it has, my fault. This project has turned me into a virtual recluse. I'm happy to be breaking out of it."

As Peckham swished hot water inside a china cup to warm it, poured the water into a small sink and put tea leaves in a silver tea infuser, Tunney perused the contents of his desk. There were journals of interest to collectors, the latest copy of *Smithsonian*, the monthly magazine sent to members of the Smithsonian Institution, a wooden box filled with precious and semi-precious stones, two rare, leatherbound books, invoices, correspondence and other items common to any office. In the center of the mess was a solid gold, ten-inch-tall pendulum suspended from a pyramid of three gold sticks. The ball of the pendulum was a large, deep green emerald.

Peckham turned and saw Tunney flick the pendulum with his finger. "An unattractive piece," he said, pouring hot water over the infuser, "but not without value. The stone is chockablock with flaws. My best estimate is that it might have come out of a Turkish sultan's collection, late eighteenth century. What do you think?"

"You're probably right, but it might be older, *early* eighteenth century. It is Turkish. The gold is finely worked."

Peckham placed the cup in front of Tunney, and they watched the gentle sway of the pendulum. Tunney looked across the desk and said, "Well, Peter, here's to seeing you again." He tasted his tea. "Good, Peter, very good."

"Thank you. Tell me, Lewis, what's new in your life?"

"Personally or professionally?"

"Personally. I keep up with you professionally through gossip. Your personal life is a little harder to track that way."

Tunney smiled. He pulled out a large, thin brown Dunhill cigar, lighted it and directed a stream of blue smoke at the pendulum. "Interesting things have been happening, Peter, professionally *and* personally, especially personally."

Peckham leaned back and raised his eyebrows. "Anyone I know?"

"Probably, but before I go into true confessions, Peter, tell me why you were so anxious to see me today."

"We are friends, aren't we?"

"Of course, but friends could have made a luncheon date, drinks at the end of the day. You sounded anxious when you called. Is there a problem?"

"Probably not, but you can help me on that. Give me a half hour, Lewis, and I think *you'll* be able to judge whether or not there's a problem."

"I'm listening."

* * *

Big Ben chimed once as Lewis Tunney got up from his chair. His youthful, smooth face was now creased. He chewed on his upper lip and hunched his shoulders, as though to force comprehension of what had been said.

"I'm sorry you're reacting this way," Peckham said.

"How else could I feel, Peter? I'd better be going."

Peckham picked up a small chamois sack the color of burnt ocher from the desk top and put it in a drawer, came around the desk and offered his hand. "When are we having lunch?" he asked. "My treat at the Audley."

"As soon as I clean up a few things. I'll call."

Peckham slapped Tunney on the back. "Call soon. I might even spring for the Connaught."

"Spring? You've become too Americanized, Peter." Tunney stood and looked down at the pendulum. It had slowed considerably and was nearing the point where friction would win out.

"Nothing is forever," Peckham said. "No perpetual motion."

"How true," Tunney said. "And too bad...Well, good-by, Peter."

"Good-by, Lewis."

Tunney leaned forward and extended his index finger into the pendulum's field of motion. The emerald stopped against it. He glanced up at Peckham, forced a smile and left the shop.

CHAPTER 2

JUNE 4

"I'M ALWAYS FASCINATED BY IT," WILLIAM OXEN-hauser, vice-president of the United States, said over the sounds of the party taking place around him. "Visitors think it's supposed to demonstrate perpetual motion, but it's not."

His wife Joline said, "I find it hypnotic."

The Oxenhauers and a small group of guests focused their attention on the 240-pound hollow brass bob of the National Museum of American History's famed Foucault pendulum. The brass bob, suspended from the building's fourth floor through large circular holes cut in floors below, moved gracefully, quietly and ceaselessly across an inlaid compass rose on the main floor. Red markers that looked like stubby candles were positioned every five degrees around the compass's 360-degree circumference and, one by one, over the course of the day, the pendulum toppled them. It was close to hitting one now.

"What *does* it prove?" a guest standing next to Oxenhauer asked.

"That the earth rotates. The pendulum's plane remains the same, but the markers, like us, are turning with the earth."

"Interesting," said the guest, his eyes watching the marker next in line to be struck.

Oxenhauer was joined at the railing by Alfred Throckly, the museum's new director. "Wonderful turnout," the vice-president said.

"Yes, sir, delightful. You should be very gratified. The exhibit was, after all, your idea."

Oxenhauer smiled, said, "I won't pretend modesty, Mr. Throckly. I gave that up the first time I asked people to vote for me."

Joline Oxenhauer looked out over the sprawling main floor where Washington's social and arts hierarchy had gathered. Most of the men wore tuxedoes, and the women were adorned in a variety of formal styles and colors. Three tuxedoed musicians performed contrapuntal fugues on a seventeenth-century harpischord and recorders, all belonging to the Smithsonian's collection of antique musical instruments. As the strains of Vivaldi blended with the tinkling of ice in glasses and the buzz of two hundred guests talking at once, Mrs. Oxenhauer touched her husband's arm and said, "I wonder when Lewis will be arriving."

Oxenhauer glanced at his watch. "Maybe his flight was delayed." He turned to Throckly, who'd just asked a uniformed waiter to refill his bourbon and soda. "Quite a surprise, wasn't it, having Lewis Tunney accept the invitation at the last minute?"

Throckly raised his eyebrows and nodded. "It certainly upset a lot of plans, Mr. Vice-President. I have hostesses upstairs right now inserting Dr. Tunney's introduction and bio into programs." Then, as though he'd suddenly been reminded by an unseen voice that the vice-president and Tunney were best of friends, he added, "But it's worth any inconvenience to have him keynote the exhibit. As far as I know, this is the first public event he's attended since going to England two years ago."

Joline Oxenhauer laughed. "Just like Lewis, packing up everything and hibernating...I wish he'd *get* here." She knew how excited her husband was at seeing Lewis Tunney again. They were old, good friends, and had spent considerable time together when Oxenhauer was teaching American history at the University of Chicago, which was before he decided to enter politics. Joline had resisted his decision to run for state office in Illinois because it meant giving up the relaxed academic life-style she enjoyed so much. Of course, neither of them imagined that he would rise quickly from a one-term Illinois state assemblyman to lieutenant governor, then win election to the Untied States Congress, from which he was selected to run for vice-president on the Democratic ticket.

Bill Oxenhauer was chosen for two reasons: he hadn't been in Congress long enough to have many political enemies, and he'd developed a national public recognition by spinning entertaining tales on leading television talk shows about the man in history he most admired, Abraham Lincoln. No one in Congress told a better, funnier story than Bill Oxenhauer, nor had any teacher of American history been as successful in bringing it alive.

The sudden emergence of a vice-president whose consuming passion was American history delighted the Smithsonian's leadership. The vice-president was, by congressional "enactment," the head of the Smithsonian's board of regents. Until Bill Oxenhauer, other vice-presidents had ignored that titular position. Oxenhauer had made time to take an active role in moving the Smithsonian Institution, and its myriad museums and programs, into a golden age, of sorts, onto center stage. When the National Museum of American History's previous director, Roger Kennedy, resigned for personal reasons, he told his staff at a going-away party, "My biggest regret is leaving now that we have a vice-president who cares, and who considers a museum to be something special. My timing, as usual, is terrible."

The waiter returned carrying a silver tray with Throckly's drink, a plate of crab balls and a small dish of horseradish sauce. Throckly picked up a crab ball on a toothpick, dipped it into the horseradish and raised it to his mouth. A dollop of sauce fell on one of his black velvet loafers. "Oh, my," he said, squatting and wiping at the stain with a cocktail napkin that bore the Smithsonian seal.

Oxenhauer looked down and smiled. He'd approved the hiring of Alfred Throckly to replace Roger Kennedy, but not without reservations. There was a foppishness to the new director which, although not alien to museum professionals, was a little too precious for a vice-president who'd once been described as a lumberjack with a Ph.D. Oxenhauer was as ruddy and beefy as Throckly was pale and delicate, his wooly, matted salt-and-pepper hair as natural as Throckly's helmet of soft gray curls was coiffured. Oxenhauer, who preferred tweeds and corduroy and who detested formal wear, was sure Throckly was content to spend every waking moment in a tux, maybe sleeping moments, too.

But the vice-president could not deny Throckly's professional credentials and stature. His background included curatorships with leading museums in San Francisco, New York and Europe. He'd been published extensively in professional journals and sat on advisory boards around the nation. Equally important, he was known as a superb fund raiser.

They moved from the pendulum to where an old-fashioned ice cream factory and parlor had been faithfully recreated, the four Secret Servicemen assigned to them never breaking their protective box as they walked.

Oxenhauer greeted Congressman Jubel Watson, who also sat on the Smithsonian's board of regents along with two other members of the House of Representatives, three U.S. senators, the chief justice of the United States Supreme Court and six private citizens. Watson was the only other member of that board besides Oxenhauer who took an interest in Smithsonian activities. He was an avid collector of art and rare books, and many of his millions were tied up in collections. Short, slender with black hair looking like patent leather, he was on the opposite end of the political and philosophical spectrum from Oxenhauer. Watson was an arch-conservative, to the right of John Birch, and proud of it. "Lovely gown, Mrs. Oxenhauer," he told Joline.

"Thank you, Mr. Watson. Actually it's quite old—"

"Like me," her husband said.

"Bill you're *not* old," his wife said, squeezing his arm. "Bill loves playing the role of the grizzled old man, but underneath that exterior is—"

"Hold it," Watson said, raising his hands. "No lurid tales out of the house of the vice-president. There's press around."

Alfred Throckly turned to a tall young man whose way into the vice-president's elite circle was discreetly blocked by the Secret Servicemen. "Ford," Throckly said, extending his hand past the V.P.'s protection, "say hello to the vice-president."

The young man was considerably taller than Throckly but looked like a younger version of the director. "Mr. Vice-President," Throckly said, "this is

Ford Saunders, administrative assistant to Chloe Prentwhistle."

Oxenhauer extended a large, calloused hand and was met with Saunders's startlingly cold, limp one. "Pleased to meet you, Mr. Saunders. I've been a fan of Miss Prentwhistle for years."

"She's said it's a mutual admiration society, Mr. Vice-President."

"Chloe and I go back a long way together. She put together the first really good Lincoln exhibition in the state of Illinois."

"Especially noteworthy since she's not from Illinois," said Throckly.

"Where is she?" Oxenhauer asked. "I haven't seen her."

Saunders looked at Throckly before answering. "Busy, Mr. Vice-President, last minute details. She'll be down shortly."

Congressman Watson now asked Oxenhauer, "Anything new on the Smithson nut?"

Oxenhauer shrugged. "I understand he's still leaving notes around, claiming to be a relation to James Smithson and threatening to blow up every museum in the Smithsonian unless he's 'recognized.'"

"The frightening thing is that he might do something drastic some day," Joline Oxenhauer said. "It's so easy to dismiss people as crazy, but then sometimes they act out."

"Let's hope he doesn't," her husband said.

One floor above, where two hundred folding chairs formed a horseshoe around a lectern, women in gowns moved through the aisles and placed an insert into programs that had been placed on the seats. The women were volunteer members of the Friends-of-the-Smithsonian, a fund-raising group dedicated to obtaining rare items for the Smithsonian's museums.

The insert had been written and reproduced at the last minute after Lewis Tunney changed his mind about attending the event and delivering the welcoming address.

It read:

DR. LEWIS TUNNEY

We are indeed honored that Dr. Lewis Tunney will personally introduce this very special and exciting exhibition of the Harsa and Cincinnati societies. Dr. Tunney, as many of you know, has established himself as the preeminent scholar of post-Revolutionary exclusive societies. His writings on the American Revolution have earned him not one but two Pulitzer Prizes in history.

Originally, Dr. Tunney's busy schedule abroad prevented him from accepting our invitation to speak, but a sudden change in his schedule has benefitted us.

We all express our appreciation for his presence here tonight, and for his willingness to share his knowledge of the subject of our exhibition.

Welcome, Dr. Lewis Tunney.

"I can't wait to meet him," one of the volunteer women said. "He's so handsome in his pictures. Looks like Alan Alda."

Another woman laughed. "You're giving away your age. Alan Alda appeals to...well, to more mature women who appreciate sensitivity in men."

"Sensitivity in men? What's that?"

They both laughed.

Sounds from the party downstairs drifted up through the Foucault pendulum's opening in the floor. One of the women leaned close to another. "I've never seen Mr. Throckly so wound up. I can't decide whether he's excited about having Dr. Tunney here or annoyed."

"Well, it did upset Mr. Throckly's plans... Come on, let's go downstairs and enjoy the party."

A long, black limousine turned off Constitution Avenue into a circular drive in front of the National Museum of American History. The chauffeur came around to open the door for his passenger but Lewis Tunney had already gotten out. He thanked the driver for a safe and pleasant ride, looked up at the building he'd once said had all the architectural charm of a stone shoe box, drew a deep breath and went to the main doors, where two uniformed guards and a Secret Serviceman stood. He identified himself, was checked off a long list and entered the building. "Hello, I'm Lewis Tunney," he said to the first person he met, an attractive middle-aged woman wearing a maroon gown.

"Oh, Dr. Tunney, welcome," she said, shaking his hand, "let me find Mr. Throckly for you. He's been worried that your flight might be delayed."

"First," Tunney said, "I'd like to see Vice-President Oxenhauer."

Before she could respond Tunney spotted the vice-president, thanked her for her hospitality and moved away. Oxenhauer saw him coming, left the circle and greeted him warmly. "Lewis, good to see you. How've you been?"

"Just fine, Bill. Yourself?"

"Considering the fact I willingly committed myself to four years inside an institution, not bad. Come, say hello to Joline. She's as excited as I am."

Joline threw her arms around Tunney, then stepped back and took him in from head to toe. "My God, more handsome than ever. How you've stayed a bachelor so long is worth congressional study in itself. You're an American original."

Tunney felt embarrassed by the open flattery. "Thanks, Joline. And you look...splendid."

Throckly, who'd broken away from Oxenhauer's group moments before Tunney's arrival, returned and said, "Hello, Dr. Tunney. I'm Alfred Throckly. We met a long time ago."

"Hello." Tunney turned to Oxenhauer. "Could I catch a minute with you?" Throckly's face reflected his annoyance at Tunney's abrupt greeting, and seeming dismissal.

"Now?" Oxenhauer asked.

"Please."

"We'll be going in to dinner soon," Throckly said. "I thought you might like to come upstairs and see where you'll be speaking. I have an audiovisual person on hand in case you want to—"

"Maybe later," Tunney said. "I'm not using my props. Would you excuse us?" He touched the vice-president's arm. Oxenhauer looked at his wife, whose expression said that she didn't understand either.

Oxenhauer and Tunney, accompanied by three Secret Servicemen, went to a corner of the museum near the main entrance, where a rural country store and post office were displayed. It had been a functioning store and post office in West Virginia back in 1861, and had literally been moved lock, stock and barrel to the Smithsonian. Besides being a popular exhibition, it also served as the Smithsonian's only working postal outlet.

Oxenhauer nodded to the Secret Servicemen, who retreated out of earshot. "Well?" he said to Tunney. "You look as though whatever's on your mind is pretty damned important."

"It is, Bill."

"Personal, something Joline and I can help with?"

"No. We can discuss my personal life later." His face was serious, hard. He put his hands on his hips, exposing a field of dark blue vest and a gold watch on a chain, looked down at the floor, then up at Oxenhauer. "Let me tell you a story, Bill. I'll make it as brief as I can."

Oxenhauer looked to where his wife stood with a cluster of young curators. "Make it quick, Lewis. We really should be getting back..."

Ten minutes later Alfred Throckly looked at his watch, then told two committeewomen acting as hostesses, "Let's try to move them into dinner. We're running behind schedule." He looked to where Tunney and Oxenhauer were talking in front of the old post office, and disappeared behind a partition.

"Lewis," the vice-president was saying, "we'd better get back to the party. I think dinner is close to being served—"

"*That's* your answer to what I've told you?"

"Of course not. I'm as sickened as you are. Look, you're staying around a few days, aren't you?"

"I planned to fly back to London tomorrow night. I have someone waiting for me."

"That gives us the day, then. I'll clear the decks. Come to my office at ten. I have some things to tell you about too."

"All right, Bill, but I still intend to refer to it in my remarks."

"I wish you wouldn't."

"Why not?"

"You could win a battle and lose a war. Besides, there are compelling reasons to hold up. Don't misunderstand, I'm as concerned as you are. All I ask is that you keep it to yourself until we get a chance to really sit down and talk."

"Ten tomorrow?"

"Yes."

Throckly intercepted Tunney as he headed for one of three bars. "We'll be going in for dinner soon, Dr. Tunney. You'll be sitting with the vice-president and with—"

"Thank you, that's fine, Mr. Throckly," Tunney said. "I'll get a drink and join you shortly—"

"Dr. Tunney . . ."

Tunney turned, and was face-to-face with a tall, gaunt woman in her late fifties. She wore a long, loose gray gown with a strip of black silk at the neck and cuffs. Her face was a montage of angles and planes, but not without a certain bright attractiveness.

"Miss Prentwhistle. Nice to see you."

"Likewise. We're all so glad you could come."

"Yes. I was on my way for a drink."

"I'll have someone get it for you."

Tunney looked past her and saw that guests were moving toward the museum's private dining rooms. "No, I'll get it myself," he said. "I need a few minutes alone . . . you know, to gather my thoughts before speaking."

"I'm sure it will be stimulating."

"I hope so. I'll see you inside. How is Mr. Jones?"

"Walter? Fine, just fine."

"See you in a few minutes, Miss Prentwhistle."

She hesitated . . . "I wonder if we could talk privately before dinner."

"I'm not sure that's necessary—"

"I think it is."

Tunney sighed and followed her to a small room that housed public telephones. They were alone. Five minutes later Tunney left the room.

A hostess asked if there was anything he needed. He told her, "Just a drink." She went to where two other women, all wives of prominent Washington businessmen, stood, and said *sotto voce*, "Just like Alan Alda, really. And never married, I understand."

Tunney took a gin and tonic from a bartender and walked to a bank of elevators. A member of the museum's security force stood in its open door. "The second floor, please," Tunney said.

"Yes, sir."

He stepped out on the next level. When the elevator doors had closed behind him he went to the folding chairs and put his hand on one of them. In front of him, rising majestically, was the "Star-Spangled Banner," the thirty-by-forty-two-foot American flag that had flown over Fort McHenry following the successful defense against British naval forces in September, 1814. A young lawyer on a ship that fateful night observed that the "flag was still there" by the "dawn's early light" which inspired him to create America's national anthem.

Tunney felt a chill as he looked up at the huge red, white and blue banner that had been so painstakingly restored by museum experts.

The room as dark except for low-wattage perimeter lights. A single spotlight illuminated the lectern. To its left were a large movie screen and two speakers. Tunney went to the lectern and looked out over the sea of metal chairs. Behind them was the opening through which the Foucault pendulum dangled.

He turned and faced the reason he was here, the Harsa-Cincinnati exhibition. In the morning the exhibit would be open to the public, another chance for Americans to touch base with their heritage. He stepped down from the lectern and entered the shadowy exhibition space. A massive oil painting of George Washington stared down at him from one side, an equally large portrait of Thomas Jefferson from the other.

He went over to a wall that had been constructed in the center of the exhibit, two glass cases housing precious memorabilia. Swords belonging to Washington and Jefferson hung vertically on either side. Behind each of the two glass windows were gem-studded medals, symbols of the Harsa and Cincinnati societies.

Tunney listened to the carefree sounds from the floor below; a woman's loud laughter cut through the din. Suddenly he looked to his left, thinking he'd heard someone.

He saw nothing.

He was conscious of the baroque music.

He took three steps forward and looked through the glass at the Harsa medal.

"I'll be damned," he said aloud to himself, and downed half his drink.

The hostesses at the party downstairs moved through the crowd and urged people to go into the dining room.

Bill and Joline Oxenhauer stood with six other people at the railing surrounding the pendulum. Another red marker was about to be toppled. Everyone laughed as Joline suggested they bet on how many seconds before the earth rotated sufficiently to bring the pendulum into contact with it.

"Want to get in on the bet?" Oxenhauer asked the Secret Serviceman nearest him.

"No, sir, but thank you," he replied, his eyes never straying from the crowd.

"Twenty seconds. I'll count," Oxenhauer said. He looked at Joline, who was staring at the ceiling. "What's the matter?" he asked.

A drop of bright red oxygenated blood hit the floor in front of him.

"My God, *look*," a woman said, pointing upward.

Now a series of red drops splattered the edge of the compass rose. The pendulum reached the side where the group stood, then swung back in the other direction, catching the marker and toppling it.

"Lewis . . . ?" Joline said.

Slowly, as though having been photographed in slow motion, Lewis Tunney's body slipped over the second floor railing and fell to the compass rose. Protruding from his back was a sword that had once belonged to Thomas Jefferson.

The pendulum reached its apex on the other side, then headed back toward the vice-president, stopping for the first time in years as it thudded into the lifeless body of the night's keynote speaker, the late Dr. Lewis Tunney.

CHAPTER 3

TUNNEY'S BODY WAS REMOVED FROM THE NATIONAL Museum of American History in a black body bag. As it passed, Alfred Throckly shook his head. "My God..." The tone in his voice seemed a blend of shock and impatience.

The man next to him said, "It takes time, Mr. Throckly. Procedures."

"What now, captain?"

"More procedures."

Captain Mac Hanrahan, chief of detectives of Washington's Metropolitan Police Department, excused himself from the museum director and went to the Constitution Avenue entrance. He stepped back to allow two uniformed policemen to carry the body bag outside, then followed. The street was choked with vehicles, some from MPD, most belonging to news media. Three large television remote trucks were parked on the sidewalk. Powerful lights mounted on their roofs turned night into day.

At the sight of Hanrahan a swell of reporters converged on the entrance.

"Take it easy," Hanrahan said, holding up his hands. "I'll have something to tell you in an hour."

"Who is it?" a reporter called out.

"The victim was not a government official, he was a private citizen."

Hanrahan saw that the officers carrying Tunney's body could not get through the crowd to a waiting ambulance. Lights and cameras were trained on the bag. "Ghouls," Hanrahan muttered, and in a louder voice: "Let them through, damn it, unless you want an obstruction rap."

"Is the vice-president still inside?" another reporter asked.

Hanrahan nodded and went inside, where Alfred Throckly was waiting.

"This is terrible," Throckly said, "beyond belief. What perverse, horrible...?"

Hanrahan saw that Vice-President William Oxenhauer and his wife were talking with his assistant, Lieutenant Joe Pearl. He went up to them. "Sorry for the delay, Mr. Vice-President."

Oxenhauer's face was ashen. The strain of Joline's earlier hysteria still showed, though she was now under control. Her eyes were red, watery. "Don't worry about us, captain, please..." Oxenhauer said, "just do what you have to do."

A Secret Serviceman took Hanrahan aside. "The vice-president should leave, captain. He has a full schedule tomorrow—"

"Yes, I understand."...."Why don't you and Mrs. Oxenhauer go home now, sir. You're not involved in this and—"

Joline looked sharply at him. "Lewis Tunney was one of our closest friends."

Oxenhauer put his arm around her. "The captain is only trying to help, darling. He's not being unkind. He's right, let's go home."

"It's wall-to-wall press out there, sir," Hanrahan told him.

Throckly, who'd joined them, said, "There's an exit through the kitchen."

Oxenhauer told a Secret Serviceman to have the limo pull around to the kitchen exit, and to Hanrahan said, "Thank you for your courtesy, captain. Could I have a word with you?"

They moved halfway around the pendulum railing. Oxenhauer checked to see that they weren't being overheard. "I learned something tonight that might have bearing on your investigation, captain..."

"Oh?"

The vice-president again looked over his shoulder. "It can wait until tomorrow...Please come to my office at ten."

"Well, sir, maybe I should be the one to decide whether it can wait, Mr. Vice-President. This is a murder we're dealing with—"

"Of course, but I'd much appreciate your allowing me to follow your earlier suggestion. I'd like to take Mrs. Oxenhauer home. She's very upset."

Hanrahan's instinct was to press the matter then and there, but Oxenhauer was, after all, the vice-president of the United States... "Thank you for your cooperation, sir. I'll be there at ten."

He watched them leave, then followed Lieutenant Joe Pearl into the dining room, where others at the party had been corralled. A team of six detectives was busy establishing the identity of each person who had been in the museum at the time of the murder, noting addresses and phone numbers, asking questions about movement during the evening and warning that they were not to leave Washington until further notice.

"Anything turn up?" Hanrahan asked Pearl.

"I don't think so. Maybe we'll put something together after we assimilate and correlate the statements—"

"*Assimilate* and *correlate*?"

Pearl picked lint from Hanrahan's lapel. "You're about to lose a button, captain."

"Yeah, I know." Hanrahan slapped Pearl on the back. His assistant was only slightly younger—Hanrahan was forty-seven, Pearl forty-one—but displayed a capacity for jargon that never failed to amuse his boss. Pearl had a master's degree in sociology. Hanrahan had graduated high school. Period. Pearl was Jewish, and relatively devout. Hanrahan's parents were Irish, and he was raised a devout Catholic, although he'd broken away from the church years ago. He'd recently divorced after twenty-two years of marriage. His mother had said at the time of the separation, "That's what happens when you marry out of your faith, Mac. You go to bed with swine, you get up with swine." Hanrahan's wife had been Baptist, which, he told his mother, hardly made her a swine.

His personal feelings about his ex-wife were another matter. She'd taken up with a man the age of their eldest son, twenty-five, in order, she said, to establish her identity as a "female being" and to catch up with the sexual revolution she'd missed out on. Hanrahan hadn't contested the divorce. He wasn't interested in competition with a damned flower child. His last words to his wife when she left were, "Remember, you go to bed with swine, you get up with swine." At least she'd laughed at that. He didn't . . .

The museum's security director, L. D. Rowland, who'd been called from his home right after the murder, asked for a few minutes with Hanrahan. They left the dining room and went to the second floor, the site of the Cincinnati-Harsa exhibition. Rowland, a black man with hair like pasted-on cotton balls, pointed to the floor.

"Yeah, we got that," Hanrahan said, referring to drops of blood leading from the exhibit area to the railing Tunney had fallen over. "Did your men see anybody at all leave the building about the time of the murder?"

"They say no, but of course it's hard to be positive about that sort of thing. I have a good staff, though."

"I'm sure you do. Let me ask you something, Mr. Rowland. Why wasn't there an alarm system on the case over there?" He pointed to where the Legion of Harsa's medal had been displayed, next to the Society of the Cincinnati's symbol. The glass covering the Harsa medal was smashed and the medal was missing.

"Museum policy now, Captain Hanrahan, not that I entirely agree with it, which is between you and me. Alarms can be triggered by a lot of things besides an actual break-in. It happened so many times in the past—short circuits, breakdowns, you name it, they decided to do away with the system. The idea is, it's sort of like sticking labels on windows warning intruders that a house is armed with a burglar alarm. It doesn't matter whether it is or not so long as a potential intruder thinks it is. I guess the museum figures people will assume these things are protected and not try anything. And at the same time avoid false alarms. I also hear talk they're thinking of installing a more sophisticated, newer system. Meanwhile..."

"Meanwhile it looks like they assumed wrong this time, or these intruders knew there wasn't an alarm." He went to the broken display case. Lab technicians had finished dusting for fingerprints and had taken photographs of the scene. The area had been roped off, including the path Tunney had staggered along from the exhibit area to the pendulum railing. Signs warning that it was the scene of the crime and that no one was to enter hung from the blue ropes. Two uniformed MPD officers stood guard. Broken glass from the display case had been carefully swept up and removed with other evidence.

"Tell me about the medal that was in there," Hanrahan said to Rowland.

Rowland shrugged. "I don't know anything about it, captain. I heard it wasn't worth a hell of a lot—"

"It was covered with jewels."

"Compared to other things in here, captain, it was nickel-and-dime."

Hanrahan leaned closer and read a card below the smashed glass.

THE LEGION OF HARSA

Created by an identified gemologist in 1794, the medal was a gift to Thomas Jefferson from original members of Harsa. It was worn by Jefferson during his term as the legion's first president, then passed down to succeeding presidents.

The medal, set with diamonds and rubies in a sunburst design symbolizing the power of God and nature, and the light under which all free men prosper, hangs from a blood-red ribbon edged with white and set in a bow. The color of the ribbon, and of the large ruby at the center of the sunburst, was to honor the blood shed by free men who steadfastly stood against what Jefferson and other founders of the legion termed "a race of hereditary patricians or nobility" as characterized by the Society of Cincinnati.

Hanrahan now read the card beneath the Society of the Cincinnati's medal, which rested securely behind glass that was intact.

THE SOCIETY OF THE
CINCINNATI EAGLE

The president-general's eagle of the Society. This badge set with diamonds was a gift to General Washington by officers of the French navy who had been admitted to the order. It was designed by Major Pierre Charles L'Enfant, and had been worn by Alexander Hamilton, Charles Cotesworth Pinckney and twenty-two other presidents of the society.

Pale blue ribbon set in a bow and edged with white; band of five diamonds leading down to the top medallion (all diamonds). In the body of the eagle is an oval of porcelain around which is inscribed OMNIA RELINOT SERVAT REMPE. On the eagle's wings are two larger diamonds on top, and smaller diamonds make up the rest of the wing. The tail is made of graduating-size diamonds and larger ones at the bottom. Upper medallion has large center diamond, two oval diamonds flanking it and smaller stones around them.

"A lot of diamonds," Hanrahan said.

"I guess maybe they were cheaper then," Rowland said.

Hanrahan walked the route Tunney had taken from the display area to the pendulum, carefully avoiding the dried drops of blood. He reached the railing and looked down into the pit, where the pendulum was once again in motion. Guests already interviewed and logged were leaving. Joe Pearl stood near the main floor railing.

"Joe," Hanrahan called.

Pearl looked up. "Yeah?"

"Finished up?"

"I think so."

"You going back?"

"Might as well. We'll get the steno transcripts of the initial statements typed. Need me?"

"No, I'll be back in a while."

"Okay, Mac." Pearl looked down at a chalk outline of Tunney's body, then walked out of Hanrahan's view.

Hanrahan turned to Rowland. "I'd like to see the entire museum again."

"Never been here before, captain?"

"Never have. Museums have always...well, I guess I just never had the time."

"I never did either 'til I started working here." His laugh was warm. "I'll send somebody with you. I've got paperwork to do, you know how it is."

Ten minutes later Hanrahan walked alongside a security guard who wore a starched white shirt, black tie and officer's cap. A leash in his hand was attached to a German shepherd.

"Been using dogs long?" Hanrahan asked as they climbed stairs leading to the second floor. He didn't want to admit it but the dog made him nervous, the way MPD dogs did.

"Yup," the guard said, "they been around here longer than me."

They started in the Nation of Nations exhibit, more than five thousand original objects and documents dedicated to the diversity of people who have come to America over the years, then moved to Everyday Life in America, where the fabric of the American character was displayed, from a classic colonial parlor in Virginia to a Victorian-Gothic bedroom in Connecticut, from a Philadelphia banker's library to a New England one-room schoolhouse.

Hanrahan was tempted to linger at some of the displays but knew he wasn't there as a sightseer. He needed to have a better sense of the building in which this bizarre murder had taken place, wanted to *know* it. "You must get to know a lot about American history," he said to the guard as they entered the We the People area—artifacts of the westward expansion, Indian wars, the Civil War, gifts to the fledgling nation from foreign powers, all based on Lincoln's words, "... government of the people, by the people, for the people."

"I don't look much at this stuff," the guard said. "I do my job, that's about it."

"I understand." And he did. It was how he sometimes excused himself for not living enough of the rich full life his ex-wife used to talk about.

Hanrahan had heard of the First Ladies' Gown exhibition. It had been written up often in the papers and was the museum's most popular attraction. Started in 1943 by renowned curator Margaret Brown Klapthor, it had steadily grown until reaching its current size, a detailed and revealing view of the women behind the great men, the nation's first ladies.

They stopped in front of one of many large, glass-walled rooms representing a White House parlor of the mid-nineteenth century. Hanrahan saw himself in the glass, touched his salt-and-pepper beard, ran his hand over baldness extending from his forehead to the crown that was bordered by fringes of what had once been a full head of black hair. Hanrahan never understood why he was balding. His father had had a full head of hair until he died at the age of eighty-four. At least he hadn't put on weight like his father. He still weighed a trim 170 pounds, about right for his six-foot frame. It wasn't that he made a big deal out of trying to stay slim, he just never put on weight. Metabolism, he figured. So nature evened things up. Bald but good metabolism. Couldn't have everything...

He shifted his focus from his reflection to the display. The mannequins, exquisite in their detail, represented the early women who'd occupied the White House. Other display rooms featured more contemporary first ladies. In this room, according to the placard, were Sarah Polk; Betty Taylor Bliss, President Taylor's daughter, who served as White House hostess in place of her ailing mother; the tall and motherly Abigail Powers Fillmore; the Victorian Jane Means Appleton Pierce; Harriet Lane, bachelor president James Buchanan's "mischievous romp of a niece," who functioned as her uncle's official hostess; the extravagant Mary Todd Lincoln; and Martha Johnson Patterson, daughter of President Andrew Johnson. Martha's mother, too, had been ailing during the White House years and had delegated hostess duties to her.

"You comin'?" the guard asked. The dog yawned.

"In a minute," Hanrahan said, drawn to the splendor in the room behind the glass—Mary Todd Lincoln's resplendent silver tea service gleaming from a marble tabletop in the center, wallpaper reproduced from a scrap discovered during a White House renovation, a white marble mantle from the Pierce administration, laminated rosewood American Victorian furniture by John Belter, a burgundy floral carpet with pink and red roses surrounded by green leaves, gilt-framed mirrors, oil portraits of the presidents and a myriad other reminders of America at another time and place.

"Let's move on," the guard said. He sounded impatient.

"Yeah, right. Sorry. It's pretty fascinating stuff."

"I guess." He jerked the dog's leash and the animal slowly, reluctantly moved with his master.

They went now to the center of the floor, where the Foucault pendulum dangled through the circular opening.

"Well, thanks for the tour," Hanrahan said. "By the

way, are there any places you know of where somebody could hide, I mean *really* hide?"

"Like whoever killed the man tonight?"

"Yeah, like him."

"Mister, there's more places to hide in this funhouse
than you can imagine."

"I figured," Hanrahan said.

As he peered over the railing, he was, of course,
unaware of a most peculiar movement in the First Ladies' exhibition. One of the mannequins, dressed in a
black velvet casaque over a gray silk skirt with black
velvet ruffles and ruche, wearing a brunette wig combed
up over crepes on the sides and adorned with velvet
ribbon, feathers and a bead clasp, took a tentative step
away from where she had posed between Sarah Polk
and Betty Taylor Bliss. The mannequin-come-alive
hesitated, listening for sounds of anyone approaching.
Hearing nothing, she continued toward a door at the
side of the exhibition room, opened it and stepped from
the room to the visitor's aisle in front of the glass.
Long, dark eyelashes lowered, then came up again. A
deep breath, a sigh, then disappearance behind one of
hundreds of partitions used to separate the museum's
backstage activities from the tourists.

"Tell Mr. Rowland we'll be in touch," Hanrahan
said to the guard. He went outside, where reporters
waited. It had started to rain. The steps leading up to
the museum were tented with umbrellas. Hanrahan
moved back under cover of a narrow overhang, pulled
a sheet of notations from his pocket, cleared his throat
and said in the best official voice he could manage,
"The deceased's name was Dr. Lewis Tunney, Cau-
casian, forty-three years of age..."

CHAPTER 4

"*Captain Hanrahan?*"

"Yes."

"The vice-president of the United States wishes to speak with you."

Hey, Mac, he said to himself, your ma should be proud of you...

"Captain Hanrahan?" asked the now familiar deep voice of William Oxenhauer.

"Yes, sir."

"You get in as early as I do."

"I didn't get in, sir, I never left."

"Oh...look, I'm sorry, captain...I can't go into details, but I'm afraid we'll have to postpone our meeting."

Hanrahan looked at his watch. It was seven-thirty. He'd intended to leave at nine for his appointment with Oxenhauer to make sure of being early. "Well, sir, may I ask when—?"

"Something brewing on the international front. I just can't get away today. I called you myself because I want you to know how much I want to cooperate with you. Lewis Tunney was a very dear friend. To both my wife and myself. If I can help you solve his ... well, I'll do everything and anything I possibly can. I want you to understand that."

"Yes, sir, when can we meet?"

"Tomorrow morning, I should think. Same time, ten. That all right with you?"

It will have to be, won't it? Hanrahan wanted to say. Instead he said, "That'll be fine, sir. But I can't let this slide. If you have something to offer, sir, I need it. Fast."

"Of course. Tomorrow morning at ten. Thank you for your patience, captain."

Hanrahan waited until his superior, Police Commissioner Calvin Johnson, arrived at MPD. He called and told Johnson's secretary that he had to see him right away.

"You'll see him soon enough, captain. He's on his way down."

Johnson was a big man, six feet three inches tall. He came from a distinguished family of black educators and had a Ph.D. in sociology. Which made him somewhat partial to Hanrahan's assistant, though he too occasionally winced at Joe Pearl's penchant for the jargonish language of his field. He had been commissioner only two years, but in that brief time had managed to establish a reputation for having gotten a handle on D.C.'s crime problem, and even some solutions for it. He had also made Washington's best-dressed list. This morning he wore a charcoal gray pinstripe suit that looked like it had been tailor-made to his lean, well-exercised frame, plus a pale blue shirt pinched at the neck with a gold bar, and a royal blue silk tie. What hair that was left on is fifty-two-year-old head was black and wavy.

"Hello, Mac," he said.

"Hello, Cal."

"You look like you've been up all night."

"Can't imagine why. You want coffee?"

"Not your coffee. It's terrible."

"Hire me a better coffee cook. Okay, you want to be filled in on last night."

"I appreciated your call at three this morning; Julia didn't."

"Give her my apologies."

"I did. What's new on this thing?"

"Nothing. We searched the museum, logged every one of the two hundred guests and asked the usual prelim questions. The lab people did their job, the press was fed a lean diet and everybody was put on notice not to leave town. It boils down to one dead historian, a missing medal and a suspect-cast of thousands."

"What about the medal?"

"It belonged to a society called Harsa. It has something to do with the Revolutionary War, and with another society called the Cincinnati."

"And?"

"And, well, I have to find out a helluva lot more. I put a bulletin out to Interpol on the medal in case they try to fence it overseas."

"Do you think the medal is what got Tunney killed?"

"As of now that seems to be the scenario, Cal. Professional jewel thieves in the act of stealing the medal, Tunney stumbles onto them, gets killed with the closest thing at hand, Thomas Jefferson's sword."

"Thomas Jefferson's sword?"

Hanrahan nodded. "Excuse me, Cal, but I really need coffee, no matter how bad it is." He returned carrying a steaming mug. "Sure?"

"More so than ever." Johnson perched on a corner of Hanrahan's desk after checking the surface for stains or splinters, touched a thin, gray moustache with the middle finger of his right hand. "Mac, what about the vice-president?"

"What about him?"

"He was there."

"Right. It seems he and his wife are old friends of the deceased, as Joe Pearl would say. His wife got hysterical, and the veep didn't look too terrific either."

"Did you talk to Oxenhauer?"

"Sure. I had an appointment with him this morning but he canceled."

"Why?"

"Something international, he said."

"Meaning what?"

"I don't know."

"Think he was trying to avoid you?"

"I doubt it. But who knows?"

"When are you seeing him?"

"Tomorrow morning at ten."

Johnson went to a window and looked down to the street. He asked without turning, "Why so interested in interviewing the vice-president? You bucking for a White House security job? Maybe Secret Service?"

Hanrahan made a sound of disgust. "You're right, Cal, this coffee is terrible. Better job? What could be better than this one? It's like going to heaven every day."

Johnson nodded, straight-faced. "It looks like rain . . . Why so much interest in Oxenhauer?"

"Because he told me Tunney said something to him before he died that might be important."

"What was it?"

"He didn't tell me."

"Why not?"

"He wanted to get his wife home. She was in pretty bad shape."

"Oh."

"That's what I said. I'll see what he has to say in the morning."

"I can see the papers now, blaming this on the 'Smithson Bomber.' What about him? Any possibility that he finally came out of the closet?"

"And killed Tunney?"

Johnson nodded, shrugged.

"I doubt it, but who knows? That's getting to be my favorite line on this case. Anyway, all we can do is wait for him to make a mistake, stick his head out of his hole. He hasn't taken credit for this yet."

"Beef up the search for him, and make a point of it with the press. The media'll play this to the hilt, turn it into a circus. God, Mac, a leading historian has Thomas Jefferson's sword rammed into his back in the middle of two hundred people in tuxedoes at the Museum of American History. Imagine what they'll do with this."

Johnson cleared his throat and moved to where a color photograph of Hanrahan, his ex-wife, two sons and a daughter stood on the corner of a cabinet. He touched the frame. "Are you over this yet, Mac?"

"Over what? The divorce? Sure."

"Must have been tough. I mean, having your wife run off with a younger man." They respected each other enough to talk straight.

"It was. It isn't anymore."

"Good. Good for you and good for this case. I'd hate to see you distracted. This is a big one, Mac. Tunney was a good man, I've heard of him . . . but our big problem is *where* he died, and the circumstances. We want to do this right. We're making some headway in this town. I'd hate to see it set back by a lot of high-level backbiting."

Hanrahan momentarily resented the pressure, even if well-intentioned, from the commissioner. Then the resentment subsided and he rolled his fingertips on the desk top. "We're on top of it, Cal. I'll keep you informed."

"I know you will, Mac. Get some sleep. By the way, what did you say that medal was called?"

"The Legion of Harsa."

"Find out more about that too. I've always enjoyed history. Like they say, we are what we were."

"Yeah, like they say, Cal." He didn't press the point that that would have made the commissioner a slave.

Twenty-four hours later, as Captain Mac Hanrahan fidgeted in Vice-President William Oxenhauer's outer office, a thirty-four-year-old woman named Heather McBean stood at the Constitution Avenue entrance of the National Museum of American History. Next to her were four suitcases. A cab driver who had driven her to the museum from Dulles International Airport offered to help her inside but she declined. "I suppose I should have gone to the hotel first," she said in a voice reflecting her weariness after a long flight from London.

"Want me to take you there?" the driver asked.

"No, thank you. I suppose they have a checkroom inside. But thank you for offering."

"Sure. You're British, huh?"

"Scottish."

"They sound the same to me."

"Sometimes to me too. Thank you."

The checkroom was immediately to the right of the entrance. Heather checked her bags, put the receipt in her pocketbook and went to the Information Desk, where a pleasant woman with blue-tinted hair smiled and asked if she could be of help.

"I'd like to see Chloe Prentwhistle, please."

"Do you have an appointment?"

"No, but I think she'll see me. It's about...about what happened here last night."

The woman's face tightened. "Yes, just a moment." She consulted a directory, dialed three numbers and told whomever answered that Chloe Prentwhistle had a visitor. "Your name?" she asked.

"Heather McBean."

"Heather McBean," the woman said into the phone.

The woman listened, looked up. "You said your last name was McBean?"

"Yes, Heather McBean." She suddenly felt faint, realized she was very hungry.

"Ms. Prentwhistle will send someone down for you shortly."

"What? Oh, yes, thank you."

Heather looked across the main floor to the Foucault pendulum, where a group of schoolchildren waited for the brass bob to fell another red marker. "I'll be over there," she said.

She joined the children. They'd grown giddy as the moment drew near and, for a second, Heather forgot about what had brought her across the ocean, the jarring jangle of a telephone in the middle of the night, the faraway voice telling her something that was, at first, incomprehensible, then still unbelievable. Could one phone call topple her from the delicious heights of the past few months, send her into the deepest despair? It could and it had.

Only weeks before, she had celebrated her thirty-fourth birthday and had never felt more alive and positive about her future. If there was a prime of life, this, she decided, certainly was it as the Mouton-Cadet Bordeaux claret and the warm outpouring of affection from her friends washed through and over her. She'd actually become tipsy that night, a rarity for her. Her uncle, Calum McBean, had once commented about her, "She looks, smells and acts like a woman, but she drinks like a man..."

The children's squeals of delight broke into her reverie as the next red marker fell. Seeing them so happy almost made her smile.

"Ms. McBean?"

Heather turned.

"I'm Chloe Prentwhistle."

"Oh, yes, I..." She looked at the children. "It's a pleasure seeing them enjoy it so—"

"Yes. How fortunate they aren't aware that it happened here—"

"What? I don't understand."

"The terrible business...Doctor Tunney...that's where he fell. The police finished up what they had to do and gave us permission to..." The face she had been talking to suddenly slipped from view as Heather McBean sunk to the floor.

"My God, she's fainted," Chloe Prentwhistle said, and called out for a guard to come help. "Immediately."

CHAPTER 5

HEATHER AWOKE ON A COUCH IN CHLOE PRENT-whistle's office. A physician stood over her, a broken vial of smelling salts in his hand. He checked her pulse. "You'll be fine, you fainted."

Heather tried to focus on his face. Her stomach was queasy; there was ringing in her ears.

"Here, my dear, take some tea," Chloe said as she placed her hand behind Heather's neck and helped her slide into a sitting position. "It's not as good as you're used to in England but it isn't at all bad. It's herb tea, hibiscus flowers, rose hips, apple . . . try it. Take a sip."

"I'll be going," said the doctor. "Glad to see you're feeling better."

When he'd left, Heather breathed in the tea's aroma. "It smells wonderful. I think I was just hungry."

"Of course. You're looking much better. The color is back in your cheeks. What would you like to eat?"

"Nothing right now, thank you. This tea will do me fine."

Chloe observed Heather closely. No doubt about her being Scottish—fair-skinned, black hair worn short and nicely framing her face, broad cheekbones and a sharp, definite nose appropriately sized to the rest of her face. She judged her to be about five four, someone who had to watch her weight.

And if her physical features weren't enough to confirm Heather McBean's Scottish heritage, her outfit surely did. She wore a red, green and white pleated skirt in the MacBean clan tartan (the "a" had been dropped years ago from the clan's spelling). Her white blouse was frilly and hugged her neck. The clan crest on her blue blazer was of a demicat, rampant and gules. The motto across the bottom of it read: *Touch not the cat bot a glove.* It meant, "Touch not the cat without a glove." The MacBeans were famous for their combativeness . . .

Heather put the cup on a table, stood up and went to a wall on which numerous framed photographs were hung. Chloe was posed in each picture with someone of note, a politician or a leading name in the arts world. In a group apparently photographed at a dinner, Heather recognized Peter Peckham. "You know Peter?" she asked.

"Peter Peckham? I met him once, at dinner."

"Did you know Lewis? . . . Dr. Tunney?"

"No, not really." Chloe paused, then said, "You're Calum McBean's daughter, aren't you?"

Heather turned from the photographs. "Niece, actually, but raised as his daughter. Did you ever meet my uncle?"

"No."

Heather returned to the couch, cradled the teacup in both hands, closed her eyes momentarily and then said, "I want to know everything about . . . how he died."

Chloe went to her desk and absently shuffled papers. She looked up over half-glasses. "Why do you have such interest in Dr. Tunney's murder?"

"Because we were engaged to be married."

"I didn't know that. That sort of news usually travels fast."

"It happened a few weeks ago, at my birthday party. We only announced it to close friends."

Chloe almost congratulated her, but caught herself in time. "I'm so sorry," she said, and joined Heather on the couch. "How terrible for you."

Heather lost her battle with the tears she'd been holding back. Chloe put her arm around her, and for a moment Heather allowed herself the comfort of the older woman's embrace. "I'm sorry," she said after a moment, "and thank you for being so understanding—"

"I can't imagine anything worse than what you're going through..."

"I've been denying the reality of it but I've got to face that it did happen. I'm left without him, he's gone... now I must at least find out *why* he was killed. I *have* to know. Somehow I feel it's all that's left for me... to make some sense of this terrible loss..."

Chloe played with a gold chain that dangled over a chocolate-colored turtleneck she wore beneath a tan pants suit. The pants drooped in the rear, and Heather couldn't help notice that there was a sizable stain on one of the front pockets. Chloe's hair was mousey brown, short and streaked with gray. She was close to six feet tall and in spite of her proportions managed to carry herself with a certain dignity. In any case, her black eyes seemed to shine with intelligence, and there was a sense of strength that some might find reassuring, or impressive, or both.

"What can you tell me?" Heather asked after a moment's silence.

"About last night? Very little, I'm afraid. It just... happened."

"Did you get a chance to talk to Lewis before...?"

"Yes, yes, I did. We chatted for a few minutes but

he seemed distracted. I suppose it was his late arrival and wanting to collect his thoughts before he spoke."

"He seemed distracted before he left London too."

"Oh? Do you know why?"

"No. I asked about it but all he'd say was that there was a problem he intended to straighten out in Washington and that he'd tell me about it when he came back. Do you have any idea what the problem was, Ms. Prentwhistle?"

She shook her head. "I wish I could help. And please, call me Chloe."

Heather nodded, forced a smile, then narrowed her eyes. "He must have been killed because of the problem he mentioned, whatever it was..."

"Not necessarily. The police are working on the theory that he accidentally came on thieves stealing the Harsa medal..."

"Oh, yes, the medal. I wanted to talk about that with you. I don't understand why it took so long to go on display after my uncle donated it to you."

"You should understand, working as you do in this field... Are you still with the British Museum in London?"

"No. After Uncle Calum died I took a leave of absence to live at the castle and settle his estate. It was a bigger and more complex job than I'd bargained for. I've been there ever since. If things go as planned it will become a museum of sorts, open to the public. I'm still negotiating with Edinburgh officials."

"Did your uncle discuss his donation of the Harsa with you?"

Heather shook her head. "May I have some more tea? It's really good... You know, I never fully understood what went on between my uncle and the Smithsonian. His letters to you were so angry..."

Chloe smiled as she took Heather's cup. "Yes, they

were, and I was on the receiving end. We were all delighted to have his donation of the Harsa but, as you know, we couldn't consider displaying it until we conducted an intensive investigation to authenticate it."

Heather nodded. "My uncle was an irascible gentleman, as everyone in the field knows, but beneath that gruff facade was a very sweet and loving person. He raised me, you know, after my mother and father died in an auto accident."

"There've always been so many stories about Calum McBean. I suppose there's never been a more ardent collector, at least not in my experience. I wish I'd had the chance to meet him," Chloe said.

"Very few had that opportunity. He was a true recluse."

"I know. That was such a bizarre year he spent before he died, disappearing like that, then reappearing. Everyone assumed he was dead."

"I knew he wasn't." Heather returned to the wall of photographs and looked at a picture of Chloe with William Oxenhauer. "Your vice-president," she said. "Lewis and he were old friends. Lewis looked forward to seeing him when he came to Washington. I wonder if they had a chance to talk..."

"I wouldn't know."

"Do you think he would see me?"

"The vice-president? I've no idea. Why don't you call him?"

"I will."

"Better yet...I'll call. How long do you plan to stay in Washington?"

"Until I know for certain why it happened, and who did it." She knew she was about to cry again, forced herself not to.

Chloe came up behind and put an arm over her shoulder. "Where are you staying, Heather?"

"At the Madison."

"Good. Why don't you call me later today. If I've gotten through to the vice-president I'll let you know. At any rate, let's keep in touch."

"Thank you. Oh, before I forget, I came across some additional Harsa papers in my uncle's files."

Chloe raised her heavy eyebrows. "Really? What are they?"

"Copies of other letters, notes taken during his year's disappearance, nothing terribly important."

"I'd love to see them. Ever since your uncle donated the Harsa to the Smithsonian five years ago it's become...well, like a part of my life." She smiled and shook her head. "Frankly, I never planned for a major exhibit, but the vice-president pressed for it and..."

"I'll make copies and bring them to you."

"I'll be happy to make the copies. Just leave them with me and I'll have the originals sent to the hotel."

Heather picked up her purse, which was the size of an attaché case, started to open it, stopped and said, "I think I'd like to keep them with me. I haven't had a chance to read them carefully, and maybe doing that will divert me for a few hours. I'll come back tomorrow, if that's all right with you."

"Whatever you say, Heather. Are you sure you're feeling well enough to leave? Would you like some lunch, or a late breakfast?"

"I'll get something a little later. Thanks so much for your interest and concern. I thought of several people to contact here but you kept topping the list. I suppose your long-time correspondence with my uncle had a lot to do with that."

"I'm sure," Chloe said. But her face, as she turned, showed a tightness she hoped she had managed to keep out of her voice.

CHAPTER 6

"*I* CERTAINLY APPRECIATE WHAT YOU'VE TOLD ME, Mr. Vice-President."

"Let me make a further point, captain. If this links to the murder of Lewis Tunney, that's one thing, but if it doesn't it could be used to reflect on one of this nation's finest institutions. I trust you know how important the Smithsonian is to me."

"I've heard."

"I don't want to hear of it in rumors, speculation, or read it in the gossip columns. I'm putting a great deal of trust in MPD's discretion."

"Well, sir, this *is* a murder investigation. I understand your concern, but it isn't exactly the sort of information under the circumstances to withhold."

Oxenhauer was clearly annoyed. Hanrahan understood, but wanted to say, and didn't, that Oxenhauer might be the V.P., but someone had just got killed. And that someone was, supposedly, his close friend. Or at least had been...

"Captain, the timing of this is extremely unfortunate."

"Like they say, there's never a good time to die,

sir. Especially if it's murder... Sorry, sir, I'm a little testy this morning—"

"Don't apologize. You have a right to be. But what I'm saying is that we're a month away from this country's most important national celebration, the Fourth of July. For the first time the Smithsonian is taking center stage, where it deserves to be. Any hint of scandal about it before the Fourth would be more than unfortunate. Especially if it proved out to be false.

"What I'm getting at, Captain Hanrahan, is that unless there's a compelling, an overriding reason for what I've told you to be made public, it shouldn't be. Can you promise me that?"

"I think so, sir. I'll sure try, but if—"

"Yes, I understand. All right, keep me informed of your progress. I've lost a close and trusted friend."

Hanrahan nodded. Chums forever... "Is Mrs. Oxenhauer feeling better?"

"She's coming to grips with it, I think. We all have to do that. Well, thanks for stopping by, and again, sorry about canceling out yesterday. It couldn't be avoided."

Back at MPD, Hanrahan was about to go to a meeting of detectives assigned to the Tunney case when the desk sergeant called. "Captain, there's a woman here to see you. She says it's about the Tunney murder."

Hanrahan rolled his eyes up and reached for a Tums. It was about to start, the procession of crazies offering useless information and theories to match. The city was crawling with them, the lonely and slightly unbalanced, no one to talk to, nobody to give them a sense of importance. They called phone-in radio talk shows to report their latest encounters with men from Mars, or their personal miseries with uncaring relatives, stone-hearted social agencies, ex-spouses, and so forth.

Recently, a demented young man claiming to be a nephew of James Smithson—the Smithsonian was named for him—had been leaving notes in Smithsonian museums threatening to blow them up if he didn't receive his "rightful recognition." So far no bombs had gone off, but it had become a nagging pain in the neck for Hanrahan.

Hanrahan now told the desk sergeant, whose name was Arey and who had a reputation for confusing phone messages, "Get her number and tell her we'll call her back."

"She says she came all the way from Scotland, captain. She says she's the deceased's fiancée."

"Tunney's fiancée?"

"That's what she says."

"What's her name?"

"Heather McBean."

"Let me talk to her."

"Hello," Heather said.

"Hello. I'm Captain Hanrahan. You were Dr. Tunney's fiancée?"

"Yes."

"You just arrived from Scotland?"

"That's right."

"Do you know anything that you think might help us?"

"Do *you* know anything that might help *me*, captain? I was engaged to be married to Lewis Tunney. He's been murdered in your city, in a leading museum, in a cold-blooded brutal fashion. The wedding is off, captain, but I intend to stay here until I get some answers that..."

Hanrahan had to smile to himself. She sure was Scottish. The anger and the brogue were thick. He told

46

Sergeant Arey to have someone escort Heather McBean to his office, hung up and called Joe Pearl, telling him to put the meeting off an hour.

"Why? Everybody's here."

"*I'm* not there, and I won't be for an hour."

"*Okay*, Mac, whatever you say."

Heather sat in the chair Hanrahan offered and crossed what Hanrahan noted were shapely legs, well muscled like a ballet dancer's, or a woman who lived in a hilly city like San Francisco.

"Is Edinburgh hilly?" he asked. It was the only city in Scotland that he could think of offhand.

"Why do you ask?"

"No special reason. I've never been there."

"No, it isn't especially hilly. Windy, though. It's in the Gulf Stream." She smiled, and so did he. Hanrahan, she thought. No doubt about being Irish. Black Irish her uncle would have said, black hair, fair skin and green eyes in nonstop motion.

"So, Miss McBean, you were engaged to marry Lewis Tunney. I'm most sorry for your loss."

"Thank you, captain... We hadn't been engaged long, only a few weeks..."

"I'm sure that makes it especially tough," Hanrahan said, unsure of what to say. "Did you work with him, I mean in the same field?"

"Yes, in a way. I was a museum curator."

"Which museum?"

"The British Museum in London."

"I thought you were Scottish."

"Being born Scottish doesn't mean lifetime prohibition from traveling."

He sat back. This one sure had spirit. The question was, would she help or backbite. "Did you meet Dr. Tunney through your work?"

"In a manner of speaking. He'd been friendly over the years with my uncle, Calum McBean, who was one of the world's leading collectors. They shared an interest in secret societies from post-Revolutionary War America. They didn't see much of each other, though. My uncle was a recluse. But they were fond of each other."

"And your uncle introduced you to him?"

"No, Dr. Tunney stopped by the museum one time and introduced himself after he'd visited my uncle. You see, captain, my parents died when I was an infant and Calum raised me as a daughter."

"Sounds like a good man."

"I adored him, and he adored me."

Hanrahan could believe it. He was impressed with her clear-skinned beauty and eyes that never let you go. By now his overall impression was that this lady was legit, no games, told you straight out what she thought but wasn't out to offend. He liked her. "What about Dr. Tunney's activities before he flew here from London, Miss McBean? It might help us to know that."

"Nothing very unusual. He was busy organizing his life after having spent two years on a research project that came a cropper. He was glad it was over, and surprisingly enough after spending two years chasing some rainbows, he was in quite good spirits."

"What about just before his trip here? Did he indicate anything that might have some bearing on what happened to him?"

She told him what she'd told Chloe.

"No names?" Hanrahan asked. "Did he say who he planned to see in Washington to solve the problem?"

She shook her head. "He was anxious to see your vice-president, Mr. Oxenhauer. They were old friends."

He scribbled notes on a yellow pad. "There was also a theft that night. Did you know that?"

"Yes, I did. My uncle Calum was the one who donated the Legion of Harsa to the Smithsonian."

"Oh?"

"Oh, yes, and it caused quite a good deal of upset in his life. He'd sent it to Chloe Prentwhistle at the Smithsonian's Museum of American History. She accepted it but wrote back that it would probably take years of investigation to find out whether it truly was the Harsa. That, to put it mildly, angered my uncle. He wrote her and said, among other things..." She laughed. "I recall this line so vividly. He said that if her 'pompous, arrogant and haughty attitude was any indication of the basic American character he was glad to never have visited her country and would see to it that he never did.'"

"Sounds like a man who knew his own mind... How long will you be in Washington?"

"Until whoever killed Lewis is brought to justice."

"That might take a long time."

"I don't care."

"Where will you be staying?"

"The Madison."

"I'll be in touch... you know, some aspects of this case are over my head."

"What are they, captain?"

"The museum world, the missing medal, background on Dr. Tunney that might relate to his death. You could help me."

"I'll do *anything* you ask."

"I appreciate that, Miss McBean. Here's my card. I'll put my home number on it. Call any time, day or night."

She put his card in her blazer pocket, and he walked her downstairs and watched her disappear around a corner.

Ten minutes later he was sitting in Commissioner Johnson's office.

"How'd it go with the vice-president, Mac?"

"Not bad...Tunney told the veep something interesting just before he was murdered."

Johnson sat forward.

"Oxenhauer claims that Tunney told him he had proof of a major scandal in the Smithsonian that, like they say, could blow its lid off."

"And?"

"The veep says he doesn't know what the scandal is."

Johnson sat back. "How could he *not* know if Tunney told him?"

"According to Oxenhauer Tunney never got specific. They made a date for the next morning but, as we know, Tunney didn't show up."

"Do you believe Oxenhauer?"

"He's the vice-president."

"He's also a politician."

"Then let's say I half believe him. I just talked to Tunney's fiancée, a girl named Heather McBean. She says pretty much what Oxenhauer told me...that Tunney knew about something brewing at the Smithsonian. He wouldn't tell her the specifics, either, promised to do it when he got back to England."

Hanrahan filled Johnson in on more of his conversations with Oxenhauer and Heather, including Oxenhauer's urgent request that nothing be made public unless it was absolutely important for the case.

Johnson shrugged. "He didn't tell you anything worth making public, did he?"

"Just that there's an unspecified scandal. Maybe we'll find out more when we dig into Tunney. I know one thing, Cal, my initial theory that Tunney just stumbled on a theft in progress doesn't hold much water.

If Tunney knew something and was about to announce it to Oxenhauer and to the world, there's a museum full of people who might have wanted to shut him up."

Johnson went to the door. "Fill me in at the end of the day."

Hanrahan shook Tums from a bottle into his pocket and headed for the meeting with his assistants.

Johnson returned to his office and took a call from Vice-President William Oxenhauer.

CHAPTER 7

HEATHER CHECKED INTO THE MADISON HOTEL AT Fifteenth and M Streets. She emptied her bags and arranged toilet articles in the bathroom, then mentally flipped a coin—a nap or food? Her stomach prevailed, and she called room service. Twenty minutes later her meal arrived; grilled fresh sea trout, fresh green beans and parsley potatoes. She ate slowly, hardly tasting the food. All she wanted to do was wipe from her mind, even for a few minutes, the nightmarish reality of what had happened.

She finished eating, changed into a robe and fell asleep. She woke up at four, showered, dressed and went to the lobby where she bought the day's Washington *Post*. There it was...on the front page a story about Lewis's murder. There was a picture of him, an old one they'd found in the files. Seeing it was like being jabbed in the stomach with a hot poker. She breathed hard and went outside. It was overcast; hot and sticky. She walked south along Fifteenth Street, the newspaper clutched under her arm. She did not have a destination at the moment, or in her life anymore, it seemed. The best thing that had ever happened to her, Lewis Tunney, was no longer in her future.

She stopped and looked at the Treasury Department. Behind it was the White House. She sat on the steps and read the *Post*'s account of the murder. Now, the words and the picture represented only a black-and-white record of a crime. There was no mention of her in the article. Why should there be? She wished they'd been married two weeks earlier instead of just getting engaged. At least then there would be some acknowledgment, some record that she'd existed in his life, and he in hers.

She tore the front page from the paper and stuffed it in her purse. At least there was more room in it now...she'd checked much of its contents with the hotel clerk, including the Harsa papers she'd brought from England.

She reached the Washington Monument, looked to her left and realized she was at the Mall, along which the Smithsonian museums were strung. Her spirits lifted a bit. As far back as she could remember a museum had provided her a place of tranquility and for reflection. It was one of the reasons she had become a curator. Museums were like friends, places to turn to when she felt troubled.

She walked the length of the East Mall; twelve square blocks, her guidebook said. On her left was the museum she had been in this morning, the Museum of American History, followed by the Museum of Natural History, and then the skating rink. To her right was the Freer Gallery with its world-famous collection of Oriental art; the original Smithsonian "castle," now the administrative center; the Hirshorn Museum and Sculpture Garden and finally the very modern National Air-and-Space Museum. Across from the Air-and-Space were two buildings housing the National Gallery of Art. The first, the West Building, was more traditional in its architecture than the newer East Building. According to what Heather had heard, their collections reflected their architectural concepts.

She paused in the West Building's rotunda—columns quarried in Tuscany, Italy, the floor of green Vermont and gray Tennessee marble; Alabama Rockwood stone, Indiana limestone and Italian travertine on the walls. "God...it's beautiful," she said aloud.

She tried to decide which exhibit to visit first. She loved Venetian and North Italian art, although her specialty at the British Museum was eighteenth-century British art, particularly the works of portraitists Thomas Gainsborough and Sir Joshua Reynolds.

She went to the Venetian section and immersed herself in Bellini, Giorgione and Titian. Rather than take in another exhibit she decided to go to the East Building, get a general impression of it and then go back to her hotel.

On her way back to the rotunda she paused in a gallery featuring Florentine and Central Italian Renaissance art. She stood all but transfixed in front of Leonardo da Vinci's "Ginevra de Benci." Finally she glanced at her watch. Eight-thirty. Signs proclaimed that the museums closed at nine.

She exited the West Building and looked across a cobblestone courtyard at two massive pink marble triangles that formed the new East Wing. It was now almost totally dark, and a threat of rain hung in the humid air. Few people were in the courtyard, most visitors preferring to use an underground concourse that linked the two museums. She walked to a fountain in the center of the courtyard where streams of water spewed into the air and, because there was no enclosure, flowed freely over cobblestones and down terraced concrete to a sheet of glass that formed one entire wall of the lower concourse.

Heather looked down over the rippling water to the below-ground window-wall. Children, noses pressed to the glass, looked back at her. One waved. Heather returned the greeting. The children's mother joined them.

Heather waved again and as she did wondered about the pungent odor...like a perfume?...she suddenly was aware of.

But not for long.

It happened fast. Someone came up behind her, brought a long, slender cane down across the back of her neck. At the same time a hand ripped her large purse from her shoulder.

The children and their mother gaped as Heather toppled forward, twisting as she fell, her right shoulder leading the way down the terraced steps, water splashing over her as she stumbled, legs akimbo, arms searching for an anchor.

Her body hit the curtain wall. The mother and her children recoiled from the anticipated smashing of the glass. It didn't happen. Heather slumped against the window, water flowing over and around her. She shook her head and blinked her eyes. Water swirled into her open mouth. She raised her head and looked, eyes clouded, at the faces on the other side of the window.

Two men scrambled down behind her and carried her back up to the courtyard. One of them placed his jacket over her shoulders. "Anything feel broken?" he asked.

"I...I don't know."

A police ambulance arrived. By this time Heather was sitting up and talking with museum security guards. She didn't, she told them, need to go to a hospital but was overruled and taken to the emergency room at Capitol Hill Hospital, where after an examination that revealed nothing more serious than bruises and lacerations, she was released. A uniformed officer from MPD asked whether she felt up to giving him a report.

"I think so," she said, "but I want to go back to my hotel and change my clothes. Everything's torn and wet."

"We'll take you back in the car, ma'am," the officer said.

"Could I speak with Captain Hanrahan?"

"Mac Hanrahan? He wouldn't be around this time of night."

"I have his home number. I'd like to talk to him." She pulled Hanrahan's wet, crumpled card from her blazer.

"Sure, give him a try," said the officer.

She dialed Hanrahan's home from a booth in the hall.

"Hello," Hanrahan said after the first ring.

"This is Heather McBean..."

"Oh, sure, Miss McBean, how goes it?"

"Not so well, I'm afraid," and she quickly told him what had happened.

"I'm very sorry," he said. "Why not let the officer drive you to the hotel. You can skip giving a statement tonight. Come to the office in the morning and I'll take one from you."

"That's very kind, but I would like to talk to you tonight."

"Why?"

56

"*Why?* Well, don't you think that what just happened to me tonight has to do with Lewis's murder."

"Why do you assume that?"

"Are you suggesting it might just be a coincidence?"

"I'm not suggesting anything, but I'm sorry to say muggings aren't exactly unknown in Washington. Now that you asked, I'd have to say it probably was a coincidence—"

"I was attacked by a female mugger."

"'Female'? Did you see the mugger?"

"I overheard a museum security guard tell one of your officers that a witness saw a *woman* hit me and steal my purse. And just before it happened I'm pretty sure I smelled perfume."

"Let me talk with the officer."

Heather put him on the line. "Hello, captain, Officer Scheiner here. She's right. A witness says she saw a tall woman hit Miss McBean with a cane."

"Anything else?"

"No, sir; except whoever did it ripped off her purse and took off."

"Look Scheiner, treat her nice. She's also a prime source of information in the Smithsonian murder. Take her back to her hotel—she's staying at the Madison— and don't press her for a statement. I'll take care of that myself."

"Okay, captain."

Heather got back on the phone.

"Miss McBean," Hanrahan said, "you go on back and get a good night's sleep. I'm sure you can use it."

"Yes, thank you . . ."

"Come by my office in the morning and we'll talk about this. All about it. I'm not dismissing anything. I've got an open mind." I better, he thought. There's sure as hell nothing in it at the moment to solve this thing...

"All right, thank you, captain. I appreciate it."

The two uniformed officers escorted Heather into the Madison, which of course had people turning to stare. She told the desk what had happened, adding that her room key had been in her purse. She was given a new one, told that the staff stood ready to help in any way it could, then went with the policemen to the twelfth floor. They stopped in front of her room. "I'll open it," one of the officers said. She handed him the key. He inserted it into the lock, turned the knob, stepped inside and flipped on the overhead light. "Damn," he muttered.

"What's the matter?" Heather asked, and didn't wait for an answer. She looked into the room. "Oh, my God..." The room had been ransacked. Every dresser drawer was on the floor, along with her clothes. The bed had been stripped, the drapes torn from their rods.

"Could I have Captain Hanrahan's home number again, miss?" Scheiner said. He dialed. "Captain, this is Scheiner—"

"What now, Scheiner?"

"We just brought Miss McBean to her room. It's been torn apart. Obviously somebody was looking for something—"

"Let me talk to her."

"I can't believe it," Heather said to Hanrahan. She felt herself shaking.

"Stay put, I'll be there in fifteen minutes. Tell the officers to wait with you until I get there."

* * *

Hanrahan hung up, turned off the television and went to the bedroom, where he took off his blue terry-cloth robe, dressed in what he'd intended to wear to the office the next day and got his car. It was not the way he'd planned to spend his evening. It was to be an early-to-bed night. He was deep-bone tired. His back ached, and his stomach, always on the verge, was in open rebellion.

He turned the ignition key, popped a Tums in his mouth and headed for the Madison.

CHAPTER 8

THEY SAT AT A CORNER TABLE IN THE MADISON'S lobby bar. Heather hadn't wanted to come downstairs but Hanrahan told her *he* needed a drink.

She cradled a glass of single-malt Scotch. Hanrahan had his usual gin on the rocks. (He'd ordered a martini without vermouth in the hope of avoiding a single measured shot of gin over ice. He needn't have worried. This bartender poured from the bottle no matter what the order. Real class.)

"I still don't understand the need for a policewoman in my room," Heather said.

"Indulge me. At my age I like being indulged."

Heather smiled. Hanrahan had called the policewoman, Sergeant Shippee, before he left his house. She arrived at the hotel carrying a small suitcase, told Heather that she was used to such assignments, that they'd get along fine, set about making up a pull-out couch with extra linen ordered from housekeeping.

"How old *are* you, captain?" Heather asked.

"Depends on the day. Sometimes I'm forty-seven, sometimes I'm forty-seven going on seventy-four. Then again, there are days when I just turned twenty-one."

"Today? Well, I started off feeling old. Right now I feel as though I've shed a few years." He checked to see whether she'd taken it as a line. He hadn't meant it that way, and she didn't seem bothered. She sat back, the glass in her hands. She'd changed into a tan corduroy skirt and green button-down shirt. Her hair was brushed back, and she wore no makeup. She didn't need lipstick. Altogether, Hanrahan couldn't help thinking, a delicious looking lady. He sighed.

There was silence as they sipped their drinks, looked off in different directions. Finally Hanrahan said, "Tell me about tonight. Start at the museum."

"Is this the statement you said you'd take?"

"No. We'll do that tomorrow. This is off the record."

"What can I say? I was standing in the courtyard between the East and West buildings of the National Gallery when someone hit me over the head and stole my purse."

"Did you see the person?" Joe Pearl, he thought, would have said "perpetrator."

"No."

"Any sense of anyone following you?"

"No... I felt a blow and the next thing I knew I was at the bottom of the fountains, my mouth full of water."

Hanrahan winced. "I'm sorry... Look, your uncle seems to have been important in your life, and to have been linked with some of the aspects of this case. Should I know more about him?"

She look startled, then pleased. "An interesting question, captain. Well... they called his death a suicide, which I'm sure it wasn't."

Hanrahan motioned to a waiter for a refill. Heather shook her head when Hanrahan pointed to her half-empty glass. He waited until his drink had been delivered before saying, "They say your uncle committed suicide and you're sure it wasn't? Why?"

She sighed. "I guess I will have another whiskey, after all."

Hanrahan gave the order. "You were saying..."

"My Uncle Calum did not commit suicide, no matter what the Edinburgh police claim. He'd disappeared for a year while he was investigating the Legion of Harsa. While he was gone rumors spread that he must have died. I knew it wasn't true. He'd told me just before he left that no matter how long he was gone, no matter what sort of speculation there was, he'd be back safe and sound."

"And?"

"That's exactly what he did. He came home to the castle one day, gave me a hug, said it was good to see me again and went to work in his study."

"Then?"

"A week later I found him in that same study, a bullet hole in his head, a gun in his hand."

"Did they establish that the bullet came from the gun he was holding?"

"Yes, at least according to the police. It doesn't *matter*, though. I don't care about circumstantial evidence. I *know* Calum did not kill himself. My uncle was a Scotsman through and through. We have no law against suicide in Scotland, but we do have laws against making a public nuisance of one's self. The last thing Uncle Calum would ever do is make a public nuisance of himself, or leave me that way."

He was quiet, but she sensed he wasn't overly impressed with her case against the suicide finding.

"Captain Hanrahan, I am not just saying that Uncle Calum didn't kill himself because of his Scottish character. I *am* saying that he simply was not a man who would prematurely end his life. He was killed, just as the only other man in my life has been, and I mean to sort out and find the truth if it takes me ... well, I've got the time for it." Too much, she thought.

Hanrahan knocked back the rest of his drink. "I believe you will, Miss McBean, and speaking for myself and the MPD, I'd like to help—at least where Dr. Tunney's concerned ... So let me ask you ... you told me that you'd met Tunney through his relationship with your uncle. Do *you* think their deaths might be linked up in some way? Assuming you're right that your uncle's death wasn't suicide."

"It would seem quite a coincidence, wouldn't it?"

"Let's take it from there ... What about whatever Dr. Tunney told you before he left for Washington. His problem he had to clear up. Nothing more concrete come to mind since we last talked?"

"No, I'm afraid not."

Hanrahan popped a Tums into his mouth. "Indigestion," he said. "Do this again," he told the waiter, indicating his glass. To Heather he said, "About what happened tonight in your room ... any idea who, why, what someone might be after? I have to tell you such things aren't exactly unique around here. Yes ... even in our nation's capital, as they say. A mugger finds a hotel key in a stolen purse and hightails it to the room before the victim gets back."

"Even my female mugger?" Her tone had an edge.

"Equality of opportunity, Miss McBean ... But look, let's not you and me get on each other's case ... You've been through a terrible experience, I'm the fellow who's got to try to solve it. We're natural allies."

Her eyes filled up and she fought to hold back the tears. She nodded vigorously and managed a quick smile. Hanrahan wanted to reach out and touch her hand, but he fought the impulse. Change the subject, he told himself . . . "Tell me about the Legion of Harsa."

She pulled herself together, sipped her Scotch, sat back. "All right, captain, you asked for it. Hope I don't bore you. The society was named after Gaius Terentilius Harsa, a Roman who lived back around 460 B.C. He was a critic of Rome's dictator, Lucius Quinctius Cincinnatus, who believed in an elitist society. Harsa kept pressing for a code of written laws that would equally apply to patricians and plebeians but he never succeeded. After your Revolutionary War a group was formed by officers from your army. They called themselves the Society of the Cincinnati, after the Roman, Cincinnatus, and adopted what some considered his elitist views. I suppose their purposes were honorable . . . promoting friendship, keeping going the rights they fought for and helping each other and their families. Certain people didn't see it that way, though."

Hanrahan said it sounded sort of like a veterans organization. What was the big deal?

"It was the way they *ran* the society that bothered other people, like your Thomas Jefferson and a judge named Burke from one of your southern states. They attacked the Cincinnati for limiting membership to the eldest male descendant of existing members. The critics accused them of trying to create a race of . . . well, as it says on the placard beneath the medal, 'a race of hereditary patricians or nobility.'"

Hanrahan nodded, and was impressed with her knowledge. He told her so.

"Thank you," Heather said, "but being brought up by Calum McBean was an education in itself. He was probably the world's foremost authority on Harsa and the Cincinnati."

"And Harsa was set up in opposition to Cincinnati?"

"Exactly. Thomas Jefferson was its first president,

just as George Washington was the first president-general of the Cincinnati."

"Are both groups still active today?"

"No. The Cincinnati is very much alive in America and in France. Its headquarters are right here in Washington, in a mansion donated by a former Cincinnati member, a Mr. Larz Anderson. I understand it's magnificent and is open to the public. The society does a lot of fund raising to promote education." She smiled "Your city of Cincinnati was named after the society, not after the Roman dictator the way many people believe."

"Interesting," Hanrahan said. "What happened to Harsa?"

"Dissolved over the years. That's what prompted my uncle to devote so much of his professional efforts to building a bridge of knowledge between today's scholars and Harsa's history. Lewis picked up that interest from him and got to be an authority in his own right."

"Another link between them."

"Another?"

"You, and Harsa. Are there more?"

"Not that I know of."

"You think Harsa could play any sort of role in their deaths?"

"How?"

"Well...the medal that was stolen, the Harsa your uncle donated to the Smithsonian...maybe somebody from the Cincinnati—"

"What would that accomplish?"

"Getting even with the past? Sort of crazy, but fanatics never do make much sense."

She shrugged. "It certainly would be the act of a

crazy person. The Cincinnati is a respected, worthy organization. Harsa hasn't even existed for years. That could be why they only stole the Harsa medal. It's much more valuable because the organization is extinct."

"Okay, Miss McBean, you're beat and upset and we can go on with this in the morning at my office. But be thinking some more about the Harsa medal . . . By the way, who'd buy a medal like that from the thieves?"

"Collectors? My uncle told me the world is full of unscrupulous collectors who buy through a black market."

"I'd like to know more about that black market . . . tomorrow?"

"I'll tell you whatever I can. And thank you for the drinks, and understanding . . ."

The policewoman answered the door. "Take good care of her," Hanrahan said. "I'm getting quite an education."

"You may discover, captain, that I know less than you think."

"I doubt *that*, Miss McBean. Anyway, good night to you . . . Officer Shippee will bring you to the office tomorrow morning."

Hanrahan stopped at his favorite diner on the way home, sat at the counter across from the grill, took out a notebook and, as was his careful habit, jotted down what had been said by Heather. The short-order cook, 260 pounds, redfaced and perspiring as the heat from the griddle wiped away any benefits of the air conditioning, delivered orders of fried eggs, waffles, omelettes and a hamburger. He saw Hanrahan. "The usual, inspector?"

"No, give me a hamburger, no onions, and a vanilla milk shake."

"Tum-tum acting up again?" The cook wiped his hands on a greasy T-shirt, tossed a patty on the grill and popped two halves of a bun in a toaster. Hanrahan watched him juggle a spate of new orders handed him by a waitress. He always enjoyed watching a top-notch griddleman, considered it an art form of sorts.

"Stretch a thick, white Bessie for Sherlock Holmes," the griddleman called to someone working the fountain. He quickly arranged the platter—bun, lettuce and tomato, a pickle, plopped the meat on it and shoved it in front of Hanrahan with an arm that looked like a tattooed telephone pole.

"Thanks," Hanrahan said.

"Anything for our finest." The chef returned to the grill.

Hanrahan ate slowly, enjoying the cooling sensation of the shake as it slid into his belly.

A half hour later he was home, in bed, and awash in thoughts about the Tunney case. When he eventually did drift off to sleep, his last thoughts were of Heather McBean. She hadn't been the random victim of a D.C. mugger. He was sure of that now. She was tied in with her late fiancée's murder, and he felt, sensed, knew that if he wanted to avoid another museum-connected murder he'd better pay very close attention to the lovely Heather McBean.

CHAPTER 9

CONSTANTINE KAZAKIS RODE THE ELEVATOR TO THE Museum of Natural History's third floor. He walked slowly along the circular balcony, occasionally looking down at the eight-ton African bush elephant that dominated the first-floor rotunda.

He came to a door marked *Staff Only*, opened it with a key and moved inside. Ahead of him were endless rows of white steel lockers, tall and short, wide and thin. A small bearded man had taken a drawer from one of them and was examining its contents. He heard Kazakis, glanced up over half-glasses and said, "Good morning, Constantine."

"Good morning, Sanford. You're here early."

"What time is it?"

"Eight."

"I couldn't sleep. We're reevaluating the *Gryllidae* exhibit this week."

Kazakis smiled. The box Sanford held contained a variety of crickets, which were the basis for the exhibit he'd mentioned. It was the Entomology section, where, Kazakis knew, no one ever said crickets when the term *Gryllidae* was available. It was the same in Ornithology, where a simple crossbill was always *Loxia curviorstra*.

Kazakis moved from Entomology to his section, Gems and Minerals, where he was an assistant curator. He, too, was early. This was the day the famed Hope Diamond, the focal point in the Hall of Gems for millions of visitors, was to be removed from its case for the first time in years.

The Hope had originally been cut from the 112-carat Tavernier diamond belonging to Louis XIV. It had been stolen during the French Revolution, then resurfaced in its new form on the London market in 1830. It was donated to the Smithsonian in 1958 by renowned gem collector Harry Winston.

The Hope had always been considered flawless, but Kazakis's boss, Walter Welsh, decided to bring in an outside gemologist to search for hidden flaws and to reweigh it. It was listed at 44.5 carats, but the world standard for the carat had recently changed.

Kazakis sat at his desk and read the *Post*. The Tunney murder was still front-page, and Captain Hanrahan was quoted as saying, "The department has assigned every available resource to the Tunney murder. We're looking into all possible leads." When asked whether anything new had developed, Hanrahan answered, "No, nothing concrete. This is a complex case. All I can say at this time is that we have every confidence that something positive will develop in the near future."

Kazakis put the paper down as a secretary came in. "Coffee?" she asked.

"Yes, please."

He was soon joined by other curators from the mineral and gem division. "Any bets?" one of them asked.

"About what?"

"On what the Hope weighs?"

Kazakis shook his head.

"How about flaws? I bet you five bucks, Connie, that they find at least one."

"Save your money," Kazakis said.

At ten the gemologist, Dr. Max Shilter, arrived. The gem division's staff accompanied him to where the Hope Diamond glittered from its glass-fronted vault. Ten armed Smithsonian security guards, augmented by four MPD officers, formed a circle around Walter Welsh, who, visibly nervous, unlocked the vault and lifted the blue diamond from its bed as though plucking a newborn from a cesarean section. "Let's go," he said, his face grim. The entourage went to Welsh's office, where, while others looked on, Dr. Shilter began what would be a painstaking examination, culminating in a precise weighing on a special scale.

Kazakis watched carefully. Before coming to the Smithsonian he had worked as a jewelry designer and gem cutter. Taking the assistant curator job had meant less income but there was the prestige to be considered. The way he had it figured, he would put five years into the curatorship, then return to designing and cutting, with the Smithsonian credential enhancing his fees. After all, he was only thirty-four.

Short and compact, with an upper body reflecting the weights he worked out with three times a week, and a strong, square olive face framed by black curls and even blacker eyes, he had joined Washington's long list of eligible bachelors. He had brought with him to the nation's capital the spoils of his previous career. His automobile was a silver Corvette. He had an extensive wardrobe of designer suits and expensive gold jewelry, including a seventeen-thousand-dollar Rolex watch. He lived in a Watergate apartment, which he had furnished in leather and chrome.

"Always impressive," said Shilter, who spoke with a German accent and whose fingers were like fat sausages, more the hands of a butcher than a lapidist. "The original stone must have been so beautiful. I've examined the Brunswick," he said, referring to a fourteen-carat diamond indentical in color to the Hope and presumed to have been cut from the original Tavernier gem by its thieves. "No question they came from the same mother stone."

A secretary whispered to Kazakis, "Mr. Throckly from American History is on the phone. He says it's important."

"Not now. I'll call back in an hour. Please, I want to watch this."

An hour later, after Shilter had proclaimed the Hope as flawless as its reputation and had weighed it in at 45.5 carats reflecting the change in standards, Kazakis returned the call to Throckly.

"It took you long enough," Throckly said.

"We were working with the Hope. What's up?"

"Has Walter called you?"

"Walter Jones? No."

"He said he was going to. He wants to have dinner tonight."

"I can't. I have other plans."

"Change them."

"Why?"

"You're trying my patience, Constantine, and I can assure you that Walter feels the same way."

"I don't like being at anyone's beck and call. I have a life of my own—"

"Tell Walter that when he calls."

"I will. I'm not trying to be difficult, Alfred, but these plans for tonight can't be changed. I'll talk to you later."

A few minutes afterward he received a call from Walter Jones. "Constantine, how are you?" Jones asked pleasantly in his well-known gravelly voice.

"Just fine, Walter. We examined the Hope today. Absolutely flawless, according to Max Shilter, and a carat heavier than before."

"No surprise. Is it safely back in the crib or did some ambitious young curator steal it en route?" He laughed too loudly.

Kazakis laughed too. "As a matter of fact, Walter, I did steal it. You called just as I was about to put a chisel to it."

"Just as long as you're not hung over. Connie, Chloe and I are putting together a last-minute dinner party tonight, just a few friends in for something simple. Naturally, you head our list."

"I'm flattered. What happened to the other thousand-and-one names?"

"All fleeting acquaintances. You're special. Seven?"

"I'd made other plans that I—"

"And she's young, blond, very pretty and madly in love with you, in which case she'll understand your need to break her heart for one evening. Seven?"

"I'll be there."

"Informal, just a simple get-together. Careful with the chisel, Constantine. You'd never be forgiven."

CHAPTER 10

HEATHER MCBEAN GAVE A COMPLETE STATEMENT about the previous night's attack to an MPD stenographer. When she was finished and the stenographer had left the office, Hanrahan asked, "What are your plans now?"

Heather looked at him quizzically. "I told you my plans, captain. I intend to stay here until Lewis's murderer is brought to justice."

"I knew what your plans *were*, Miss McBean, but considering what's happened to you over the past twenty-four hours, I thought you might be thinking about returning to England."

"That never crossed my mind."

Hanrahan shuffled loose papers into a pile, put a paper clip on them. "I happen to find your determination admirable, and obviously I can't force you to go home, but frankly I'd like to convince you to do just that."

"Why?"

"Because I think you'd be safer there." He sat back and folded his hands on his chest. "It would also make my job easier if you weren't in Washington—"

"I don't understand. You told me that I could be of help to you—"

"That was true when I said it, but yesterday's events have changed things. Heather McBean, I don't want to have to worry about your safety and at the same time look for Dr. Tunney's killer." He saw her stiffen in the chair. "*Try* to understand, Miss McBean. I'm not—"

"I understand, but you must understand me too. I don't *want* you to be concerned about my personal safety. I'm also fairly capable of taking care of myself. I always have been. I was careless yesterday. I admit it. It never occurred to me to look over my shoulder while I was walking your streets, nor was I thinking that someone might ransack my hotel room. I've learned my American lesson and I won't make the same mistake twice. No...I'd never be able to live with myself if I left Washington for London and sat there, thousands of miles away, waiting for news. Somehow I feel close to Lewis here. That may sound strange, captain, but that's the way it is...and Miss Prentwhistle has been helpful...And I know I'll meet others...In the meantime I'll just follow my uncle's advice."

"Which was?"

"No offense, captain, but he said 'Do it yourself if you want it done right.'"

"No offense taken, Miss McBean..." Well almost none, he thought..."but I must tell you police officers can be right once in a while, and even helpful...Well, it's up to you, of course, but if you stay you'll have to follow my orders and accept that the investigation is my territory."

"I assure you I won't be underfoot, captain, although I don't intend to pretend I'm a helpless little woman...another thing my uncle taught me was that

74

any action is better than no action, which is why I've hired a private investigator in London."

"To do what?" He didn't like the churlish tone in his voice.

"To find out what happened in Lewis's life the week before he left London. I want to know what it was that so upset him that week."

Hanrahan rubbed his eyes. "I'd say you're wasting your money, Miss McBean. I've already been in touch with Scotland Yard, they promise full cooperation—"

"Money is not exactly a problem or the point, captain."

"Yes . . . I realize that . . . who's this investigator?"

"Someone I found in the London phone directory. His name is Elwood Paley and he sounds quite trustworthy. I called him last night and he's agreed to take the case."

Agreed? Hanrahan wanted to say. What private op ever turns down a case when money's no object? Instead, he said, "If I can provide your Mr. Paley with any information, you just let me know."

"That's very kind of you. I'll keep it in mind. And you can continue to depend upon my cooperation, which you seemed to want twenty-four hours ago—"

Hanrahan's phone rang. He picked it up and heard a desk sergeant say, "Captain, the Air-and-Space Museum this time. That Smithsonian nut left another bomb threat."

"Son of a bitch," Hanrahan said. And to Heather, "I'm sorry, but—"

"Please don't apologize," Heather told him. "I'm not that delicate, and I heard much stronger stuff from my uncle . . . What is it?"

Hanrahan smiled. "The looney running around town

75

threatening to blow up the Smithsonian has left another note. He claims he's related to Smithson."

"Is he?"

"Am I? Half the people in this city have elevators that don't reach the top floor."

At first, she didn't understand, then did and smiled back. "May I come with you?"

Hanrahan stood up and took up his jacket from a clothes tree. "I don't think that would be too good an idea...Thanks very much for coming by with your statement...We'll be in touch—"

"But what if this so-called Smithson bomber has something to do with Lewis's murder? I told you, and I meant it, captain, I wanted to be involved in every phase of the investigation. I deserve that—"

"And I told you, Miss McBean, that I thought it would be best if you went back to England. This is what I do for a living...I'll have to decide..."

She understood, of course, but she didn't like it. Strangely, she *did* like him...

Hanrahan entered the Smithsonian's Air-and-Space Museum through the Jefferson Drive entrance. Two uniformed MPD officers stood with museum security guards next to "Friendship Seven," which had carried John Glenn on America's first manned orbiting flight in 1962. The note, neatly typed, was taped to a small window through which Glenn had viewed the earth as no American had ever viewed it before.

The note read:

My patience is running out. I have given you more than enough time to realize that my claims are legitimate, my threats serious. Your theft of the Smithsonian from my family is an offense to every decent person and must be corrected. Therefore, unless there is immediate attention to

*my rightful heritage and demands, I will destroy
everything that is Smithsonian. Cease taking me
lightly. I mean what I say.*

It was signed *"The Wronged."*

"You questioned your men about anyone who might
have left the note?" Hanrahan asked the museum security chief.

"Yes, sir, I did, but it's been a heavy morning. Summer, you know."

"Nobody unusual?"

The security chief shook his head.

"Keep asking."

Hanrahan told one of his men to take down the note
and take it to the lab for prints, then walked outside
into a hot, humid, festering Washington summer day.
Two reporters who'd responded to the call over the
police radio came up behind him. One of them, a pretty
young woman wearing a yellow sundress and carrying
a pad and pen, asked him if the bomber's note was
connected with the Tunney murder.

Hanrahan had no comment.

"Are you still claiming it's just a coincidence?"

"I'm claiming nothing." How could he? He knew
little more than they did.

He got in his car, slammed the door, started the
engine and turned the air conditioning to its lowest
setting. He drove around the perimeter of the Mall and
parked near the Castle, a red sandstone building with
eight crenelated towers that symbolized the entire
Smithsonian for millions of visitors. During the Smithsonian's early years it had housed all of its operations,
including a science museum, lecture hall, art gallery,
research laboratories and administrative offices. Since
the building of new, individual museums, the Castle
had become the Smithsonian's administrative offices,

as well as home for the Woodrow Wilson International Center for Scholars. It also housed the tomb of James Smithson.

Hanrahan circled the Castle to the Mall entrance, stopping to admire species of flora identified by small signs, one of which read, "Poison Ivy." He climbed the steps and paused in the lobby. Immediately to his left was the Smithson crypt.

He entered the small room and looked around. The symbol of the Smithsonian was, according to a placard beneath it, designed to represent the life of Smithson. There was a demi-lion with ruby eyes from the Smithson family coat of arms set in Smithsonite, a mineral also named after him.

Smithson, according to printed material on the walls, had been the illegitimate son of Elizabeth Hungerford Keate (Macie) and Sir Hugh Smithson, Duke of Northumberland. The younger Smithson was characterized as a gentleman-scientist in the eighteenth-century tradition, pursuing his interests in the same era as Beethoven and Mozart, Voltaire and George III, Cavendish, Priestley, Arago, Lavoisier, Lord Byron, Napoleon and, in America, Washington, Jefferson and Adams. He'd graduated from Oxford in 1786 as James Lewis Macie, and later was admitted to the Royal Society as a gentleman well versed in natural philosophy, chemistry and minerology.

Another sign told Hanrahan that Smithson's will have directed that "an establishment for the increase and diffusion of knowledge among men" be founded at Washington under the name Smithsonian Institution. His reasons were unstated, although there was speculation that he wanted to leave a name greater than his illegitimate birth had given him. The decision to establish his center of learning in Washington was especially mysterious because Smithson had never set foot in America. Again, one could only speculate, according to the placard's author, that America represented an illegitimate offspring of Mother England, and perhaps was thereby metaphorically appealing to Smithson. Distant relatives of Smithson had contested his will. It was only after a lengthy battle that the United States won. That happened in 1838, and for the next eight years Congress debated the nature of the institution; should it be a college, arboretum, library, observatory or scientific research organization? Finally in 1846 the Smithsonian was created mainly for scientific research patterned after Smithson's own life of scientific achievement. The final bit of information Hanrahan tried to take in before leaving was that Smithson's papers and personal effects had been lost in an 1865 fire that destroyed the second floor of the Castle.

Hanrahan went on to the office of the Secretary of the Smithsonian, Borden G. Costain. Costain's secretary told Hanrahan that he was in Central America supervising an archaeological dig. Hanrahan wasn't exactly sure why he wanted to see Costain. He wasn't a suspect, hadn't, so he was told, even been in Washington at the time of Tunney's murder. But Hanrahan recognized, felt an increasing need to spend more time with the Smithsonian, absorb its atmosphere, and knew he'd been avoiding it because, for whatever maybe psychological reasons, he was somehow intimidated by it.

As he drove back to MPD he decided that that better not be the case any longer. It was pretty clear that this bizarre case was all wrapped up in the memorial to the illegitimate "gentleman-scientist."

CHAPTER 11

*A*LFRED *T*HROCKLY READ THE TELEGRAM SLOWLY, FOR dramatic effect. Ford Saunders and Chloe Prentwhistle sat across the desk from him.

"*Returning in three days STOP Expect solid and positive progress in Tunney matter STOP Entire Institution at stake STOP Costain.*"

Saunders examined his fingernails. "So?"

"So?" Throckly mimicked. "He means it."

"What are we supposed to do, reach into a display case and produce Lewis Tunney's killer?"

"I wish we could," said Throckly. He sounded appropriately oppressed.

Chloe, who wore a tailored powder-blue suit, ruffled navy-blue silk blouse, patterned blue stockings, and black pumps, touched Saunders on the arm. "Relax, Ford, Borden is very much under the gun. We can't expect him to return to his domain, the scene of a murder of a leading historian, pat us on our heads and offer bonuses."

Throckly stood and paced. "This museum, *my* museum, is where Dr. Lewis Tunney was murdered with Thomas Jefferson's own sword. A precious medal has been stolen. What Costain is saying is that he wants this house cleaned by those who live in it, *us*. What I want to know is what we're going to do to accomplish that?"

"What *can* we do?" Chloe asked. "It's a police matter. Yes, it's unfortunate that the murder and theft happened here, but that doesn't make it our problem, certainly not our fault. We don't solve murders, the police do."

"Perhaps you'd like to be the one to explain that to Costain when he returns."

"With the salary and title of director come certain unpleasant tasks," Saunders said.

"That doesn't help," Throckly said.

"Sorry."

Throckly drummed his fingers on a windowpane, turned. "Look, I have other meetings. Let me ask you...do you think it would be a good idea to hire our own private investigator?"

"I think it's a terrible idea," said Saunders.

Chloe stood, tucked her large leather handbag underneath her arm and took a few steps toward the door.

"You agree with Ford?" Throckly asked.

"Yes," she said. "Leave it to the police. It isn't our business. Coming, Ford? I want to go over those plans with you for the Roosevelt reception."

If they had left Throckly's office a few moments later they would have seen a Hispanic man come up the back stairs, pause in front of the third-floor directory, then walk toward Throckly's office. He told the receptionist that he wished to speak with Mr. Throckly. She asked whether he had an appointment. He said he didn't. She told him Throckly was busy. He said it was important that he talk to Throckly right away. "He'll want to see me..." The receptionist sighed, and buzzed Throckly, explained the situation.

Throckly began to say through the intercom that he

was too busy when the man broke in, "I know where the medal is."

"Send him in," Throckly said.

The man entered Throckly's office, closed the door behind him. He wore baggy white kitchen-workers' pants, scuffed black shoes, a flowered shirt in yellow and green colors, a wrinkled, stained tan jacket.

"Well?" Throckly said.

"I work in the kitchen."

"What's your name?"

"Carlos Montenez. I wish to speak to you about the medal that is missing..."

"Go on."

"I know where it is—"

The director impatiently shook his head. "Don't play games with me, Mr. Montenez. That medal is not only very valuable, it's involved with a murder."

"I know that, Señor Throckly. It is why I've come to you. You must want it back very much."

Montenez sat in a chair and lighted a cigarette. "I will tell you where it is for money."

"Blackmail?"

Montenez shook his head. "A reward. When something worth a lot of money is missing, the owner must pay to have it returned."

"I'll call the police—"

"If you do that you will never see it again."

"How much do you want?"

"Five thousand dollars...and I know it is worth a lot more."

Throckly hesitated, then, "How did you get it?"

"It does not matter."

Maybe it didn't, Throckly thought..."I'll have to talk to someone else about this. I don't have the authority to pay rewards for stolen items. I'll be back in ten minutes."

Montenez snubbed out his cigarette. He obviously hadn't planned for this. It was taking too long. "Five minutes," he said.

"All right, all right." Throckly quickly moved into the reception area, then into the hallway and hurried to Chloe Prentwhistle's office. She was with Ford Saunders. "You won't believe this," Throckly said, "but there's someone in my office who claims he has the Harsa."

Saunders and Chloe looked at each other. Chloe said, "Who is he?"

"A Spanish kitchen worker. Look, it doesn't matter, he says he can lead us to the Harsa for five thousand dollars—"

"That's impossible."

"I know but—"

"I don't mean *paying* him is impossible, Alfred, I mean his having the medal. Where did he get it?"

"I don't know, I think we should call the police—"

"God, no," Chloe said. She opened her purse and took out a checkbook. "*I'll* pay him."

"With a check?" Saunders said.

"I'll go to the bank if he insists."

"Chloe that's—"

"Calm down, Alfred," she said. "Think a moment. Costain wants us to clean our own house. If we call in the police, this man in your office might well panic and run. Then what do we have? Nothing. But if we can actually get the Harsa back in our hands, we'll have the satisfaction of having accomplished it ourselves, and we'll *have* it. That's what counts..."

"There's only one thing to do," Saunders said, "and that's get the Harsa back. Chloe's right. We'll worry about the rest later—"

"But what if *he* stole it? What if he's fronting for someone—?"

"Alfred, this is no time to play what if. Let's not lose this chance."

Back in Throckly's office, Montenez was on the verge of bolting. "Too late, too late, good-by—"

"Wait, Mr. Montenez," Throckly said, "it means you may get what you want."

Chloe told him to sit down. She stood over him, checkbook in hand. "I understand you want five thousand dollars for the Harsa medal. Do you have it with you?"

"No."

"Where is it?"

"I will tell you when I have the reward."

"Do you think we'd turn over five thousand dollars to you without the medal?" Saunders asked.

Chloe motioned him to be quiet, turned to Montenez. "We'll go together to the bank and I'll cash this check."

They left the museum, drove in Saunders's red Chevy Citation to a suburban branch of Chloe's bank, where she cashed the check, then drove to Florida Avenue near Fourteenth Street, one of Washington's ghettos.

Saunders reluctantly pulled up to the curb. Two men drinking wine from bottles in paper bags scrutinized them as they got out and stood in front of a decrepit four-story building. The ground floor was occupied by a plumbing supply company. The windows were dirty; pipes and fittings strewn about on a carpeted ledge were barely visible.

"The medal is upstairs?" Chloe asked.

"*Si.* Come in."

They entered a small foyer, noted a scribbled sign over a mailbox: *Montenez*.

They climbed a shaky staircase to the second floor where a man was asleep in a corner.

Chloe asked Montenez which apartment.

Montenez went to a door, knocked, said something in Spanish. When no one responded he took a key from his pocket and opened the door. The others followed him inside. "Betty," he called. No reply. He went to a bedroom at the rear, Chloe at his heels. An unmade bed took up the center of the room. Montenez went to the room's only closet and pulled out boxes.

"Well?" Chloe asked.

"It's gone."

"The medal?"

"*Si*. She took it."

"Your wife?"

"*Si*."

"I knew this was wrong," Throckly said. "We should have called the police—"

"Where is she?" Chloe asked Montenez.

He shrugged and threw one of the boxes across the room.

"Are you sure she has the medal?"

He answered by cursing in his native language and slapping a dress against the window.

"Let's go," Chloe said. They left the apartment and proceeded to drive back to the museum.

"Do you think he was making it up?" Saunders asked as he eased into the flow of traffic.

"It seems *obvious*, doesn't it?" Throckly said, wiping his face with a handkerchief. "Don't you agree, Chloe?"

"It was worth the chance," she said. "And at least we didn't make fools of ourselves publicly by calling the police. This murder has had enough terrible publicity without adding to it. By the way, when this is over, make sure that man is fired."

Betty Rodriguez sat across the desk from Mac Hanrahan. On the desk was the Legion of Harsa. Hanrahan stared at it as though it were alive. Two other detectives stood behind him. A court stenographer was poised in a corner, waiting for something to record.

Hanrahan looked at Betty, who wore a white nurse's-aide uniform beneath a tan raincoat. Her thick, black hair was short and neatly combed.

"You realize, Miss Rodriguez, that this medal was stolen from the scene of a murder?" Hanrahan said.

"I know that," she said. "Carlos found it that night and brought it home."

"Carlos is your husband?"

She shook her head. "We live together as man and wife. His name is Carlos Montenez."

"And he works at the Museum of American History?"

"Yes, in the kitchen."

"He's a chef?"

"He washes dishes."

"Where did Carlos find the medal?"

"He told me he found it in the garbage when he was leaving work."

"The same night as the murder you've heard about?"

"Yes."

Hanrahan turned to one of the detectives. "Get me that list of people interviewed that night." Then to Betty Rodriguez: "Go on, there's nothing to be afraid of, you did the right thing by coming here."

"I *told* Carlos to bring it back to you. He said he would, but that he wanted a reward."

"From the police?"

"From the museum. He said that they would pay a reward for something so precious."

The detective came back with the list. Hanrahan looked it over. There was a section for kitchen personnel, and Carlos Montenez was on it.

"Did he tell you exactly when he found the medal,

Miss Rodriguez? Was it before or after the police questioned him?"

"I told you...he said he found it when he was leaving the museum. He said he walked out the back door and saw something shiny in a garbage can."

"A *garbage* can?" one of the detectives muttered. "Doesn't make sense, Mac. Why would somebody go to the trouble of stealing it, then toss it in the trash?"

Hanrahan ignored him. "Betty, you said that your husband—Mr. Montenez—brought the medal home and showed it to you. You also said that you told him to return it but that he wanted a reward. How did you end up with it?"

"When he left the apartment this morning to see the people at the museum, he told me to leave the medal where he hid it in our closet. I thought about it. It's been there since the night the man was killed, and every night I could not sleep thinking about it. After he was gone this morning I cried. Carlos is a good man but sometimes he thinks in ways that are wrong. Like many men."

"Who did Carlos plan to see?"

"I don't know, someone very important at the museum."

"The director?"

"He didn't tell me. When he was gone I decided that the right thing was to bring it to the police. Carlos had done nothing. He only *found* it, in the garbage."

"He withheld evidence and harbored stolen goods," a detective said.

Hanrahan gave him a look..."Do you have something to do?"

"Me? Whatever you say, Mac."

"How about going outside. Tell the desk to have my car brought around in front."

"It's right downstairs in the garage."

"Yeah, I know, but my leg's bothering me."

"What's wrong with your leg?"

"Get the car."

"Sure." He leaned close and whispered in Hanrahan's ear, "I don't buy her story, Mac."

A regular Sherlock Holmes, Hanrahan thought, and sighed. When the detective was gone, Hanrahan got up and walked into the bullpen outside his office and put through a call to Commissioner Johnson. "Cal," he said, "I think I've got a break in the Tunney case sitting in my office."

"What is it?"

"That's later. I want a lawyer here before I do any more questioning."

"Who are you questioning?"

Hanrahan gave him a thumbnail sketch of Betty Rodriguez. When he was through Johnson said he'd send someone over in fifteen minutes.

"Would you mind waiting a few minutes?" Hanrahan asked Betty when he returned.

"I have to be to work."

"Use my phone. Call them."

"I don't want to lose my job. I started only two weeks ago."

"They'll understand."

Fifteen minutes later a young, short, pudgy and pasty attorney from Legal Aid arrived. He was introduced to Betty, who said, "I don't need a lawyer. I didn't do anything."

"I know that, I believe that," Hanrahan said, "but it's better for everybody to have one here." He was not about to blow a lead because of some legal technicality. He'd done it before...

The attorney's name was Michael Petrella. "Have some Danish and coffee, counselor," Hanrahan said, then turned back to Betty Rodriguez. "Let's continue, Miss—"

"No...I brought this to you because I did not want Carlos to be in trouble. He has never been in trouble before. He did not steal this thing." She waved her hand at the medal on Hanrahan's desk as though it were an evil talisman.

"I told you I believe you—"

"Is she being charged?" Petrella asked, his cheek bulging with cheese pastry.

"No," Hanrahan said. "Get me Alfred Throckly at the museum on the phone," he told the remaining detective.

"What's his number?"

"Jesus." Hanrahan found Throckly's number in his files and dialed it himself.

"I was just about to call you, captain," Throckly said, having decided, in spite of Chloe, that he should tell the police. After all, he had *his* reputation to worry about too. "An incredible thing happened here this morning—"

"About Tunney?"

"Yes...a man walked into my office, said he knew where the Harsa was. He wanted a reward. I went with him to where he lives but the medal was missing. He claims—"

"That his wife took it."

Thank God, Throckly thought, that he'd volunteered the information..."How did you know that?"

"She's sitting with me. With the medal. Where's Mr. Montenez?"

"We left him at his apartment."

"How long ago was that?"

"About twenty minutes."

"What adress?"

Throckly gave it to him.

"You should have called me, Mr. Throckly."

"Yes... I see that now... but his story seemed so farfetched, we didn't want to seem foolish, bring more bad publicity on the museum—"

"Stay near the phone."

Hanrahan hung up and told the detective to go with a tactical unit to Montenez's address.

"To arrest him?" his wife asked.

"To bring him in for questioning."

"He found it, I swear."

"I'm sure he did. Does your husband have a gun?" She shook her head. "He's never hurt anyone."

"Bring him in," Hanrahan repeated to the detective, "but go *easy*."

"Coffee, Mr. Montenez?" Hanrahan asked.

"No, no coffee." Montenez sat next to his wife Betty. She'd put her hand on top of his.

"This is Mr. Petrella, Mr. Montenez. He's a public defender and is here to act as your attorney."

"I don't need a lawyer, I did nothing."

"Okay, but we'd like to hear from you what did happen this morning. It could help us, and maybe you too." He asked the detective if Montenez's rights had been read to him. The detective said they had. Hanrahan looked at the stenographer, then at Montenez. "The officers read your rights to you, Mr. Montenez, when they came to your aparment?"

"*Si.*"

Petrella, who'd been perched on the edge of the table containing the food, pushed himself away. "Mr. Montenez, you don't have to answer any questions if you don't want to. Are you charging him?" he asked Hanrahan.

"Maybe."

"For what?"

"Possession of stolen goods, maybe blackmail. I might hold him as a material witness, depending on what we find out here this morning."

"As your attorney, Mr. Montenez, I again tell you that you're not under any obligation to answer questions."

"Okay, Mr. Montenez," Hanrahan said, "please tell me as carefully as you can how you found this medal, what you did with it since finding it and what you planned to do with it this morning."

When Montenez had finished his story, Hanrahan said, "You say you had no idea when you picked it out of the trash that it had been stolen or was valuable?"

"*Si*, that is *right*."

"That was the same night Dr. Lewis Tunney was murdered. You didn't know about that either?"

"I knew that. The cops questioned me in the kitchen, like the others, but I didn't know about the medal."

"Didn't it seem strange that something with diamonds and rubies was in a garbage can?"

"Guess so..."

Betty Rodriguez put in, "I told him the next day that it was in the papers and that he should return it right away."

"Why didn't you, Mr. Montenez?"

"I wanted a reward. Why not?"

"And the people at the museum got the money for you this morning and went with you to get the medal?"

"*Si*."

"Who went with you besides Mr. Throckly?"

"I don't know their names."

Hanrahan leaned back in his chair and rubbed his eyes. "Mr. Montenez, you may be telling the truth, but I've got to make sure." And to Petrella, "We'll hold Mr. Montenez as a material witness and for possession of stolen goods—"

Joe Pearl came in. "Mr. Throckly from the museum is here, Mac. He's in my office."

"Good, I want to see him. Excuse me." Hanrahan and Pearl left as Montenez was led away for booking.

"Captain·Hanrahan," Throckly said. He stood and enthusiastically extended his hand. "What wonderful news. The Harsa is here, safe?"

"That's right, Mr. Throckly. No thanks, I might say, to you and your colleagues. Who was with you on your little junket to the Montenez apartment?"

Throckly hesitated.

"Who, Mr. Throckly?"

"Miss Prentwhistle and Ford Saunders."

"And nobody called the police."

"Please, Captain Hanrahan, try to understand—"

"I *do*, Mr. Throckly. Believe me, I *understand* . . ." He shook his head in disgust.

Throckly sighed and pressed his lips together. "Could I see the medal, captain?"

"It's on its way to the lab."

"Lab?"

"Examination, prints."

"When can we have it back?"

"When this case is solved."

"But we must have it back sooner than that. The exhibition is built around it—"

"Forget it."

"Can I at least see it?"

"Maybe in a few days."

"That's crucial, captain. We must ascertain whether it's the authentic Harsa—"

"It had *better* be, Mr. Throckly, or we're all going to look like asses. I'd like to speak with Miss Prentwhistle and Mr. Saunders."

"Oh? When?"

"This afternoon. Please arrange for the three of you to be at the museum at three o'clock."

By one that afternoon MPD was crawling with press. Radio and television were reporting a major break in the case and had even identified poor Carlos Montenez as a prime suspect in the Tunney murder case.

Hanrahan and Joe Pearl interviewed Prentwhistle, Saunders and Throckly at three. Their stories were the same. They all agreed they'd made a foolish mistake in judgment because of the excitement over the chance to recover the Harsa and, as Chloe said, "having a chance to clean our own house."

"I think they're telling the truth, Mac," Pearl said as they drove back to headquarters.

"You're probably right, Joe," Hanrahan said. "Damn it."

At four that afternoon Calvin Johnson came into Hanrahan's office. "The judge denied Montenez's bail," he said.

"Why?"

"The material witness aspect. I think it was right. I'd hate to lose Montenez too soon—"

"He didn't kill Tunney. I don't think he even stole anything. he's just a poor—"

"It's good to have *any* suspect around, at least for a few days. Takes some of the pressure off, and it won't kill him. He correctly read Hanrahan's expression. "It'll take pressure off you, too, Mac."

"What else can I do for you, Cal?"

"Two things. First, I just got off the phone with Vice-President Oxenhauer. He wants the Harsa returned to the museum so that it can be placed on display again."

"Impossible, we can't pick—"

"Nothing's impossible when the vice-president requests it. The Fourth of July is coming up and Oxenhauer wants things back to normal at the Smithsonian. Once the lab has gone over it I don't see anything wrong with giving it back. It's probably safer there than it would be here. Make sure they beef up security, that's all. It'll look good for us, Mac. We've gotten it back, and the place will be crawling with people wanting to see it. By the way, what are you doing for dinner tonight? Julia is preparing something special, we thought you'd like a home-cooked meal."

"What do you think I eat every night?"

"I know, Mac, you're a gourmet cook, but you haven't been over in a while. We'd love to have you."

"Thanks, Cal, but I planned an early night. Raincheck?"

"Sure. Think about the Harsa and the V.P.'s request, Mac. I'll check in with you in the morning."

"Okay. By the way, what do you tell the press when they ask why the jewel thieves would go to the trouble of stealing a valuable medal from a major museum, then toss it in the garbage?"

Johnson smiled and slapped him on the back. "The way we always answer those questions, Mac, by not answering. All we know is that through diligent, astute police work a major break has occurred in the Tunney case."

Hanrahan didn't smile in appreciation at such ingenious police p.r.

Ten minutes later Hanrahan received a call from Heather McBean. "Is it true," she asked, "about the Harsa?"

"Yes."

"That's wonderful . . . but what does it mean . . . I mean, in terms of Lewis's death?"

"Hard to say."

"Could we meet? I'm anxious to hear all about it. May I see the Harsa?"

"No, not yet, at least for a few days. About getting together, well...tell you what. I planned a quiet evening alone with some good food, wine, peace and quiet. If that appeals to you, you're invited. Do you like chicken?"

"Chicken? Is there a restaurant in Washington that specializes in chicken?"

"Yeah, my house. In all modesty, Miss McBean, there isn't a better cook in Washington than yours truly, and when the going gets tough, as it is now, I cook. I guess it relaxes me, makes me think I'm something I'm not and puts decent food in my cop's delicate stomach. Look, I'm not some lecherous old guy chasing pretty Scottish lassies. I'm a cop who likes to cook. What do you say?" Did he really mean all those disclaimers...?

"I say all right."

"Seven. I'll be at the hotel."

Hanrahan decided the entree for the evening would be chicken with dill. What he'd told Heather was at least partly true. He did love to cook, had taken courses in some of the city's best cooking schools and could lose himself in a kitchen the way some other people could in travel, movies, or museums. It also beat a sour-stomach marriage.

On the way home he picked up chicken breasts with the skin on, fresh dill and parsley, scallions and cherry tomatoes. He had the rest of the ingredients at home—half-and-half, mayonnaise, salt and white pepper. He arranged for everything in the kitchen, showered and headed for the Madison. It wasn't until he pulled up in front that he had his first twinge of doubt about the evening. She was British, and everyone knew that the

British were not exactly connoisseurs of gourmet food. She was a lovely young thing, and he felt for her, but . . . well, of the many things in life he couldn't tolerate, high on the list were doctors, lawyers, politicians, sexually liberated women who couldn't stop talking about it and insensitive palates. Put that last first.

CHAPTER 12

CONSTANTINE KAZAKIS STOOD AGAINST F. SCOTT'S black and chrome art-deco bar and sipped a Buck's Dream—kahlúa and Chambord blended with a scoop of French vanilla ice cream. He knew the young, attractive oriental girl next to him. She was with a well-dressed young man and was saying, "... and I'm really into love, romance. Did you read that article in Esquire on the death of sex? It was so right. Sexual liberation has destroyed love and romance."

Kazakis smiled. Three months ago, after they'd become acquainted at the bar and had gone to his Watergate apartment, she'd quoted another magazine about how love was insipid and she was "into my body," and so forth. What was it Emerson had said that he remembered from school? "... A foolish consistency is the hobgoblin of little minds." Ralph Waldo never met this lady ...

Just then he spotted Janis Dewey coming through the front door, watched her look around, catch his eye and make her way through a knot of dancers fumbling through a vintage Sinatra recording. She kissed him on the cheek, nestled the small of her back into the bar and closed her eyes.

Kazakis placed his hand on her arm. "Tough day?"

She opened her eyes and smiled. "Yes, very. You?"

"Like any other day in Washington's answer to Disneyland. Did you see the piece on the weighing of the Hope?"

"Yes. I looked for your name."

He laughed. "I'm the silent force behind the scenes. What are you drinking?"

"White wine. Are we having dinner? I'm starved."

"I'd planned on it."

"Here?"

"Why not?"

She smiled. "Because I always feel like an extra in a Busby Berkeley movie in here."

"Still watching old movies?"

"I like them. The new ones disappoint."

She took her wine from the bar, tasted it, grimaced. "Bar wine."

"We're fresh out of Taittinger blanc de blanc..."

"Sorry, Connie," she said. "I'm uptight—"

"About the other night?"

"Among other things."

"I enjoyed it, watching the aging contingent of the Smithsonian hobble about on their canes."

"Did you? Don't answer, of course you did."

"They do have their amusing sides."

"There are also sides that are anything but amusing. Amusing...I hate that word. It's too damn arch. Phony."

"Pardon me, keeper of the language and all things pure. Look, if you'd rather go home. I'll find something else to do."

"Maybe you should. I'm not your typical date for the evening."

"You're not my date at all, Janis," he said. "You

called me, remember? You suggested we get together and talk. Remember?"

"Let's get a table."

He ordered steak tartar, she had agnolotti in a rich cream sauce. They said little as they waited to be served. After the food arrived Constantine Kazakis said, "I have the impression that the cool and calm Miss Dewey might be on the verge of a collapse—"

"Don't be ridiculous."

"What's bothering you, Janis? It was a pleasant get-together at Walter's house. The pâté was good, the wine a cut above table variety and the conversation... well, the conversation was what it generally is, inside and competitive and—"

"You know I'm not referring to the usual chitchat, Connie. There are things Walter and Chloe said that bothered me."

"Such as?"

"Do I have to repeat them? They applied to you, too."

"You and I look at this whole thing differently, that's all. Relax, it'll blow over."

She squeezed her eyes shut and pressed her lips together. He reached across the small table and took her hand. "Easy, Janis, you're turning the molehill into a mountain." Her beauty suddenly hit him—creamy skin, a mane of auburn-bordering-on-red hair reaching down her back, full, red lips and intense greenish eyes, a tall, lithe figure with full breasts.

She opened her eyes, pulled her hand free. "I'm *frightened*, Connie, and I think I have reason to be."

"Frightened people make mistakes. All we have to do is not make mistakes and it'll be a thing of the past... eat your pasta, it'll get cold...

"Look Janis, you knew what you were getting into, and so did I. Sometimes nice simple things get complicated, and the key to handling them is to get back to basics...that's what Walter was saying. Remember? Lord, you should see yourself. You look like you've seen your mother's ghost. Relax, pull yourself together and let's get on with it."

"I may leave."

"Leave the museum?"

"Yes."

"Bad move. Only invites questions...do you want your pasta heated?"

"No, I want to go home. I'm sorry Connie..."

Kazakis returned to the bar after Janis left. The young oriental woman was now alone. "Hi," he said.

"Hello."

"I'm embarrassed, your name is..."

"Tina. Your name is funny. Greek. Connie, right?"

"Right, for Constantine. Where's your date?"

"How've you been?"

"Terrific. You?"

"Great."

"Where's your date?"

"He wasn't my date. He's my boss. He went home to mama. Where's yours?"

"Home to bed...Had dinner yet?"

"No."

"Want to?"

"Didn't I see you eating?"

"I nibbled. Come on, let's get out of here. I feel like Chinese."

He said it with a straight face.

CHAPTER 13

Hanrahan stood at a podium in MPD's main briefing room. In front of him were a dozen members of the Washington press corps. He read from a statement prepared by Commissioner Johnson, who stood next to him.

"A team of experts from the Smithsonian has examined the medal recently recovered by this department. The medal, known as the Legion of Harsa, was presumed to be the one stolen from the Museum of American History the night of Dr. Lewis Tunney's murder. The Smithsonian team has reported that the recovered medal is, in fact, that same medal. The Legion of Harsa has been returned to the Museum of American History for public display. A police laboratory analysis of it has, however, failed to shed any evidential light on the Tunney case. Nonetheless, we consider the recovery of the Legion of Harsa to be a significant move forward in our investigation. The man who had the Legion of Harsa, Carlos Montenez, has been charged with possession of stolen goods. He's free on bail. He is considered a material witness in the ongoing Tunney investigation." He did not add that he had ordered a twenty-four-hour surveillance on Montenez. What else could he do?

Questions came from the floor. Hanrahan held up his hands. "Sorry, I can't answer questions at this time." He looked to Johnson, who nodded. "The commissioner will take your questions."

Hanrahan then pushed through the crowd to the hallway, where he motioned for Joe Pearl to follow him. They went to the basement garage, where Hanrahan's car was parked. "Joe," he said, "I want somebody to go undercover at the museum."

"What capacity?"

"Capacity?... You mean disguise... well, somebody to fit into the kitchen."

"I suppose we could work something out with the catering manager—"

"No, I don't trust anybody over there."

"That makes it tough."

"Then get some undercover people working shifts as tourists. Have them keep an eye on the Harsa exhibition and rotate them."

"Okay, Mac. Where are you going?"

"The museum. I want to see that medal again."

Pearl smiled. "If this case goes on much longer you'll get cultured, Mac. I mean, beyond your stomach."

"I'm ready. Hell, I even own a tuxedo."

A large crowd was waiting to get into the Harsa-Cincinnati exhibit. Hanrahan stood patiently in line and listened to comments around him. The theft of the Harsa and its return was good for business. Almost everyone he eavesdropped on was talking about it. One matronly woman told her husband, "I've heard it's cursed, like the Hope Diamond. That's why that man was killed." A young man wearing jeans, rubber thongs and a T-shirt that read "No Nukes" told his girl friend,

"Maybe Thomas Jefferson got sore at the state of the union and came back to life." She thought that was a *riot*.

Eventually Hanrahan arrived at the Harsa-Cincinnati display case, where the two medals shone brilliantly from behind glass. He looked closely and noticed a sliver of wire with a pressure-point against the lower right corner of the Harsa pane. He was glad to see it. The case was now, finally, electronically alarmed, which it should have been in the first place, never mind all the fancy rationalizations of the staff.

A museum security guard stood six feet away and surveyed the crowd. Hanrahan thought of the Smithson bomber and thought that he could be standing next to him. All the attention given the Harsa would probably stir up the bomber's interest, maybe even prompt him to leave his next note there. Hanrahan at least felt good that he'd ordered undercover officers to keep an eye on things.

He strolled away from the exhibition and went to the railing that Tunney had fallen over. He looked down. The pendulum swung back and forth, slowly. A large group of people pressed against the first floor railing, waiting for the next red marker to be struck.

Hanrahan thought of the night Tunney was killed and of his tour of the darkened museum. He looked toward the archway leading to the First Ladies' Gown exhibition, walked through it until he stood in front of the display room he had admired that night. He stared through the glass for several moments. "Damn it . . ."

He proceeded to Chloe Prentwhistle's office. Her secretary, young, blond and almost attractive, nodded toward a closed door and told him that Miss Prentwhistle was in conference. "Would you like to speak to Mr. Saunders? He's Miss Prentwhistle's assistant."

He nodded. A few minutes later Ford Saunders appeared from an inner office, decked out in royal blue velvet jacket, gray slacks, black Gucci loafers, a white silk shirt open at the neck and a crimson ascot.

"Captain Mac Hanrahan, MPD," Hanrahan said, offering his badge. *This* guy had culture? A damn fop, Hanrahan thought.

"What can I do for you, captain?"

"Well, Mr. Saunders, I'm a little confused about one of the display rooms in the First Ladies' exhibit."

"What confuses you?"

Hanrahan glanced over at the blond secretary, who was obviously taking in every word. "Could we talk privately?"

Saunder's office was, not surprisingly, a symphony in antiques. The carpet and drapes were crimson, the walls stark white. Saunder's desk was an 1810 mahogany pier table with a skirt of crotch veneer and tapered, reeded legs. Against one wall was a Queen Anne slant-front desk on a turned frame, circa 1730. Its walnut, maple and pine sections were deeply burnished, and bat's-wing brass pulls were polished to glittering perfection. Prints with brass frames adorned the walls. The desk was bare. Not even a fingerprint marred its surface.

Hanrahan openly admired the desk.

"A perk of the museum world," Saunders said. "We have so many pieces *not* on display that we borrow them to decorate our offices. Please, sit down." He pointed to two cherry Chippendale chairs. Hanrahan sat; Saunders remained standing behind his desk. "Well, captain, what was it that confused you about the First Ladies' exhibition?"

"The number of mannequins in it, Mr. Saunders."

Saunders raised his eyebrows. "I don't follow."

"I counted seven today, Mr. Saunders, but the night of the murder I counted eight."

"Very mysterious," Saunders said, propping up his elbow and touching his mouth with the upraised hand, like the late Jack Benny, Hanrahan thought.

Hanrahan was put off by Saunder's manner, but this was no time for character commentary. He pressed on...."Is it possible that there *were* eight mannequins the night of Dr. Tunney's murder?"

"No, captain, I'm really afraid not. No disrespect intended, but there have been seven First Ladies in that room for years, unless one of them had a visitor and didn't tell us about it." He laughed. "You just must have been mistaken. I'm sorry..."

"Could be... I've been wrong before. Still..."

"Did you actually count them? Forgive me again, captain, but I've never heard of anyone actually standing there and counting the mannequins—"

"You have now." He realized, though, that Saunders made sense... but he was a man conditioned by years of attention to detail. It was in his bones.

"I didn't mean to—"

Hanrahan stood. "Thanks for your time, Mr. Saunders."

"I don't envy you, captain."

"For what?"

"For having to find a murderer in this, so to speak, haystack. Any leads, as I believe you call them?"

"A few."

"Call me if I can be of help."

"Sure. You bet." God, he really did dislike this guy.

He left Saunder's office and saw that Chloe Prentwhistle's door was now open. And standing just inside it were Chloe and Heather McBean. Chloe was smiling and had her hand fondly on Heather's shoulder.

Hanrahan waited in the hall until Heather came out. "Hi," she said, "what a surprise."

"Same here. I wanted to see Miss Prentwhistle, you seem to have gotten to her first."

"Captain...I wouldn't put it that way. Anyway, what did you want to see her about?"

"A couple of loose ends."

As they walked toward the elevators Heather said, "I just gave her the Harsa papers I brought with me from England."

Hanrahan stopped dead. "What papers?"

She told him about having found additional documents in her uncle's files.

"Why didn't you give them to me? Where are they?"

The elevator arrived, and they rode in silence to the main floor. As they stepped off, Heather said, "I had them in the hotel safe."

He didn't bother to point out that she'd only answered one of his questions. "Where are you going now?"

"I'd planned to see the Harsa, now that it's back on display. Chloe gave me a special pass to avoid the crowds."

"I just came from it, but I'll go with you, if you don't mind."

She looked at him. "So formal, captain. I like you better as a cook. And by the way, that meal was altogether as advertised."

He shrugged, masquerading his pleasure. At least the lady had good taste.

This time Hanrahan used his shield to gain entry to the exhibit. He and Heather admired the medals. When they were leaving the exhibit he asked if she'd like a cup of coffee.

"No, but tea would be fine."

They took a table in the public ice cream parlor

attached to the old-fashioned ice cream factory exhibit. She ordered Darjeeling tea; he had a butterscotch ice cream soda.

"I'd like to hear more about the papers," Hanrahan said.

"There's not much to tell. Actually they aren't very important, not at all, compared to the main body of documents my uncle sent to the museum when he donated the Harsa."

"Did you make copies?"

"I thought of it, then decided not to bother."

"Did anyone know you had those papers the day you were attacked? That was the same day your hotel room was broken into and searched—"

"My Lord, I can't see there'd be any connection...I mean, as I told you, those papers aren't important, they have no value."

"But someone who knew the papers existed might have assumed they were important."

She thought of mentioning Chloe, but decided not to...Hanrahan would jump to conclusions, and she simply wasn't going to be responsible for putting Chloe through needless grief, however momentary. She'd had enough, and she'd been very kind...Mac Hanrahan was doing his job and she respected him for it. Indeed, she was grateful to him for it...they both, after all, were after the same thing, and besides, except for his occasional grumpiness, he really was quite a decent man...very decent...but she was a big girl, it was her fiancé who was dead, and there were some things she could and would use her own judgment about...She finished her tea. "I suppose you could be right, captain, and I'm certainly not trying to tell you how to run your investigation...though"—and she smiled—"at times I suspect you think otherwise, but I honestly doubt it.

Anyway, the tea was delicious. How is your ice cream soda?"

He looked at her. She was a difficult lady to stay mad at.

"It's very good...it's tough finding a good ice cream soda these days." Along with, he thought, a good five-cent cigar and a good woman...

They left the museum through the Mall entrance. Outside, workmen were erecting sound stages and booths in preparation for the opening of the Smithsonian's annual Festival of American Folk Life, which would run from June 24 through the Fourth of July weekend. This year's festival was a salute to the artists, musicians and craftsmen of the British Isles and the state of Arizona. A strange twofer, Hanrahan thought.

"It's exciting," Heather said.

"Yeah, this is a good time to visit Washington." Hanrahan pointed to the 556-foot-tall Washington Monument. "You ought to go up in it while you're here. You ride an elevator up and walk down. They say that in really hot weather there's so much condensation that it actually rains inside, but you can't prove that by me. I went up in winter..."

"It's beautiful," she said, and there was a catch in her voice.

"Tallest building in Washington. Well, I'd better get back. Can I give you a lift?"

"No, thank you..." And there were tears in her eyes. Hanrahan wanted to put his arm around her, but held back. "I'm sorry, I should be past tears by now...it's just something that takes over and...I know you understand..." She turned, hurried down the steps and headed east along the Mall.

Hanrahan went inside the museum, and on to Chloe's office. She was on her way out when he got there.

"It'll only take a minute," he told her.

Back in her office, he said, "Miss McBean told me she gave you some documents or papers that related to the Harsa. I'd like to see them."

Chloe looked annoyed. "You know, captain, we *are* all on the same side here. Sometimes I get the feeling you don't feel that way." She picked up an envelope from her desk and handed it to him, obviously trying to hold back a blast of her indignation. "I just went through them. They're quite meaningless, sad to say, although it's always nice to have anything connected with a display."

"Can I take these with me?"

She gave him a look. *"Certainly.* May I also copy them first? It will only take a minute. I shan't smuggle them out." She told her secretary to make the copies. "Anything else, captain?"

"Well, I know you're annoyed with me, Miss Prentwhistle, and maybe I even sympathize with how you feel. In my work you do and say things that don't win popularity contests. Anyway, yes, there is something else..." And he proceeded to tell her about his confusion over the number of mannequins in the First Ladies' Gown exhibition the night of Tunney's murder.

She laughed a genuinely hearty laugh. "I don't wish to make light of your powers of observation, captain, but I assure you that there have never been more than seven first ladies behind that glass since Margaret Brown Klapthor put the whole concept of the exhibition into motion."

Hanrahan smiled more pleasantly than he felt. "I guess you're right, Miss Prentwhistle. It's been driving me crazy, that's all. I'm usually pretty good at counting heads."

The secretary returned with the photocopies for

Hanrahan. He quickly compared them to the originals, handed them back to Chloe Prentwhistle and left the museum, feeling frustrated, vaguely angry, and a little foolish.

CHAPTER 14

"How are you this morning?" Hanrahan asked Heather. He'd called her at the hotel and from the sound of her voice had apparently awakened her.

"Fine, thank you..." She yawned. "I don't much care for your television but stay awake until ungodly hours watching it."

"Join the club," Hanrahan said. "By the way, I hear you raised so much hell with Officer Shippee she's about to ask to be relieved from her guard duty."

"It all seems so *silly*. Things have calmed down now. No sense spending your taxpayers' money needlessly, and I honestly do feel uncomfortable with her being about—no reflection on the woman, of course."

"I'm sure. We'll see though. This is really our business...well, anything I can do for you?"

"I don't think so. Chloe Prentwhistle has arranged a meeting with your Vice-President Oxenhauer for me. I'll be seeing him at two. I'm pretty excited about that."

"Good. I'd be interested in hearing what he has to say."

"To look for anything that contradicts what he said to you?"

"That would mean I didn't trust my country's second highest elected official."

"Do you? I thought everybody was open to suspicion."

"Give me a call when you're through."

"I will..."

Joe Pearl, sitting in Hanrahan's office, asked him, "How do you evaluate her, Mac?"

"Evaluate? Joe...Joe...how you do go on." Hanrahan propped his feet up on the desk. "If you're asking what do I think of Heather McBean, I think she's a nice, straightforward young woman. I think she's been shocked by Tunney's murder, that she has a mind of her own and is determined to hang around until the murder is solved... What did you come up with on Ford Saunders?"

"Not exactly a plentitude. He's thirty-nine years old, single, never married, worked in other museums before coming to Smithsonian four years ago. Why the special interest in him?"

"Among other things, I don't like him."

"I didn't either when I interviewed him."

"What'd he have to say?"

"That he'd gotten sick and left the party early."

"Left Tunney's party early? You didn't interview him at the museum the night of the murder?"

"No. We picked up his name from the guest list, saw that he wasn't there when Tunney was killed and called him the next day."

"Where'd he go that night?"

Pearl consulted a typed sheet from a thick purple file folder. "He claims to have gone to a friend's house in Georgetown, guy named Norman Huffaker."

"And?"

"Huffaker confirms that Saunders showed up, said he wasn't feeling well and spent the night in the guest room."

"How'd the timing work out?"

"Fine for Saunders. Huffaker places him at his house about a half hour before Tunney was killed."

"What's the story on this Huffaker?"

Pearl leaned forward. "Mac, do you know you've got a hole in your right shoe?"

Hanrahan looked at it, thought of the late, great Adlai Stevenson, who as a presidential candidate displayed such a homey touch as well. "I'll get it fixed." What the hell, he thought, I'm no Adlai Stevenson.

"Yeah, you should. It's almost all the way through."

"I *said* I'd get it fixed, Joe. What about Huffaker? You believe him?"

"He seems okay, a little swishy but what's new?"

"You figure he and Saunders are lovers?"

"Maybe. Why?"

"Lovers lie for each other, have for centuries."

"If they're lying they got their stories straight."

"Anything else about Saunders?"

"Such as?"

"Instincts, Joe. Gut feelings. What are yours about him?"

"That he's gay, bright and probably too scared to lie. There's an interesting linkage between Saunders and some of the others, though. We picked it up by going through the personnel files at the museum."

Hanrahan burped, reached for the Tums bottle. "What linkage?" he asked as he dumped tablets in his hand, chose an orange one and put the rest back.

"Saunders's major reference for his job at the Smithsonian was Walter Jones."

"Jones? Oh, yeah, the art dealer and appraiser. So . . . ?"

"Somebody else who was at the party got her job with Jones as a reference too."

"Who?"

He checked the file. "Janis Dewey. She works at the National Gallery of Art."

Hanrahan stared at him.

"Mac, I always look for link-ups, the way I was taught. Jones is evidently tight with Chloe Prentwhistle."

"How tight?"

"Well, I checked around. It seems Jones and Prentwhistle—hey, what a funny name—Jones and Prentwhistle have been going together for thirty years. What struck me was that Jones has no official connection with the Smithsonian but he apparently gets these people jobs there."

"A benefactor?"

"If you say so . . . what's next?"

"What struck *me* was one of the curators at the party, a guy named Kazakis. He's a gem curator at the National History Museum."

"I remember his name."

"He used to design jewelry too, and was a pretty good gem cutter. And *he* used Jones as a reference, too."

"Interesting." Pearl stood.

"Where are you going?" Hanrahan asked.

"We're running everyone who was at the party through the computer. You know, the usual inputs to see what else ties them together. How they interface—"

"How they *what*? Jesus, I can't stand that computer jargon. It gives me indigestion. Okay, let me know what comes up."

"Will do. By the way, Mac, you could use heels on those shoes too."

"Get out, Joe."

"Just trying to be helpful."

At four that afternoon Hanrahan received a series of phone calls.

The first was from his former wife Kathy, who asked that they get together for, as she put it, "a serious talk."

"You in trouble?" Hanrahan asked.

"Of course not, but things have changed in my life recently that I wanted to discuss with you."

"Like what?"

"Please, Mac, it's been long enough for the bitterness to have gone. All I want to do is have dinner, or lunch, and talk. Is that so terrible?"

"Depends on what we talk about. All right, when do you want to get together?"

"How about tonight? Feel like whipping up one of your gourmet meals?"

"No."

"Name the restaurant."

"Café de Paris."

"Are you still going there?"

"I am. It's honest, the food is good, the prices are right. What time?"

"Seven?"

"See you there."

There was a moment of silence. "Mac," she said, "please come with an open mind. Leave the anger for a few hours. Okay?"

"I'll do my best..."

The second call was from Alfred Throckly. "You called, captain?"

"Yes. I wanted a list of the people who verified the authenticity of the Harsa."

"That list was submitted before we were allowed to come to headquarters to see the medal."

Hanrahan didn't try to hide his annoyance. "Give it to me again, if you don't mind."

"Just a moment." He came back on the line. "Chloe Prentwhistle, Ford Saunders, Constantine Kazakis and, of course, myself."

"Anybody from outside the museum?"

Throckly paused. "Yes, as a matter of fact there was. Mr. Walter Jones. It's standard procedure to bring in outside experts."

"Anyone else?"

"No."

"Well, Mr. Throckly, I'm glad you got the Harsa back. Thanks for returning my call."

The third call was from Heather. She sounded excited. "...he's such a nice man, your vice-president. I didn't realize how close he and Lewis were. He actually filled up when he talked about him."

"I gathered they were good friends. Did he say anything about what had upset Dr. Tunney before leaving London?"

"No. He told me that he and Lewis talked briefly and that they'd planned to meet the following morning. I wish they'd had a chance to talk. If they had, maybe, maybe..."

And somebody, Hanrahan thought, obviously didn't want the vice-president to hear what Tunney had to say... "Don't torture yourself, Heather..." It was the first time he'd called her that, and it came out so naturally neither of them seemed to notice.

She smiled quickly. "I'm sorry, seems I'm always going teary on you. By the way, Vice-President Oxenhauer pledged the power of his office to help get to the bottom of things...and when I returned to the hotel I had a really most pleasant surprise."

"Which was?"

"Evelyn Killinworth." She pronounced the first syllable of the first name "*Eve*."

"Who's she?"

"*He*. Dr. Evelyn Killinworth. I met him years ago when he was professor emeritus of Anglo-American history at Oxford. Evelyn and my uncle had struck up a friendship, as much of a one as Calum would ever allow. At any rate Evelyn left Oxford to take a professorship at Georgetown University and has been here ever since. I'd made a note to call him but never got around to it. Just as well; he's been in California for a month as guest lecturer at Stanford University. Now he's back, and actually was at the hotel waiting for me."

"That's nice," Hanrahan said. For some reason the news of another male in the scene annoyed him.

"You must meet him, he's very charming and I'm certain he could help sort out things—"

"Sure, well, I suppose I can use all the help I can get. Look, I have to go. Call me in the morning and maybe we can set up a meeting with this...how do you pronounce it—*Evil-in*?"

"Dr. Evelyn Killinworth."

"Give me a call."

"I will. And thank you. I mean that..."

Before leaving to meet his ex-wife, Hanrahan called Joe Pearl into his office, picked up a purple file folder from his desk, looked at it, winced. "Why are we using purple folders in the Tunney case?"

Pearl smiled. "I guess they got a good deal on them in purchasing. Why? You don't like purple?"

"It's not a matter of liking purple or not liking purple, Joe. It's just weird, that's all."

Pearl shrugged. "I kind of like it, Mac. The manila

ones are boring. You know, the same. It's nice to have some color in the files."

Joe Pearl, color coordinator, thought Hanrahan as he left the office.

"You look good, Kathy."

"So do you, Mac. I like the beard."

"You see much of the kids?"

"More than before. I think they're forgiving me...How about you?"

"Forgiving you?"

"Yes."

"No."

"I could never understand that about you, being a Catholic. Your religion is based on forgiveness."

"That's religion. We're real life."

"I know that, and what happened to us was real life too."

Hanrahan shifted in his chair and picked up a menu. He looked over it. "What are you having?"

"The usual."

"What's that?"

"You don't remember?"

"No."

"A fish broiled with garlic and a couscous salad."

Hanrahan told the waiter, "Broiled fish filet with garlic, two couscous salads and a shore dinner."

They shared a bottle of white wine. Hanrahan looked across the table at the woman he'd spent twenty-two years with, the woman who'd been mother to their three children. She looked no different than when they'd separated, all blue-eyed innocence, face shaped into a cameo defined by soft, natural black hair that reached the shoulders of her fuzzy, teal-blue sweater. She always looked so damn vulnerable. It was unfair. Hanrahan knew that underneath was a will of iron, a female survivor at all costs. Bet on it.

"Mac," she said, "I want to come back."

"Why?"

"Because it's where I belong, with you."

"You didn't feel that way a couple of years ago."

"I was wrong. I made a mistake . . . We do that, you know."

"Who?"

"Us human beings."

The waiter delivered their dinners. Kathy held up her wine glass. "To a new beginning?"

Hanrahan left his glass on the table.

She leaned closer. "Please, Mac, at least consider it." She put her glass on the table, he lifted his.

"Couldn't we even explore it? I'm sorry, Mac—"

"So am I. But that's as far as it goes . . . Eat, before it gets cold."

Over crème brûlée and coffee Hanrahan asked, "Where's the guy you took off with?"

"Bill?"

"Whatever."

"I don't know. We realized it wasn't working and decided to go our separate ways."

"What went wrong?"

"Everything." She laughed. "*It* was wrong."

"Made you feel old?"

"No, just foolish."

"Well, Kathy, I've got bad news, or good news, depending on your point of view. I've gotten over it. It took a while, wasn't easy, but I did. Right now I'm fairly happy as a bachelor. I have a pretty good life. There's no room in it—"

"For me? Or for anyone?"

"Not for you, maybe not for anyone. Who knows?" Only briefly did Heather flash in his head, but she *was* there for a moment. It surprised him, startled him. "Statistics say we men are getting married again right away because we can't cope with laundry and meals and stuff like that. I always handled routine things pretty good. As the months go by it's easier being alone. Maybe that's dangerous, but right now I'm what you could call contented...lonely at times, but content."

She touched his hand, he took it back.

"Mac, I'm sorry—"

"Don't be. You did what was right for you. Getting back together isn't right for me. Real life. Nothing to do with forgiveness. Or guilt."

"But what if it *did* work? What if we found we could have all those good times again?"

"That's a possibility, until..."

"Until what?"

"Until the next bearded flower child comes along who turns you on. Kathy, let's let it *go.*"

"I have to, don't I? I don't have a choice."

"I guess you don't. Look, I have an early day tomorrow..."

He walked her to her car. He wanted to hold and kiss her. She seemed so alone, in need of him. He fought back the urge. The fact was that she didn't need him for the reasons he needed to be needed.

"Good night, Kathy. It was good seeing you again. Take care."

"You, too, Mac. Thanks for dinner. It was good."

"I'm glad. No kidding..."

"I know...well, so long, Mac. We all sleep better knowing Hanrahan's in charge." She was smiling when she said it.

CHAPTER 15

THEY SAT AT A BANQUETTE ON LA BRASSERIE'S SEC-
ond floor, opting for air conditioning over the outdoor
café. Most people had chosen to be outside; the tiny
room was less than half full.

Across from them was a wall tiled in orange. Behind
their heads was French provincial blue and pink wallpaper. A small gas lamp on their table stood next to a
slender vase containing a single red rose and a frond
of leather-leaf fern. French accordian music was a
background.

Evelyn Killinworth shifted his six-foot, 300-pound
body on cushions upholstered in flame-stitch fabric.
He seemed too big for the room, like an oversized piece
of furniture in a dollhouse. He'd acknowledged it when
he and Heather were shown to their table. "They didn't
have me in mind when they designed the room," he'd
said pleasantly, "but they surely did when they created
the menu." He'd recommended the bourride, creamy
seafood bisque under a top hat of flaky, buttery pastry
that crumbled into the soup as they ate it. The salad,
another of Killinworth's suggestions, was salade Ray-
mond, crunchy walnuts and blue cheese with endive
and watercress. Heather fought against the notion of

dessert, but Killinworth prevailed, saying that the crème caramel was very good, which, Heather had to admit, it was.

"You're uncomfortable," she said as coffee was served and he shifted, as he had several times before, to accommodate his bulk.

"The price one pays for gastronomic indulgence." He laughed, causing his immense jowls to quake. His cheeks were unnaturally pink; a tatoo artist might have created them with needlepoint. The hair remaining on his head was stringy, inadequate for the dimensions of what was there to cover. His mouth was small and round, and he worked it even when not chewing. He wore a double-breasted blue blazer over light gray slacks, a custom-made white cotton shirt and red silk tie.

"I'm glad you're back from California," Heather said. "I'd thought so many times of trying to reach you but this has been such a dreadful week and..." Tears flowed in spite of herself, as they had earlier.

He took her hand, patted it. "You have every right to cry. 'Heavy the sorrow that bows the head, when love is alive and hope is dead.'" He delivered the words in deep, near-stentorian tones.

Heather dabbed at her eyes with a handkerchief. "That's lovely. Shakespeare?"

"Gilbert, *H.M.S. Pinafore.* You cry all you want, dear. Get rid of it, let it drain from you."

"It's so good to see an old friend."

"Of course." He placed his arm around her, and she buried her face in his shoulder.

When she pulled away, Killinworth took out a long, thick black cigar. "Do you mind?"

"No. Actually I like the aroma."

He lit it, being careful not to allow the flame to touch the tobacco, blew smoke into the air, grunted with pleasure, turned to her. "Any notion who killed Lewis, Heather?"

The directness of the question took her aback. She raised her dark eyebrows, shook her head. "I'm afraid not."

"I assume you've spoken with the police."

"Yes. There's a Captain Hanrahan who's in charge of the case and who's been very good to me. As a matter of fact, I'd like you to meet him."

"Fine. People at the museum? Have you spoken to Chloe Prentwhistle?"

"Yes. She's nice, a little odd but very decent."

He drew on his cigar and released its blue smoke.

"Do *you* know anything that might help?" Heather asked him.

"No, not any more than I could factually disprove the absurd theory that your Uncle Calum took his own life."

A tiny smile came to her lips. "That's right, you always shared my view that he hadn't killed himself. I believe that's the last time we talked."

"Exactly so. Now, let's get back to Lewis's death. I know it's difficult for you constantly to be reminded of it, but we must get to the bottom of things."

"You sound determined."

"Aren't you?"

"Of course I am, but I assumed your interest would be . . . well, more as a friend than a colleague."

"Why?"

"Maybe because I need a friend at this point more than I need a partner."

"I am your friend, Heather, but I hope that doesn't exclude me from caring about seeing Lewis's killer brought to justice. I think I can be of help. I know many of the people in the field. I understand them.

Lewis, I'm sure, was murdered by someone involved with his career and interests."

"Oh . . . ?"

"Why would you think otherwise?"

"I don't know . . . I suppose it's easier accepting the act of a demented person, a thief caught in the act, an irrational human being who acted on impulse rather than someone who'd thought it out ahead of time."

"Heather, what's important right now is for you to tell me everything you've learned, from any source, for any reason. I'm going to take notes . . . I'm afraid note-taking is a way of life with me. Please, proceed. Share your information with me and we can begin working together. You know, Heather McBean, your Uncle Calum always said that if you want to accomplish anything in this world, you must do it yourself."

She nodded, managed a smile. "I recently quoted him to that effect myself. All right, this is what's happened to date . . ."

After she'd filled him in on the details, he put away his notepad and said, "You must leave the hotel."

"Why?"

"After what you've told me, Heather, I'd say your own life is in jeopardy. Captain Hanrahan apparently thought so too. Whoever killed Lewis will be uncomfortable with you on the scene."

"But—"

"I insist. When I came to America I bought a quite handsome house in Georgetown. You're familiar with that portion of this city?"

"Yes, I've—"

"I live in the bottom half. Until leaving for California I rented the upstairs to a professor of linguistics at Catholic University. Frankly I think he was in the employ of the government, possibly the CIA, but that's neither here nor there. He was a delightful chap, very popular with the ladies if my ears served me right. At any rate, he's gone, Arizona or Utah—I'm afraid they all tend to be the same to me—and the apartment is furnished, clean and vacant. I insist you stay there for the duration of your stay in America."

"I couldn't."

"Why not?"

"I don't know, it would be taking advantage of a friendship and—"

"And your sense of propriety makes you uncomfortable sharing a house with a man? Nonsense. In the first place, I am like a father to you. In the second place, I stopped pursuing the opposite sex years ago, more's the pity, but there it is. In the third place, I have a splendid Victorian housekeeper who blushes at Walt Disney cartoons and who will see to your every need. No further discussion. Here." He handed her a key. "You'll come and go as you please. I shall never intrude on your sanctity unless summoned. Please, do this for me, and for Calum. He'd be horrified at the thought of you staying alone in a hotel. They're not safe, as you've found out, even the best of them. And they cost money, something that was very dear to his Scottish heart."

Heather looked at the key, then at Killinworth. "All right. Thank you."

"Splendid. We shall go to the Madison immediately, transport you and your belongings in my automobile and have you tucked in within the hour."

"I don't know what to say, Evelyn."

"Say nothing. You are a stranger in a strange city. I am your friend, the closest thing you have to family in this grand experiment known as the United States of America. Come, my dear."

* * *

When Mac Hanrahan called Heather at the Madison the next morning he was told that she'd checked out.

"Where'd she go?"

"We don't know, sir."

She called him later that afternoon, told him about accepting Killinworth's offer. "You must meet him, captain."

"Yeah, I'd like to meet him. Very much."

They made a date for lunch the next day.

CHAPTER 16

". . . AND SO, CAPTAIN, I'D SAY IT'S IMPOSSIBLE, AT
least from a professional's point of view."

"I appreciate your expert opinion, Mr. Kazakis,"
Hanrahan said. He had stopped at the Museum of Natural History on his way to lunch with Heather and
Evelyn Killinworth. He and Constantine Kazakis had
spent a half hour talking about the Harsa. Mostly Hanrahan wanted to know whether it would be possible to
create a good copy of the Harsa.

"You see, captain," Kazakis said, "it isn't a matter
of duplicating the craftsmanship. That's easy, if you
know what you're doing. The problem is in the stones.
When the Harsa was designed and assembled, jewels
were cut in a distinctly different fashion from the way
they are today. The difference would not be discernible
to a layman . . . but it would be to me."

"And you're certain the medal that's been returned
to the Museum of American History is, in fact, the
original Harsa."

"No question about it."

"Any dissenting votes?"

"What do you mean?"

"Was it a unanimous decision that it's the real McCoy?"

"Yes."

"How about Mr. Jones?"

"Walter? He concurred. Why do you ask?"

"Just curious. Well, thanks for your time, Mr. Kazakis."

"My pleasure, captain. Any progress on the case?"

"I'm optimistic. Let's leave it at that."

Heather had told him to meet her and Killinworth at Le Lion d'Or on Connecticut Avenue. Hanrahan knew that the restaurant was as expensive as it was good from having celebrated a few special occasions there over the years with his wife. He stopped thinking about that when Killinworth, after being introduced, said in full voice, "What a pleasure to have an esteemed law enforcement officer to lunch."

When they'd been seated Hanrahan ordered Gordon's gin on the rocks. Heather and Killinworth had wine, a Robert Mondavi 1974 Cabernet Sauvignon Reserve. It was obvious to Hanrahan that Killinworth was well known and welcome at Le Lion d'Or.

"Before we get down to the unpleasant business of discussing the death of Dr. Lewis Tunney," Killinworth announced, "allow me to suggest that we might order. If bear were in season I'd heartily endorse it, but since it isn't, the lobster stew, anything in puff pastry, duck breast with black currant sauce or venison are guaranteed to please." He looked at Heather and Hanrahan for their reactions. "The shrimp in basil sounds good to me," Heather said.

Hanrahan was tempted to order anything except what this *Eve*lyn Killinworth had touted, but he remembered once having had a great striped bass in pastry. He ordered it. Killinworth insisted on their sharing an appetizer of hot rabbit pâté.

"Well," Killinworth said to Hanrahan, "I don't envy your trying to sort out this nightmarish business. Needles in proverbial haystacks, it appears."

"Not quite that bad," Hanrahan said. "Heather tells me you might be able to help."

Killinworth, who'd tucked his napkin into his collar, delivered a modest laugh and shook his head in Heather's direction, then said to Hanrahan, "Modesty precludes me from admitting that what you've said might be true, captain. But the truth is, it could well be."

Hanrahan was now wishing he'd declined the invitation. He found the whale of a man across from him to be a monumental bore. But he reminded himself that the reason he was there was to get a line on Killinworth's relationship to Heather. He felt a rush of annoyance...possessiveness?...at her for trusting *Eve*lyn to the extent of moving in with him. All right so he was older, a friend of the family, but he'd come across a few of those that were also dangerous and dirty old men..."Go ahead, Mr. Killinworth," he said, "I'm listening."

"It's Dr. Killinworth," Heather said.

"Sorry...what do you think, doctor? What's your diagnosis?"

"I don't have one...thoughts, yes. Diagnosis, as you put it, no. I understand the Harsa has been returned."

"That's right."

Killinworth raised heavy, bushy eyebrows. "And you are confident it is, in fact, the Legion of Harsa?"

"According to experts at the museum, it's authentic, the same one stolen the night of Dr. Tunney's murder."

"You and your men are to be congratulated, captain. Retrieving the Harsa is a major coup."

"Minor compared to solving Dr. Tunney's death."

"Of course. What is a medal compared to a life?

Frankly, though, I would have assumed that the Harsa would never be seen again."

"Why?"

"Priceless icons have a way of disappearing once they end up in the wrong hands."

"Go on."

Killinworth dabbed at his mouth with his napkin. "Dessert?" he asked.

Heather and Hanrahan passed, Killinworth ordered a giant flaming orange soufflé. "Sorry, captain, but I can't pass up this soufflé. There's just none better. You must taste it... Now, we were discussing how valuable works of art and historic treasures tend to disappear once in the hands of the less-than-honorable. Obviously, all stolen goods have their channels of disposition, but with works of art, these avenues of distribution are... how shall I say it?... well, more esoteric, more difficult to follow. The buyer hides it along with his other illegally obtained items."

"I realize that fencing a precious jewel or historic medal is different than fencing a stolen TV set. Do you have any idea who might have bought the Harsa, if it had been fenced?"

Killinworth laughed, setting his corpulent body into motion like a giant jello mold. "Hypothetical, wouldn't you say, captain? No one, of course, bought the Harsa. It was stolen by an Hispanic dishwasher—"

"No, that's not so."

"The papers..."

Hanrahan leaned close to Killinworth. "I really enjoyed the lunch, Dr. Killinworth, and I've enjoyed meeting you, but I have a notorious short attention span. My ex-boss used to preach that any lunch not resulting in progress in a case was a wasted lunch." He looked at Heather to see whether she was offended. She didn't seem to be, maybe a little uncomfortable...

Killinworth, too, checked Heather for a reaction, then sat back, removed the napkin from beneath his chin, pursed his lips. He looked to Hanrahan rather like a large, pouting baby. His feelings had, Hanrahan realized, obviously been hurt, and Hanrahan was almost sorry for what he'd said. Almost.

Killinworth leaned the elbow patches of his gray tweed jacket on the table. He spread the fingers of his right hand across his lips. Hanrahan noticed that his fingernails were lacquered.

"Look, Dr. Killinworth, I didn't mean to offend you but—"

The fingers left Killinworth's lips and he waved them in front of Hanrahan. "No apologies necessary, captain. I was, I confess, a bit overbearing. Apologies should come from me."

"Forget it."

"Absolutely not. We've been fencing. You're here to scrutinize this stranger who's suddenly entered the picture, especially where Miss McBean is concerned. I assure you that I am Miss McBean's friend. As I was her uncle's. My intentions are honorable, my motives familial. I hope that reassures you..."

Hanrahan thanked him for lunch. He stood up and looked at Heather. "Glad to see you're in good hands, Miss McBean. Keep in touch."

Later that afternoon, Hanrahan received a call from Heather. She hoped he hadn't been offended at Killinworth's manner... "He's overbearing, I know, but brilliant and well meaning. He was very impressed with you. And it's true, he's like family to me. He—"

"I don't know why you're going through all this"— he didn't like the churlish sound of his own voice— "Killinworth doesn't seem to have anything to offer the investigation. I've no interest in him. But if *you're* comfortable with him, that's what counts. Like I said, keep in touch."

After hanging up, and telling himself he's sounded like a jerk, Hanrahan called Joe Pearl into his office. "A Doctor Evelyn Killinworth," he said, "I want to know everything there is to know about him, down to the color of his oversized shorts and whether he has holes in his socks."

"Why?"

"Why? Because I don't like him. He's too fat, pompous, arrogant, knows too much about stolen art, has conned the McBean girl into moving in with him and, on top of all that, manicures his fingernails, for Christ's sake. I *hate* men who have manicures. Color me prejudiced."

"Well, Mac, there's no arguing with cool, professional logic. Especially if it comes from one's boss."

CHAPTER 17

"GOT ANYTHING ON KILLINWORTH?" HANRAHAN asked Joe Pearl, who'd just entered his office carrying an armful of purple file folders.

"Working on it, Mac. We do know he taught at Oxford, then at Georgetown U. He—"

"Yeah, yeah, I *know* all that."

"Testy. Bad night?"

Hanrahan looked up, ran his hand over his beard. He had stopped to have it trimmed on the way to the office and had gotten the usual line from his Italian barber of many years... "I charge you for the beard, not the haircut. There's more hair on your face than on your head." Hanrahan had laughed, as usual, but his heart wasn't in it. For some reason his creeping baldness seemed more pronounced this morning than on other days. And it bothered him more.

"No, Joe, I did not have a bad night. In fact, I had a very good night. I made veal scaloppine in apple-lemon sauce."

Pearl raised his eyebrows. "That's wonderful. Company?"

"My mother stopped over."

"Oh." No wonder he was testy. "Mac, two things.

First, a guy from San Francisco called after you left last night. He said it wasn't important enough to bother you at home. He left his number." He handed a slip of paper to Hanrahan. On it was a name, Arthur Detienne, and a San Francisco area code and number.

"What'd he want?"

"He's an art dealer in Frisco, said he'd learned something that might interest you. He wants to speak with you directly."

"What else?"

"This." He pulled a sheet of lined yellow paper from one of the folders and put it on the desk. Hanrahan picked it up, squinted, looked up. "I can't read your damn handwriting."

"Sorry. I didn't get a chance to type it up. It's about Chloe Jones." He said it almost casually.

"Chloe *who*?"

"Chloe Jones. Chloe Prentwhistle was married to one Walter Jones in Maryland twenty-nine years ago."

"No kidding. I wonder why they keep it secret."

"Who knows...it's more fashionable to live together these days than to be married."

"I'll ask them. I'm going out to her house at eleven."

"*Their* house."

"Whatever. Got anything else?"

"I've got four undercover people on two-hour shifts at the museum, and I talked to the Smithsonian's insurance company. The Harsa would have been covered under the Smithsonian's umbrella policy even though it hadn't been added to the rider as a piece on display."

"Why hadn't it?"

"They hadn't gotten around to it. Evidently things grind slowly at the Smithsonian. It probably would have been on display for a week before the listing went to the insurance company."

"I see. You said it would have been covered anyway. Why?"

"Because it *was* on public display."

"Those are the only things covered?"

"No, but display items' coverage is much larger. The stuff in the back is valued at considerably less."

"So when the Harsa was in the back room, its insurance value was less than what it is right now?"

"True."

"The insurance people must be damned happy it was returned."

"You bet they are, but according to the guy I spoke to they never argue with the Smithsonian over claims. Its track record is solid."

"For things on public display."

"Right."

"What about things stored backstage?"

Pearl shrugged. "I don't know."

"Check it out for me. See how many things have been reported stolen from the back rooms and paid for by the insurance company."

"I'll get right on it."

Pearl started to leave the office. Hanrahan said, "Joe, put top priority on the Killinworth background check."

Before leaving the office, Hanrahan reviewed the Prentwhistle and Jones files. Jones's address was different than that listed for Chloe Prentwhistle. A detective had interviewed Jones at the address listed for him.

As Hanrahan drove toward the Rivercrest section of Northwest Washington and crossed the Potomac on the Chain Bridge his thoughts lingered on Killinworth's relationship with Heather and on why Chloe Prentwhistle and Walter Jones would marry but keep it a secret. He'd have a chance to answer the latter question himself. He hoped Joe Pearl's efforts would throw some light on Killinworth and Heather.

Chloe Prentwhistle lived in a modern, redwood-and-glass home set into a hillside, affording a view of the river, American University and the MacArthur Reservoir. As he drove into a circular driveway Hanrahan estimated it must be worth two hundred thousand dollars. Once he was inside he upped that by one hundred thousand.

Chloe greeted him at the door. She wore a madder-lake caftan and slippers with toes that curled up, and a pink bandana.

"Come in, Captain Hanrahan," she said pleasantly.

"Thank you. Nice place you have here."

"It's comfortable." She led them through a large foyer that was more an art gallery. Massive pieces of Calder, Haber, and Brancusi sculptures were pin spotted from the ceiling, and Matisse, Picasso, Braque and Hogarth paintings were handsomely displayed against white walls.

They went to a study at the east end of the house, where Walter Jones sat on a long, chocolate-colored corduroy couch. He was reading an art magazine, which he put down as Hanrahan entered the room.

"You've met Walter Jones," Chloe said.

"Yes," Hanrahan said. They shook hands.

Hanrahan looked at Chloe, who was straightening a small Graham Sutherland engraving. "Appreciate being able to see you on short notice, Miss Prentwhistle."

She turned. Gray light coming through a window made her appear, for a split second, to be a statue herself, Hanrahan thought.

"What can I do for you?" Chloe asked, and glanced at Jones. "Walter was just leaving..."

"Yes, yes, I was…" Jones said. He crossed the room and kissed Chloe on the cheek. Hanrahan tried to look at them as man and wife. They were the same height, both thin, a matched pair of storks. Jones was immaculately dressed in beige slacks, brown herringbone sport jacket, blue oxford button-down shirt and brown knit tie. He'd allowed the hair on his temples to grow longish, which gave him the appearance of having horns. Judging from his mottled skin, alcohol was not exactly alien to his life-style.

"You don't have to leave on my account," Hanrahan said.

"I was planning to anyway, captain. I just dropped by to catch up on a few things. Well, have a good chat. By the way, captain, any progress in the case?"

"Some. Small victories."

"Better than no victories." He started for the door.

"Mr. Jones—"

Jones stopped, turned. "Yes?"

"Before you go, I've something to ask both of you. I hope you won't mind." When neither of them spoke, Hanrahan went on, "I understand you're married, and have been for years."

Chloe managed a smile. "Why should you ask, captain?"

"No need for concern. Last I heard, marriage was still considered an honorable institution." If a damn near impossible one, he added to himself.

Jones went to a portable rolling bar and poured himself whiskey from a glass decanter.

Chloe seemed to have come to grips with the situation, carried a pleasant smile on her face, managed a nonchalant pose. "As you said, marriage *is* an honorable state, and, I assume, not yet against the law."

"I guess I'm just nosy by habit and profession. I wondered, though, why two people like yourselves would marry and not announce it, not live together as man and wife. I understand Mr. Jones has his own home."

"For tax purposes," Jones said, "if you must know." He'd returned the couch and was busy twisting fringe on an orange throw pillow.

"Tax purposes? How does—?"

"What business *is* it of yours, captain, how we choose to structure our personal lives?" Chloe said. "I emphasize *personal*. Does it, for example, have a bearing on the Tunney case? If so, please tell us how. If not . . ."

"You're right," Hanrahan said. "Like the press is always telling us, I've exceeded my bounds."

Her tone shifted. "That's quite all right, captain. Since it's come up . . . Walter and I decided when we married to maintain distinctly separate identities for professional reasons."

"I don't think I understand. Professional . . . ?"

From the couch Jones said, "You continue to exceed those bounds, captain—"

"Walter, aren't you going to be late for your appointment?" Chloe said. And then to Hanrahan, "Walter and I have been in the same field for many years, captain. Matter of fact, that's how we happened to meet. I have a responsible position at the Smithsonian, Walter is considered the most accomplished and knowledgeable appraiser in Washington. I often call him in on museum matters. I choose to do so because of his expertise, *not* because we are man and wife. However, too many people are unable to separate those relationships. You know, the wife or relative is hired because she or he is highly qualified, but everyone else raises eyebrows and speculates otherwise. We prefer to avoid the situations. When we married we knew we faced complications. We could have avoided all of them by not marrying, but we're not of the new generation that considers living together synonymous with the vow of marriage. All of which makes us rather hopelessly old-fashioned, perhaps anachronistic, but that's the way we are, and I must say we're proud of it."

"I trust you are now satisfied, captain?" Jones said, his face tight with anger.

"Walter, you really will be late for your meeting," Chloe said.

He stood, finished off his drink and went to the door. "I'll talk to you later, Chloe."

After he was gone Chloe, seated on the couch, said, "You must excuse Walter, captain. He's been under great strain these past few weeks."

"Since... but may I ask why?"

"Business, I'm afraid. And the Tunney situation has contributed to it. Walter was a great admirer, you might almost say a fan of Dr. Tunney's scholarship. His death has affected him."

Hanrahan nodded. "I can understand that. Well—"

"Drink?" Chloe asked quickly.

"A little early for me."

"You don't mind if I do, do you? I've been up since dawn, which tends to push up the acceptable time for the first cocktail."

Hanrahan watched her walk to the bar and pour bourbon into a tall glass. She added a splash of soda, turned and held up the glass. "To a successful resolution of this dreadful business."

"I'll sure drink to that," Hanrahan said, holding up his hand as though it contained a glass.

She joined him on the couch again. "So, captain, what can I do to help in this difficult job of yours?" Her manner had changed now that Jones was gone.

"You could tell me who killed Lewis Tunney?" he said with a straight face.

For a moment she was taken aback, then relaxed and shook her head. "That's your job, captain. But believe me, if I find out you'll be the first to know. Can I ask you to do the same? We make light to get through the gruesomeness of this, but I assume we do *not* take it lightly."

Hanrahan nodded. "I appreciate that, Miss Prentwhistle.

"Well, I have to be going. Thanks for seeing me, and for being so frank with me. I understand it hasn't been easy."

As they stood at the front door, Chloe said, "You're an interesting man, captain. I almost said attractive."

"Thank you."

"Still sure you won't stay for lunch?"

"Maybe another time."

As he drove back to MPD he thought that if he had stayed for lunch he possibly could have ended up in bed with her. Not that he would have. Beside not wanting to take unfair advantage—for all her facade she was clearly upset, vulnerable—he had a rule never to become involved with anyone connected with a case. That was rule number one. Two, he never messed with a married woman, no matter how unconventional she was or how much she pleaded marital miseries. Third, she wasn't really his type, although it did occur to him that with her *he* would be the younger one. He thought of Kathy and her twenty-five-year-old lover—and then of Heather McBean, and then quickly of rule number one. Too bad . . .

By the time he was back in his office he had decided that everything—the case, Kathy, Heather, Commissioner Johnson, Carlos Montenez, the press—was too damn much. He needed a break.

That evening he spent three hours making a lasagne Bolognese with chicken livers and béchamel sauce from a recipe he'd picked up on a trip to New Orleans the year before. He did not eat until ten, but by the time he did, fortified by a couple of extra dry straight-up martinis, no lemon twist or olive or onion, he felt a little better about the world. He cleaned up, packaged a portion of the meal to deliver to an aged widow the next morning who was on his parish's neediest list, had a cognac while watching a late-night talk show, then climbed into bed and promptly fell asleep. The only dream he could remember the next morning was one in which a life-sized Legion of Harsa medal occupied a king-sized bed. Surrounding it were Chloe Prentwhistle, Walter Jones, Heather McBean, Evelyn Killinworth and other unidentified persons. They were all naked. Instead of diamonds, the medal was studded with purple grapes, and everyone in the bed plucked them from their settings and fed them to one another. Hanrahan saw himself in the dream standing on the side and observing through metal mesh, which prevented him from joining in. He wore a loincloth. The last thing he remembered about the dream was that he had a full head of curly black hair, and that his thickening midsection was slender and tight. Dream on, you Irish idiot...

"Bless you, Mac," the aged widow said when he delivered the foil-wrapped meal the next day.

"Enjoy," he said.

"Chicken livers?" she said.

"Yes."

"I don't like chicken livers."

"You can pick them out." he said, kissing her cheek.

CHAPTER 18

"ANY DEVELOPMENTS?" COMMISSIONER CALVIN Johnson asked Hanrahan over lunch.

"Yeah, matter of fact there is, Cal. I got a call the other day from an art dealer in San Francisco. Name is Detienne. I called him back this morning. He tells me that there've been inquiries about the Harsa medal."

"What sort of inquiries?"

"People putting out the word that if it comes on the market, they'd be interested in buying it."

Johnson finished the dim sum on his plate, smacked his lips. Hanrahan had finished his meal long before. Calvin Johnson was the slowest eater Hanrahan had ever known. After sipping his tea, Johnson said, "Why would anybody look to buy that medal? It's back in the museum, isn't it?"

"That's what I said. Dietienne says the inquiries came up right after it was stolen, although one of them was brought to his attention the day he called me."

"Anybody we know?"

"As a matter of fact, yes. At least know of."

"Who?"

"Jubel Watson."

"The *congressman*?"

"None other, according to Detienne."

"A congressman interested in a medal connected with a murder? Jesus."

"That's what I thought. He's a big collector, it seems. How do you want to handle this, Cal?"

"He's a congressman. Any proof beyond what Detienne told you?"

"No, but I can ask around. The question is, am I free to confront Watson about it?"

"Of course."

"All right, I'll call him this afternoon—"

"Well . . . hold up a day or two. Let me evaluate the situation before we jump."

Hanrahan felt a sour lump in his stomach, although he could have predicted the commissioner's reply. As they drove back to MPD from the Golden Palace he brought up the subject of vacation time due him.

"Now now, Mac," Johnson said, "not in the middle of this thing."

"The problem is, Cal, I promised my sister in New Orleans I'd come down for her twenty-fifth wedding anniversary. I hate to miss it. She's my favorite."

"Not now, Mac."

"I'm committed. I won't take a full week, just a couple of days. Besides, I need it. A few days away and I'll be able to look at the Tunney thing a little clearer. I hope."

Johnson walked Hanrahan to his office. "Okay, go, but make it quick."

Afterward Hanrahan debated calling Heather to tell her he would be away, then decided against it. For some reason he felt annoyed with her . . .

But the moment he was on the plane two days later he regretted the decision. "Childish," he told himself. Am I jealous of that pompous old bird?

He called her from his sister's house. She told him

she was happy that he managed to get away for a few days, then added, "I'm thinking of a trip myself."

"Where to?" he asked, hoping he sounded more indifferent than he felt.

"London, then to Edinburgh. Evelyn has to go back on business, and it would be a good time for me to tidy up loose ends and talk with Mr. Paley about what progress he's made."

"When would you go?"

"No definite plans yet. I'm sure you'll be back before I leave."

"Sure... well, if I'm not, have a good trip."

"It's Captain Hanrahan," he heard her say to someone in the background. And then he heard Killinworth's booming voice say, "Give him my best."

Whatever that is, Hanrahan thought.

CHAPTER 19

Hanrahan returned to Washington the night of June 19, a Friday. There was a message on his desk from Heather McBean. He called her.

"Nice trip?"

"Yes."

"Welcome back."

"Thank you. Are you still going to London?"

"Yes, on Sunday."

"He's going with you?"

"Evelyn? Yes. It was his idea."

"Oh? Look, when you get back, call me. Maybe things will have broken by then . . . Is there some place I can call you if I need to while you're away?"

"We're staying at the Chesterfield in London. It was Lord Chesterfield's home and—"

"Okay, okay. Maybe I'll be in touch."

"After that we'll be in Scotland. I suppose I'll stay at the castle."

"Your uncle's?"

"Yes. It's dank and cold, like a castle is supposed to be, but it was home to me for many years."

"Well, take care. How long will you be gone?"

"Less than a week, I expect."

Hanrahan next placed a call to the offices of Congressman Jubel Watson and was told that Watson was out of town and would not return until the following Tuesday. Hanrahan wasn't sure what he would have said to Watson had he been there, because of Commissioner Johnson's hedge about time. Still, he felt it was okay to find out where the man was.

He worked in his office on Saturday and Sunday. Joe Pearl worked Saturday too, and together they pored over every available scrap of information on the Tunney case, looking for some discrepancy, inconsistency, indiscretion, *any* damn thing that might trigger or at least open up a new avenue of investigation. There weren't any, aside, that is, from what had already aroused Hanrahan's interest. They went over that list:

a. Evelyn Killinworth. Hanrahan didn't like him, which of course hardly made the man a murderer, or crook. It didn't disqualify him either.

b. Prentwhistle and Jones secretly married. Was there more to it than the explanation he got?

c. Jones getting jobs for Ford Saunders. A connection, but so far no significance.

d. Ford Saunders. He left party early, was vouched for by possible homosexual lover Norman Huffaker. No crime there either. Unless somebody was lying.

e. Harsa medal examined and validated by "insiders." Hanrahan added the quotes after he'd listed the item.

f. Hanrahan's count of mannequins in First Ladies' exhibition. Was he seeing things?

g. Vice-President Oxenhauer's relationship with Tunney, and his being the driving force behind the Harsa-Cincinnati exhibit.

h. The attack on Heather, followed by the search of her hotel room. Connected?

i. What Tunney knew before leaving London that upset him, and how much of it he told Oxenhauer in spite of the veep's denial.

j. Carlos Montenez and the Harsa being dumped in a garbage can. "Professionals?"

k. Possible link between Heather's uncle's alleged suicide and the Tunney murder?

l. Killinworth's knowledge of an art black market.

m. Killinworth in general. See *a*.

n. Congressman Watson alleged by Detienne to be looking to buy the Harsa through illegal connections.

o. Who's Evelyn Killinworth? See *a* and *m*.

Hanrahan spent Sunday doing what he usually ended up doing in a difficult case, creating possible scenarios. Pearl had suggested a few, and Hanrahan had come up with another half dozen. None of them played worth a damn. He packed up his briefcase at eight and went home, settled into a black recliner and took out Joe Pearl's report on Evelyn Killinworth. It was complete, and inconclusive. The item that did catch his eye had to do with Killinworth's finances. According to what Pearl had come up with, Killinworth's only source of income was his teaching and lecture fees. Hanrahan thought of the lunch at Le Lion d'Or, of Killinworth's general expansiveness: "Owns a house and doesn't need the rent from the other apartment... Well known at expensive restaurants... Flies off to London... Dresses expensively."

At midnight he received a call from his mother, who said, "I understand you had dinner with Kathy."

"That's right."

"So?"

"So what?"

"What did you talk about?"

"Things."

"Be careful."

"Of what?"

"Of her. Remember what I told you when she left."

"How could I forget?"

"People are strange, my dear. They seem to be one thing in the bright sunlight, but when night falls all sorts of strange sides come out."

"I didn't know that."

"Don't talk fresh to your mother."

"I'd never be fresh with you, mama. I'm a dutiful, loving son."

"I know you are, and that's why I want you to watch your step. Women like Kathy are out for what they can get, no matter who gets hurt."

"Mama, she's the mother of your grandchildren."

"And, she's Baptist."

"I've had a tough day, ma. Thanks for calling."

"Just be careful, Mac, that's all I ask."

Hanrahan smiled. "Are you sure you're not Jewish?"

"Don't be fresh. You may be grown up but I still remember you in diapers."

The image made him feel the same way. "Go to sleep and stop worrying."

"Give me a reason."

"Because it's late.

"I woke you. I'm sorry. Are you still working on that murder at the museum?"

"Yes."

"Look for the woman."

"Huh?"

"They say he was handsome, brilliant, rich, the sort of man a woman would kill for."

"I'll make a note."

"Good. Call me once in a while."

"I'll do that. I love you, ma. Good night."

"Good night, son. Be a good boy."

CHAPTER 20

"BRITISH AIRWAYS FLIGHT 276, DIRECT SERVICE TO London, is now ready for boarding through Gate Number Three. Passengers traveling with small children may board first."

Heather glanced at her watch as she put coins in a phone booth. Eight-twenty. Their flight would depart Dulles at 8:45, arriving the following morning at 8:45, London time. Killinworth was across the terminal buying a newspaper. He wore the largest tan trench coat Aquascutum made, and a red plaid rain hat that was too small for his head. From the rear, it occurred to Heather that the effect was like a cherry atop a mound of coffee ice cream.

"Hello, this is Heather McBean," she said when her call was answered. "Is Chloe Prentwhistle there?"

"No, she's not," Ford Saunders said. He told her who he was.

"Oh, yes, Mr. Saunders...well, I wanted to ring her up to say good-by before leaving for London."

"Did she know you were going?"

"I told her I intended to but wasn't definite. My flight leaves in twenty minutes."

"I'll certainly tell her. Should I say how long you'll be gone?"

"A week at most, I imagine. I'll be staying at the Chesterfield in Mayfair in case she needs to contact me. I plan to spend a few days in Edinburgh the end of the week, at my late uncle's castle, but I should be back by next Sunday."

"Well, have a safe trip. I'll tell Chloe when—"

"*British Airways Flight 276 is now boarding...*"

"I must run, Mr. Saunders. Thank you."

Heather and Killinworth walked through a door leading to a large people-mover that took them to a waiting 747. A male flight attendant showed them to their seats in the Super-Club section, which represented a compromise. Killinworth had wanted to fly first class, where the seats would better accommodate his bulk, but Heather considered it an unnecessary extravagance since the club seats were just as large. "*Chaip*," he kidded her, using the Scottish idiom for cheap. "*Wastrie*," she'd responded. They sat two abreast. "*Twa in a raw*," she said in Scottish, smiling.

The aircraft began its takeoff run, slowly at first, then gaining speed until it groaned into flight, eventually reaching its transatlantic cruising altitude of 39,000 feet. The captain announced that their arrival would be ahead of schedule because of a 155-mile-per-hour tailwind.

"Will you be staying at the castle?" Killinworth asked

after an hors d'oeuvre of garnished smoked Scottish salmon on buttered brown bread had been served.

"I'd like to," she said, "although now that the conversation is under way for public access there's just Agnes and she's only there from time to time. I'll see how the loneliness sits."

"I might be able to get up for a day, perhaps an overnight," Killinworth said. "Hard to say. It depends on how things go in London."

"You never told me what business you're on," Heather said.

"Nothing of much importance," he said, sipping white wine. "Are you certain you want to see this Paley chap?"

"Yes, I want to know what he's found out about Lewis's activities before he left London. I can't help believing that that has some bearing on his death...I think Captain Hanrahan agrees with me."

"Really? Well, frankly, Heather, I don't much like that chap, although I must admit a certain bias against anyone who wears a badge."

"That's cynical."

"Perhaps. But I can't help thinking of your uncle's alleged suicide, and the handling of it by the Edinburgh police. That was enough to turn even an optimistic soul like myself into a cynic."

The captain announced that they were about to encounter air turbulence and that seat belts should be securely fastened. Killinworth fingered his belt, which was extended to its maximum length.

Heather looked out the window and watched the giant aircraft's wings flex in the choppy air. She realized how much she missed London and Edinburgh. It would be good to be home, no matter what the circumstances or how short the stay. She needed to touch base again with friends, many of whom she'd met while working at the British Museum, and once again to experience familiar places that had provided such warmth and pleasure. Her only reservation was agreeing to stay at the Chesterfield. Its bar and restaurant had long been particular favorites of hers, and it was in the Chesterfield's private octagonal salon where she, Lewis Tunney and ten of their friends had gathered to celebrate her birthday and, it turned out, their engagement. At first she'd balked at Killinworth's suggestion that they stay there. It would be too painful, she told him. But he convinced her that "the best thing to do after falling off a horse is to climb right back on. Besides, the Chesterfield has been like a home to you in London. I insist that we stay there..."

During the movie, which neither of them wanted to see, Heather napped. Killinworth read a succession of magazines provided by the flight attendants. Heather awoke as Killinworth struggled to leave his seat to buy something from the inflight duty-free shop—a five-pack of Henri Winterman half-corona cigars for himself, and L'Air du Temps perfume for her.

"How did you know I liked this brand?"

"A keenly honed sense of smell and an appreciation for the more genteel fragrances of life. Actually, my dear, I noticed it in your purse."

Killinworth retrieved his double-breasted blue blazer and trench coat from the overhead rack as the captain announced they would be landing at London's Heathrow Airport in twenty minutes. He struggled to get into them and was perspiring and breathing heavily when he sat down and buckled his seat belt.

"Are you all right?"

"The world was designed for midgets and skinny people," he grumbled. "Yes, I'm all right. You?"

"In grand fettle."

He looked at her and shook his head. "You should

discard any remnants of your Scottish linguistic past, my dear. It sounds too quaint."

She laughed. "One thing Uncle Calum couldn't stand was someone who speaks pan loaf."

"What the devil does *that* mean?"

"An affected English accent. Calum was very proud of being Scottish, you know. He insisted that I be too."

"You haven't disappointed him."

"I hope not." She thought of her uncle...he *was* quintessentially Scottish, a highlander by birth, a Midlothian most of his adult life after moving to Edinburgh in his teens, proud and stubborn, hard as nails, often caustic and seemingly cold, but as Heather knew better than anyone, with a wide and deep vein of kindness, and love, that showed itself at odd times and in odd ways. She knew she was about to cry, took a deep breath and said lightly, "Allow me my Scottish phrases, Evelyn, at least in Calum's memory."

"Of course, my dear."

They rode a moving sidewalk at Heathrow to Baggage Claim and Customs. Heather had suggested in Washington that they rent a car, but Killinworth had vetoed it. "In this world of chaos, confusion and man's lack of civility toward his fellow man, the London taxi remains a linchpin of civilization. Of the myriad things I miss about London, it is the taxi that heads the list." He'd even quoted a poem by Ogden Nash:

The London taxi is a relic
For which my zeal is evangelic.
It's designed for people wearing hats,
And not for racing on Bonneville Flats.
A man can get out, or a lady in;
When you sit, your knees don't bump your chin.
The driver so deep in the past is sunk
That he'll help you with your bags and trunk;

Indeed, he is such a fuddy-duddy
That he calls you Sir instead of Buddy.

And so they rode a black London cab from the airport to Charles Street, in Mayfair, where Heather was warmly greeted by members of the Chesterfield's staff. They were shown to their rooms, Heather's on the second floor, Killinworth's on the third. After unpacking they met for a drink in the library, a handsome, paneled room where guests could order from room service twenty-four hours a day. Heather said little. Killinworth seemed fired up over being back in London and indulged himself in a monologue on the role of Britain in the world community and the reasons for its decline. He might have gone on for a second hour if a group of Americans had not come into the library and sat down on couches across from them. The new arrivals obviously found Killinworth amusing, not only because of his bombastic, pontifical speeches but because he'd come from his room wearing a red-and-green oriental dressing gown over his trousers and shirt, plus red carpet slippers.

"I think I'll get to bed," Heather said. "I want to feel fresh tomorrow."

"You go ahead, my dear," Killinworth said, rising and gesturing toward the door. "Sleep well. We'll breakfast together?"

"What time?"

"Nine."

They had breakfast in the Buttery.

"One of those bloody Americans actually had the cheek to ask whether you were my daughter," Killinworth said.

Heather smiled. "What did you say?"

155

"I said you were my sixth wife and the mother of my tenth and eleventh children."

"You didn't."

"No, but I should have."

"Well, time to get started," Heather said. "Will I see you later on?"

"Depends on where you and I are later on. I suppose we could rendezvouz for tea. What time are you meeting with the private peeler, Paley?"

She looked blankly at him.

"Private eye, gumshoe. Surely you know that bobbies were originally called peelers, after Sir Robert Peel. Why they changed it from his last name to his first is beyond my comprehension. It's precisely the sort of thing I was talking about last night when we were interrupted by those Americans. Such changes in a people's traditions, minor as a slang term for police officer might be, are typical of what erode the underpinnings of a society. If you go back in time you clearly see that . . ."

She listened until he paused to finish his tea, quickly stood and said, "I really must go, Evelyn. Will we meet here for tea?"

"No, the Dorchester. I prefer its traditional approach. You didn't answer my question about your meeting with Paley. When does that take place, and where?"

"I don't know. I'll call him later this morning. Now don't worry about me."

"Well," he said as they walked through the lobby and headed for the street. "if you change your mind, leave a message with the desk. I'll call in."

Heather insisted that he take the lone cab parked in front of the hotel. "I could use the walk," she said. She watched him drive off, then proceeded briskly to Curzon Street, went north on Park Lane, the Dorchester and Grosvenor House hotels on her right, the vast stretch of Hyde Park greenery on her left. She reached Marble Arch, where she was almost run over because she looked left instead of right before crossing the street. She had had the same problem in reverse in Washington, and had just gotten accustomed to being a pedestrian in a right-hand drive city when she left.

She reminded herself to look in the appropriate direction as she walked east on Oxford until reaching Tottenham Court Road in Bloomsbury. A few minutes later she stood in front of the neoclassical facade of the British Museum, Britain's vast and most celebrated storehouse of past cultures and peoples, millions of items consecrated to the benefit of millions of yearly visitors.

She was hesitant about climbing the steps, just as she'd been reluctant to return to the Chesterfield, another scene of happy times and promise of more that had been destroyed with one fast, cruel thrust of Thomas Jefferson's sword.

She entered the building beneath sculptor Sir Richard Westmacott's Victorian frieze and looked to her right, where over ten million volumes, manuscripts, music scores and philatelic collections were stored and displayed in the galleries of the British Library, including the Magna Carta, Shakespeare's first folio and the Gutenberg Bible. Directly in front of her was the British Library Reading Room, open only to scholars with special credentials. She rode the lift to the upper floor and meandered through galleries containing medieval, western Asiatic and Egyptian collections until she reached the prints-and-drawings section where she'd worked before Calum's death.

"Heather," a male voice said. She turned to see Bryan Mills approaching. They'd worked closely together, and he was one of her favorites. They shook hands, saying nothing until Mills said, "I'm sorry, Heather, about what happened."

"I know you are, Bryan. Thank you." She forced lightness into her voice. "Well, what's new at the B.M.?"

He shrugged. "Not much, really, at least up here in Prints. We did a Michelangelo drawings special that wasn't too well received. They're fighting now over whether to mount a special on Rubens or Lorrain. Lampl's carrying a brief for Lorrain but Mrs. Markham queered his pitch and is pushing Rubens. She usually wins, as you probably remember."

Heather looked around the large room. "Yes, I remember, Bryan." She remembered many things. Too many.

"Free for lunch?" he asked.

"Yes, but first I need to make a couple of phone calls."

"Use the office."

She found Elwood Paley's number in her purse, dialed it. He answered on the first ring.

"It's Heather McBean, Mr. Paley."

"Oh, yes, how are you, Miss McBean?" He had a thick Cockney accent and vocal cords that sounded as though they'd been filed down with a rasp.

"I'm in London. Could I see you?"

He cleared his throat. "Well, I suppose we could, but I don't have much to report. Of course I'm still working on it day and night."

Her heart sank. *"Nothing?"*

"Not quite that bad, luv. You can judge for yourself."

"When can I see you?"

Another long pause and a stutter-step start. "Can't be today, I'm afraid. Terribly busy."

"Look here, Mr. Paley, if you've discovered anything, *anything* at all, I must know about it. I won't be here long. I'm flying to Edinburgh in a day or two, then back to America."

"Well, I suppose I could this evening but it would be bloody thin time—"

"Just tell me *where* and *when*."

"I've urgent business in the East End. If you don't mind treking over there I could—"

"What *time*?"

"Eight. It's a pub called the Quid, on Cable Street."

Heather knew the street and the area, although she hadn't spent much time there. The East End was a tough, waterfront district, Jack the Ripper's territory. She'd visited a pub in that area a few times, the Prospect of Whitby, directly on the Thames and created from an abandoned coastal sailing ship in the eighteenth century. Drinkers used to watch hangings on Execution Dock from the pub's windows, where the tide drowned chained victims, including Captain Kidd.

"I'd prefer the Prospect of Whitby," Heather said. "It's nearby, on Wapping Wall."

"Wouldn't set foot in such a tourist trap, ma'am. Urgent business will have me at the Quid. Best I can do."

He was certainly damnably independent. But right now she didn't feel in any position to quibble over protocol. "I'll be there at eight."

Moments after hanging up on Paley she felt even more angry at his treatment of her. She was, damn it, paying him. But she forced herself to forget about it and spent the rest of the morning talking to Mills and other staffers who'd been at the museum during her employment. Four of them went to lunch at a nearby pub, where in spite of heroic attempts to steer clear of Tunney's murder the conversation eventually got around to it. At first, Heather had great trouble talking about it. Then she told everything she knew, and even gave a chronological account of her Washington experiences. In the end, she felt a little better.

Evelyn Killinworth, too, had lunch, but not in a pub. He shared a table at the Savoy, overlooking the Thames, with a tall, attractive blond woman in her mid-forties. Killinworth had spent a portion of the morning at a branch of the Barclay Bank, where he maintained a sizable account. He had gone on to Lewin on Jermyn Street to order four custom-striped dress shirts, then to Nutters, his favorite tailor on Savile Row, where after receiving a warm greeting from Tommy Nutter himself he ordered two suits costing seven hundred pounds each.

Killinworth and his companion left the Savoy at two-thirty. They stood on the sidewalk, and she handed him a set of keys. "You really are a despicable bastard, Evelyn," she said.

He laughed. "I prefer to think of myself as simply being astute, brilliant and knowing which buttons to push. Besides, you ought to be a little more selective with whom you sleep. Have a splendid day, and thank you."

He hailed a passing taxi. The driver pulled down the window. Killinworth said, "Belgrave Place in Belgravia, please."

He sat back in the spacious comfort of the immaculately clean black Austin taxi and watched London slide by his window, tiny side streets chosen by the driver to avoid Trafalgar Square's congestion, down Piccadilly to Wellington Arch and then into the quiet, refined section of London known as Belgravia, stately foreign embassies flanking elegant private townhouses, one of them the scene of the popular British television program, "Upstairs, Downstairs."

Most of the buildings were of off-white stone, and the taxi stopped in front of one of them, three stories tall, on Belgrave Place. Four fluted columns defined the entryway. Large black gilt-decorated doors with ornate brass knockers were formidable, as was a high black wrought-iron fence with sharp spikes that flared out in two directions, making entering *and* leaving difficult except for the most athletic of intruders.

Killinworth paid the cabbie, tipped him ten percent, received a polite "thank you" and went to the iron gate. He pressed a button. Curtains on a window to one side of the door fluttered, then hung still. The door did not open. Killinworth pressed the button again. Now the doors opened and a short man of obviously Arabic origins stepped onto the small, curved top step. "Killinworth?" he asked in a singsong voice.

"Of course it is, Ashtat. If you weren't sure, you'd never have opened those bloody doors and exposed your crown jewels to the world. Buzz this gate open. It's starting to rain."

Ashtat looked up into a thickening gray sky. A drop of rain hit his eye. He blinked, reached inside the door to a button that controlled the gate. There was a soft buzzing sound as the gate quietly, slowly glided open. Killinworth stepped through and extended his hand to the Arab. The Arab hesitated, took it, quickly turned and went inside the house, Killinworth at his heels.

Rashad Ashtat wore a tight-fitting black silk suit, white shirt and black tie. His face was pockmarked. His left eye, as a result of a childhood injury, perpetually looked to the side. He went over to a large, richly furnished living room, turned and waited for Killinworth to join him. Killinworth had stopped in the foyer to look at the paintings on the walls: a Girtin watercolor of early London, an unsigned medieval religious egg tempera and gesso, a Monet, a Cézanne and a small Gainsborough portrait.

"I especially like the Gainsborough," Killinworth said as he joined Ashtat in the living room. "His brushwork always impresses me."

"A minor piece, Killinworth, of little value."

Killinworth saw that one end of the living room contained six steamer trunks and numerous suitcases. "Taking a holiday?"

"Yes."

"Evidently an extended one."

"I don't know how long, Killinworth. And it is business."

Killinworth laughed. "Yes, I'm sure it it. Where are you going?"

"That is not your concern."

"Of course it isn't, but I'd like to know."

"I'm going home, to visit family."

"That's *difficult* business, Ashtat."

"Business and pleasure."

Killinworth shrugged and admired the living room's art.

"Why are you here?" Ashtat asked, his voice rising even higher in pitch, testifying to his anxiety at this unannounced visit.

"Just a friendly call, my friend," Killinworth said, not looking at him, "but while I am here, perhaps you can help me."

"I don't have much time, I must finish packing and I have an important dinner engagement."

Killinworth turned and extended his hands, palms up. "And I wouldn't dream of standing in your way, my friend. Tell me something, Rashad, what's the local gossip about Lewis Tunney's murder?"

"Why would I know?"

"You did hear about it, I presume."

"Of course, but that is all I know, that he was murdered—"

"Startling, wasn't it?"

"Killinworth, I have much to do and your visit is...ill timed."

"Not unusual for me."

"Is that all you wanted, to ask whether I had heard about the Tunney murder?"

"No, Ashtat, that's *not* all."

"Then tell me and leave. I do not wish to be rude but—"

"I've never seen you rude, Ashtat. Devious and calculating perhaps, but never rude. I'll come to the point. I am in London representing a very wealthy and, I might add, famous person. This person, whose name you would immediately recognize, which is why the person shall remain nameless, wishes to purchase a certain artifact."

"And?"

"And," Killinworth said with an exaggerated sigh, "you came immediately to mind as someone who could fulfill the person's request."

"What does this rich and famous person wish to purchase?"

Killinworth smiled, laid the fingers of his right hand on the palm of his left, examined his nails, then said without looking up, "The Legion of Harsa."

Ashtat started to laugh, stopped, started again, then uttered a series of short, rapid sounds like an ack-ack gun, or an automobile with ignition problems. "The Harsa is not on the market, Killinworth. It has been returned to the Smithsonian."

"Rather," Killinworth said, moving to a large Velázquez original illuminated by pinspots in the ceiling. "How fortunate Velázquez was to have Philip IV as a

163

patron. Think of what Holbein might have done if he hadn't been strapped as court painter to Henry VIII."

"I am not in the mood, Killinworth, to discuss the relative merit of dead artists."

"But you will admit that Velázquez had a sense of composition unparalled in western art—"

"Please leave, Killinworth."

"I shall, but keep in mind that my client is quite serious about wishing to obtain the Harsa, if, of course, you *should* ever hear of its availability. You will then give me first opportunity?"

"Yes, yes. Now, please, *go*."

"Good chap. Delightful seeing you again. Enjoy your holiday with your family. As one gets older it becomes increasingly important to maintain family ties. Life is so transitory, and one of the saddest conditions is to lose someone without having, how shall I say, resolved the relationship. *Assalamoo ahlaykum*, my friend."

"Peace be with you, *too*, Killinworth."

Killinworth thanked the Arab and went to the street, where he waved down a passing taxi. "The Dorchester," he said.

As Killinworth stood at the bar in the Dorchester drinking double gins without ice, Heather was walking down Davies Street. She stopped in front of the shop bearing the sign—*Antiques, Peter S. Peckham, Prop. By Appointment Only*. She pressed the bell and heard the musical triplet chime from inside. She pressed it a few more times, then knocked repeatedly on the door. There was no response.

She went to a red phone booth and dialed a number written on a piece of paper. She let it ring twenty times before hanging up. "Where are you?" she muttered as she took a final look at the name on the paper, *Peter Peckham (Home Number)*. She walked down Audley

Street to the Dorchester, and found Killinworth in the main lobby, where tea service was set up at elaborately dressed tables attended by waiters in black swallowtails. They compared their day's activities over diamond-shaped tea sandwiches of salmon, cucumber, ham and egg. Killinworth told her about his purchases, and said he'd enjoyed a fine lunch at the Savoy. When Heather asked him whom he'd lunched with he told her it was no one she knew, just an old crony.

"And you, my dear, what did you do your first day back in London?"

"Spent time at the B.M., had lunch with friends, browsed some shops. I tried to contact Lewis's friend Peter Peckham but had no luck."

"What about the Paley chap?"

"I rang him up. Unfortunately he had nothing to report." She had decided not to mention her appointment with Paley that evening, not wanting him to pressure her into having him accompany her. This was something she wanted to do for herself, by herself. Evelyn was so helpful, but enough was enough. She wasn't, after all, totally helpless.

"Just as well," Killinworth said as the waiter brought a silver platter heaped with tarts, meringues, eclairs and slices of obscenely rich Black Forest cake. "Would you be good enough to leave the tray?" he asked the waiter. Then to Heather again: "What's the plan for this evening?"

"I made a date with an old friend," Heather said.

"Oh? Someone I should know?"

She shook her head. "A school chum." She was getting annoyed with his curiosity . . . however well intentioned.

"I see. Well, I'm tied up this evening too, but not for long. Will you be having dinner with your school chum?"

"No."

"I'm not engaged for dinner either. Shall we meet later?"

"Yes, I suppose that will be all right..."

"Good. Nine-thirty, at the hotel?"

"Yes, that—" And then she shook her head. "I'm not sure I can handle the restaurant, Evelyn. The hotel was difficult enough, but we had my birthday celebration in the restaurant the night Lewis and I..."

"The night you announced your engagement. I understand, Heather, believe me I do. But you must face up to it. In fact, I insist that we dine there. Nine-thirty. You'll honor me."

"Yes, all right," she said in a near-whisper.

They returned to the Chesterfield at five. As Heather napped, then showered, and as Killinworth made phone calls while room service delivered gin to his rooms, a tall, well-dressed woman stood in line at Customs at Heathrow airport. Her flight had arrived moments earlier. The Passport Control officer took her U.S. passport and scrutinized the name and photograph. *Linda Claire Salzbank.* "Business or pleasure, Miss Salzbank?"

"Overnight, a last-minute business obligation," she said.

"Have a pleasant evening," he said, handing her her passport and looking to the next non-British citizen in line. She proceeded to a waiting line of cabs. It was raining heavily, and a dense fog had rolled in, enveloping everything in a gray, wet cocoon. She gave the driver an address, sat back and tightly gripped an oversized combination attaché case and overnight bag that was her only piece of luggage.

Heather came down to the Chesterfield's lobby at seven-thirty. She chatted with one of the desk staff, then went to the front door and peered out. The rain had intensified; buildings across Charles Street were vague, fluid shapes. She gingerly stepped through the doors and saw Killinworth on the corner, an umbrella over his head, his attention on the busier Curzon Street a block away.

"Evelyn," Heather called.

He turned and shouted, "Bloody rain." A few moments later a taxi responded to his frantic waving. Killinworth again looked at Heather. "Share it with me?"

"Yes, thank you."

When they were together in the taxi, Killinworth told the driver, "Belgrave Place, Belgravia." To Heather he said, "I'm running a little late. Hope you don't mind my being dropped off first."

"Not at all."

A few minutes, and eighty pence later, Killinworth told the driver to stop at a corner in Belgrave Square. He handed him two pounds and said to Heather, "Getting off here. See you at nine-thirty."

"Yes. All right."

As he opened the door the blowing rain whipped inside the cab. He slammed the door behind him and disappeared into the fog.

"Where to now?" the driver asked.

"The East End, Cable Street, please, a pub called the Quid."

"Don't know that particular pub, ma'am."

"We'll find it as long as we get to Cable Street."

"As you say, only that's not the sort of spot I'm comfortable dropping a proper lady at."

"I appreciate your concern, but it's quite all right."

"Yes, ma'am."

Fifteen minutes later, as the driver circled the Tower of London and turned onto Cable Street, he said,

"There's a very nice pub, ma'am, close to here called the Prospect of Whitby. I'd recommend it over the spot you've chosen."

Heather smiled. "I know that pub, but I'm meeting someone at the Quid. Thank you, though, for the suggestion."

He pulled up in front of the Quid. The area was dominated by project housing and warehouses. The lighted signs were blurred images through the fog and rain. Heather paid the driver and ran to the protection of a small ledge overhanging the front door. Raucous female laughter cut through the general male din inside. She watched the taxi pull away, then opened the door. An oval bar in the center of the room was crowded with drinkers, several of whom turned to look at her. An Irish jig played loudly through a speaker suspended in a corner. The floor was covered with chipped red-and-gray tiles. The barstools were red vinyl, and there were ripped tan vinyl benches along the walls.

To the rear of the pub two men played darts. One was tall and heavy; his nose and cheeks were plum-red. He wore a green plaid shirt and heavy workman's trousers. His sandy hair was thick and unruly. His opponent was a much smaller man, sallow-faced and bald except for a fringe of gray hair. He wore a black raincoat over a rumpled brown suit.

Heather told the bartender, "I'm looking for Mr. Elwood Paley."

"That'd be him over there," the bartender said, pointing to the smaller of the two dart players.

Paley spotted her, assumed who she was and waved for her to join him. She walked to the fringe of the dart playing area. He held up a finger. "One minute, luv. I'm up."

Heather watched him throw his three darts, putting them in a tight bunch around the triple-twenty section.

His score was written on the board as he turned to Heather, extended his hand and said, "Elwood Paley at your service. Glad you found it. I'd have come over to your neck of the woods but like I told you on the blower, I'm tied up here tonight."

Heather wondered if his main business wasn't drinking and dart playing. She asked if they could sit down and talk.

"Just as soon as I teach this bloke what darts are all about. Go on over there and have yourself a bitter on me. I'll join you shortly."

Heather sat on a bench, and Paley told the bartender to see that his "lady-friend" was served "half a bitter."

Heather sipped it and watched the finish of the game. Paley lost, she was rather glad to note, and handed his opponent money. He came to the table and sat down next to her, evidently sensing what she was thinking when he said, "It might not seem work to you, mum, but I keep in with the locals. Good sources of information, if you catch my drift."

"I suppose," Heather said, not wanting to prolong the conversation in recriminations. "What have you found out, Mr. Paley?"

"About your fiancé?"

"Of *course*."

"Well, now, Miss McBean, I'd be lyin' in me teeth if I said I learned very much, be handin' you a bag a hooey. I've gained my reputation by bein' honest to a fault—"

"That's admirable, Mr. Paley."

"Only way to work. Tell too many lies and you find yourself in the Thames tryin' to swim with blocks on your feet and hands."

Heather sighed. "What *have* you learned?"

"Well, now, let me see." He pulled a dog-eared pad from his raincoat pocket and turned pages until he found what he was looking for. "First of all," he said, "I've not been able to find Mr. Peter Peckham, which, I might add, is cause for concern, and I'm not the only one feelin' this way. The gent seems to have disappeared, which isn't regular for someone like him."

"You have no idea where he might be?" she said, her voice reflecting her concern.

"Not a clue, ma'am. I come up with a few people who knew him but they've not seen hide nor hair of him for more 'n a week."

"I see." Heather sipped from her mug and stared at the scarred tabletop. Two drunken longshoremen came into the pub. One of them made a mildly suggestive comment to her as they passed. "Don't mind them," Paley whispered in her ear. "Nothin' to fear as long as you're with me."

Heather did her best to ignore everything and everyone around her. "What about Dr. Tunney? Did you learn anything about his movements before he left for America?"

Paley flipped through a few more pages. "Yes, I did, ma'am." He placed his hand over the page, cleared his throat. "You'll be payin' me the balance of my fee this night, I take it."

"That depends."

"On what?"

"On whether you've earned it."

He slipped the pad back in his pocket, got up, went to the bar and bought himself another bitter. He returned to the table, downed half the dark brew, and turned a stare on Heather that was altogether unpleasant. He had a small face, pale and soft, but there was now an unmistakable hardness, cruelty, that made Heather lean away from him. He smiled, exposing yellowed teeth. "I'm not accustomed to havin' my work questioned, Miss McBean. I've got me a good reputation. Like I told you when we first talked, there's no guarantees in this business. I do my best. If I come up with something, that's ducky. If I don't, that's hard beans but I get paid one way or the other."

"I'll pay you what I owe," Heather said. "Now please tell me what you can about Dr. Tunney."

Paley waited until she'd dug into her purse and extracted his remaining fee in pounds. He counted them, put them in his pocket, withdrew his pad and returned to the page he'd stopped at earlier. "Let me see," he said, squinting at his writing. "Ah, yes, I did discover, with some difficulty, I might add, that Dr. Tunney did talk with the missing Dr. Peckham during that week."

"You're certain?"

"Yes, indeed. I never report anything that ain't certain."

"Where did they meet?"

"At Mr. Peckham's shop on Davies Street. Someone saw a gent fittin' Dr. Tunney's description go into the Peckham establishment one day about noon and come out of it about an hour later."

"What else?"

"That's the size of it."

"Where else did Dr. Tunney go that week?"

"I don't know. I come up against a blank wall, if you catch my drift."

"Yes, I catch your drift. You've told me everything you know?"

"For now. Of course, I can keep on the case—"

"For another fee."

"I'm a workin' man, luv. I get paid for my services like everybody else."

"No, Mr. Paley, I won't be needing your services any longer."

"As you wish, ma'am. If I can be of any further assistance in the future, just ring me up. Care to linger a bit? I was about to get me a bite to eat. I'd be happy to have you join me and my friends—"

"Thank you, no."

She pulled her raincoat tighter around her, stood up and went to the door. The rain was falling as hard as when she'd arrived. She considered going to a phone and calling for a cab but her need to escape the pub was overwhelming. She stepped out into the rain, opened her umbrella and walked up Cable Street. She was on the edge of tears over the lack of information Paley had given her. Her frustration turned to anger, and she walked faster. At Dock Street two local yobbos stood in an abandoned building's doorway. One of them said, "What have we got here, a dolly-girl out lookin' for a grind in the rain?"

His friend laughed and stepped into Heather's path. "Pretty bird, ain't 'cha? You wouldn't mind if I grabbed your arse, now would ya?"

"Get away from me," Heather said, hoping she sounded more confident than she felt.

The other, ferret-faced and red-eyed, joined his friend in front of her. "I ain't seen you before," he said, cocking his head and leering.

"Get out of my way—"

One of them reached out and grabbed at her breasts through her raincoat. "You got nice titties, luv." he said. The other one made a move to circle her.

Heather didn't hesitate. She brought her foot up into the crotch of the one in front of her as hard as she could. He doubled over and moaned, "She got me in the cobblers." Heather rammed the tip of the umbrella into the other one's face, opening a gash on his cheek. He howled and lunged for her. She used the umbrella to keep him away, dropped it, turned and ran toward the Quid. She heard them chasing after her and she ran blindly, the rain stinging her eyes, her feet sloshing through deep puddles on the uneven sidewalk.

The lights of an automobile came around the pub's corner, illuminated Heather and her pursuers. Heather waved wildly at the driver, who stopped, pulled down the window of his cab. "What's the matter, miss?"

"They're after me—"

"Get on your way, you little bastards, before I warm your lugs for you," the driver said. The punks swore, reviled Heather, but turned and disappeared into the night.

"Thank you," Heather said.

"Don't be thankin' me, ma'am, but you'd better get in if you don't want to drown yourself."

She retrieved her umbrella and rode the cab back to considerably more genteel Mayfair and the warmth and security of the Chesterfield. The driver insisted on escorting her into the lobby, where Heather thanked him profusely. "You saved my life..."

"Just a case of comin' along at the right time. You get yourself into some dry clothes, and if you don't mind my givin' advice, keep away from places such as you've been tonight. It's not safe for a lady on those streets."

"I'm convinced," she said, and thanked him again. When she asked if she might give him something, he told her no, it was his pleasure. It was a lovely moment she wouldn't soon forget.

In her room she stripped off her wet clothes, drew a hot bath, wrapped herself in a robe and checked her watch. Nine-fifteen. She was to meet Evelyn in fifteen minutes.

As Heather was finishing dressing, Killinworth was coming through the lobby carrying a paper bag and an envelope addressed to his Savoy luncheon companion containing the keys she'd given him. He gave the en-

velope to the desk clerk to mail and went directly to
his room, double locked the door behind him, placed
the bag on the bed, opened it. He removed a small
chamois sack the color of burnt ocher. The top was
secured with a leather drawstring. Killinworth loosened it and slipped his hand inside, fondled something,
withdrew his hand, tightened the drawstring and put
the sack in the bottom of a suitcase, which he put in
the rear of a closet. He tossed the paper bag in a waste-
basket, washed his hands and face and combed his
hair, checked himself in a mirror and went to the restaurant, where Heather had just been shown to a table.
"I'd hoped to be here first," he said, "to help you
through the ... initial difficulties."

"After what's happened to me tonight I had very
little problem with it." She told then about her meeting
with Paley and being attacked on the street.

"How dreadful for you," he said, patting her hand.
"I should have been with you ..."

"Yes, well, it's over now ... how was your meeting
in Belgravia?"

He smiled noncommittally and ordered for them—
smoked salmon appetizers, steak au poivre for him,
Dover sole for her. "Routine business, nothing of im-
port," he said. "Turned out, in fact, to be a bore and
damnably unproductive." ...

After dinner she said, "I'm exhausted Evelyn. I'd
like to get to bed."

"Of course. I might tarry in the bar for a cognac.
Positive you won't join me?"

"Positive, but thank you. I'll see you at breakfast."

Killinworth ordered a double cognac, nursed it for
ten minutes, then said to the bartender, "I'll be
back ... forgot something in my room."

Where he went was to the hotel's basement, where

there were two public phone booths. He wedged his frame inside one of them, put fifty pence in the slot and pressed seven numbers. Moments later his call was answered with, "Scotland Yard."

Killinworth spoke through a handkerchief he had placed over the mouthpiece. "I wish to report a murder on Belgrave Place, in Belgravia, Number Seven."

"Who's the victim?"

"Number Seven Belgrave Place."

"Your name, please."

"Good night."

He stopped to polish his custom-made Church's shoes on a machine provided for hotel guests, returned to the bar, finished his cognac, bid the bartender a pleasant good night and went to his room, where he promptly fell sound asleep.

CHAPTER 21

"I'M SORRY, CAPTAIN, BUT MR. SAUNDERS ISN'T IN the office and won't be back for two days."

"Is he away on business?" Hanrahan asked.

"Yes, sir. He's in New York attending gallery openings."

"Thank you. By the way, is there some way I can reach him in New York?"

"He didn't say where he's staying."

"What gallery opening is he attending?"

"There are several. He didn't say which, I'm afraid. He usually doesn't."

"Please have him call me when he returns."

Next on Hanrahan's list was Congressman Jubel Watson. Watson was in committee but returned the call at noon. "Thanks for getting back, congressman. I wonder if I could have some of your time this afternoon. It's about the Tunney case."

"The Tunney case? There's nothing I could possibly tell you about that, captain. I gave my statement the night of the murder. I was there, along with two hundred other people. That's the extent of my knowledge."

"I realize that, sir, but I'd still appreciate a few minutes."

"Well, let me check my schedule . . . is four all right?"

"That'll be just fine. At your office?"

"Make it my suite at the Hay-Adams."

"I'll be there."

Hanrahan had lunch in his office and pored through transcripts of interviews in the Tunney case, making notes as he went. He left MPD at one-forty-five for a two o'clock meeting with Borden G. Costain, the Smithsonian's secretary, at the administrative center in the Castle.

Costain was not what Hanrahan had expected. After spending as much time as he had with the Smithsonian's hierarchy, Hanrahan had developed a museum archetype for himself. Costain didn't fit. Tall and broad shouldered, he looked more like a former all-American college football player than the head of the nation's leading museum empire and tourist attraction. He wore a double-breasted gray blazer and khaki slacks, pale blue button-down shirt and a dark blue tie with tiny gold emblems which, on closer examination, proved to be the Smithsonian's emblem. Thick, bushy salt-and-pepper hair was short and grew close to the temples, almost a crew cut. His face was deeply tanned and etched. His eyes were deep blue and lively.

"Good of you to see me, Dr. Costain," Hanrahan said after he'd been ushered into a spartan office.

"Sorry I wasn't here earlier," Costain said. "Coffee? A drink?"

"No thanks."

"I think I will."

The Russian vodka Costain poured looked good. Hanrahan changed his mind and joined him. "Here's to finding the bastard who killed Lewis Tunney," Costain said, raising his glass in a half-hearted toast.

"That's worth drinking to," said Hanrahan, surprised at Costain's choice of words. "I understand you were away at the time, supervising an archaeological dig?"

Costain nodded and opened blinds on the window. "That's right. A lot of people don't realize how involved the Smithsonian is in archaeology and anthropology around the world. There isn't a day goes by that we don't have a team in remote places trying to find answers to our origins. But that's not why you're here, captain."

Hanrahan finished his drink. "No, it isn't, but it's sort of interesting. They've been kidding me ever since this case broke about my suddenly becoming cultured. At any rate, the reason I wanted to see you was to get whatever ideas you might have about the Tunney murder."

Costain shook his head, went to a file cabinet and picked up a shrunken head that had been tossed on top of loose files. He held out the head to Hanrahan for closer examination. "See this, captain? It's Jivaro Indian from Ecuador." He handed the head to Hanrahan, who took it and ran his fingers over its leathery surface. The head was small and black. The eyelids were closed but bulged unnaturally. The lips were sealed with three pins of chonta wood that had string hanging from them.

"Headhunters?" Hanrahan said.

"Yes. We know it here as Item Number 397,131. You can read it on the tag...The Jivaros are interesting people, captain. It takes them about twenty-four hours to prepare a head once they've severed it from a victim. They slit it up the back and skin it. They use a special herb from a vine known as chinchipi and boil the head in it until it shrinks. Then they fill it with hot rocks to continue the shrinking process, and then use hot sand. It's very important to them that it be done right. The head is, after all, a tangible symbol of their recent success, a source of pride, satisfaction. After it's shrunk to the right size they smoke it over a smudge to achieve this nice color. They shine it up like you and I buff our shoes, then bring it home with them."

"That's sure fascinating, Dr. Costain, but I wonder what—"

"It's not worth a hell of a lot, captain. One of our people bought this head, Number 397,131, in 1930 for twenty bucks."

"The point, Dr. Costain?"

"The *point* is that I can understand a Jivaro Indian cutting off a head and preserving it as a trophy, but I can *not* understand some sick son of a bitch coming into the Museum of American History, ramming a sword belonging to Thomas Jefferson into the back of a leading scholar and walking away scot-free."

Hanrahan handed the head back to Costain, who returned it to the file cabinet with enough force to send papers scattering. He turned. "Dr. Tunney's murder has reflected on this entire institution, captain, and the failure to resolve it reflects further on everybody involved, including, if I may say so, the MPD and yourself."

"Dr. Costain, *we* don't exactly enjoy unsolved murders either—"

"What progress has there been?" Costain's voice was edged with frustration, anger and pain. He sat behind his desk and rubbed his temples. "Ideally this business should have been taken care of internally. I'd hoped for that. Unfortunately it hasn't worked out that way."

"I understand how you feel, Dr. Costain. But I also have to tell you that it looks like the answer to Dr. Tunney's murder might be right here inside the Smithsonian."

Costain looked as though he'd tasted something sour.

"I hope to hell you're wrong. Let me explain something to you. The Smithsonian is at a crossroads. We have a vice-president who believes in it, which, I might add, represents a distinct departure from the past. There's a major funding bill in Congress right now that would provide important money for the Smithsonian. It would mean the world being brought into the Smithsonian. If what you suggest turns out to be true, all this could be lost."

And you'd go down in history as the man at the helm, Hanrahan thought. "Could you spell that out for me?" He thought he knew the answer, but he wanted to keep Costain talking. Who knew what he might drop...

Costain sat back, made a tent with his fingers. "The nature of Congress and its elected officials... The arts have never exactly been at the top of the priority list when it comes to budgets. Usually, especially in hard times, we have to lobby like a cornered badger just to sustain our appropriations, let alone get them increased. But this time around we have a vice-president who's in our corner, and we have a champion in Congress who can use the vice-president's leverage in committee."

"Congressman Watson?"

"Yes." Costain seemed surprised that Hanrahan knew.

"I have an appointment with him later on."

"That right? Why? Does he have something for your investigation?"

"Who knows? In my business you check out everything, everybody. That's the boring way we sometimes even get results."

Costain nodded, said he understood. Hanrahan thanked him for his time and for the drink. As he was about to leave he asked, "You don't happen to know an Evelyn Killinworth, do you?"

"Yes, why?"

"What can you tell me about him?"

"Eccentric, a maverick in the field, good teacher, some say unconventional in his approach, personally and professionally. Why do you ask?"

"Just curious. I met him a little while ago."

"In connection with the Tunney murder?"

"No, not really...well, again, Dr. Costain, thanks for seeing me."

Hanrahan waited in the lobby of the Hay-Adams until four-fifteen, when Congressman Watson finally arrived.

"Sorry I'm late." They stepped into an elevator and Watson pushed the button for the top floor. "I'm afraid I don't have much time, captain," he said as he watched the floors light up on a panel. "I've got to be at an embassy reception at five."

"I'll try to make it brief," Hanrahan said.

They rode the rest of the way in silence, the diminutive Watson bouncing up and down on black alligator shoes and fiddling with his tie. He led the way into his suite, which was spacious and airy and dominated by works of art on every wall and table surface.

"Excuse me a moment," Watson said as he disappeared into a bedroom. His housekeeper, an elderly black woman in a starched gray uniform and white apron, came out of the kitchen. "Can I get you something, sir?"

"Oh, no, no thanks," Hanrahan said. He was standing where Watson had tossed his briefcase and the day's newspaper on a trumpet-leg lowboy. The paper was open to an inside page, from which a headline stared up at him: "VICE SQUAD RAIDS GEORGE-

TOWN PARTY." Hanrahan picked up the paper and read the story. He'd heard about the raid that morning. There was some joking about it around MPD, although no one seemed to have many details. All Hanrahan knew was that the MPD's vice squad, acting on complaints from Georgetown residents, broke up what was reputed to be a monthly gathering of well-heeled Washington transvestites. Such raids had occurred before, and Hanrahan had been skeptical about the value of them. It was one thing to get the word out to such groups that there had been complaints, another to bust in, list names and expose them to public ridicule. He was glad to see that names had not been included in the newspaper account.

Watson returned from the bedroom. He'd taken off his dress shirt and wore a T-shirt. "I need a shower and shave," he said. "What can I do for you? Drink?" Before Hanrahan could answer Watson called into the kitchen, "Get my guest a drink." He excused himself and returned to the bedroom.

The housekeeper asked Hanrahan what he wanted.

"Gin," he said, "and ice."

"Plain gin?"

"Yup."

She brought him a glass filled with ice and a bottle of Beefeater. Hanrahan poured his own drink and took it with him as he toured the living room. Two items side by side on the wall caught his eye. They were hung over a Ming dynasty chest; neatly printed cards inside each frame explained what they were. One contained a painted enamel badge set in a star of pastes that was, according to the card, from the "Noble order of Bucks, an eighteenth-century convivial society that had features in common with freemasonry." In the other frame was a medal from the "Anti-Gallican Society, formed in 1745 to oppose French imports and influence." The medal was fashioned from faceted rock crystals and two painted enamels.

"Like them, captain?" Watson had reappeared.

Hanrahan turned, "They remind me of the Harsa and Cincinnati medals."

"Not nearly as important or valuable, but significant."

"I never realized how many societies there've been."

"Hundreds. Some had an impact, like Cincinnati and Harsa, others were just clubs for some good ole boys, sort of like a poker club or local firehouse. You know, a chance to get away from the wife for a night with the excuse of an important meeting." He laughed. "So what's new?" When Hanrahan didn't join in the hilarity, Watson said, "Well, I've got to get dressed. What's on your mind, captain?"

"The Tunney murder."

"What about it?"

"The Legion of Harsa..."

"I don't understand."

"I understand you'd like to own it."

Watson frowned. "That's a damn peculiar thing to say."

"Well, sir, I was talking to a—"

"Is there anything wrong in appreciating an historically valuable item, captain?"

"No, but—"

"I'm fascinated with early secret societies, as many people are."

"As Lewis Tunney was."

"He was more than interested, he was a leading expert."

Hanrahan put down his glass. "Congressman, do you know an art dealer in San Francisco named Detienne?"

Watson thought for a moment. "No, can't say that I do. Should I?"

"Probably. He told me you'd made it known that if the Legion of Harsa came on the market you'd be interested in buying it."

"That's damn nonsense. Now look here—"

"Just asking. Information comes from many sources, congressman, and I follow up. That's my job."

"This...Detienne says that *I'm* looking for the Harsa? Which, as I understand it, has been recovered."

"That was the rumor."

"And you put credence in ridiculous rumors?"

"Depends."

"Captain Hanrahan, perhaps you aren't aware of the fact that I am the Smithsonian's leading advocate in Congress."

"I know you're behind a bill to increase funding for it."

"Yes, and the murder of Lewis Tunney on its premises has damaged the public's perception of this nation's finest and most revered public institution. Nowhere else in the world has such a collection of history been gathered under one..."

As he went on with his speech Hanrahan thought that he sounded as though he were filibustering on the floor of Congress. When he finished lecturing on the virtues of the Smithsonian and his love for it, Hanrahan said quietly, "Thanks for your time, congressman. Enjoy your reception." Watson made a move to escort him to the door. "No need," Hanrahan said. "I can find the door."

He no sooner had reached the lobby when his beeper went off. He called from a booth and was told that the Smithsonian bomber had left another note, this one at the Arts and Industries Museum, next to the Castle.

Just what we needed, Hanrahan thought as he drove

to the scene of the latest threat, "The Jupiter," an eight-wheel, thirty-six-inch-gauge wood-burning passenger locomotive that dominated one of the display galleries that radiated like spokes from an octagonal rotunda. The locomotive had been built by the Baldwin Locomotive Works of Philadelphia for the Santa Cruz Railroad of California. A maroon gas lamp trimmed in gold sat atop its front; a maroon cow catcher flared out below it. The note was Scotch-taped to the gas lamp.

Hanrahan tore it down, using his handkerchief to avoid smudging prints.

This is the final warning. I have acted as a gentleman should, have given you ample time to consider my demands before an unfortunate incident occurs. You have twenty-four hours to introduce a bill in the Congress of the United States of America to return to me, as the rightful heir to James Smithson, the Smithsonian Institution and its belongings. Time has run out, sirs.

"Do you know what I'm going to do to this nut when we nail him?" Hanrahan said to a uniformed officer.

"What's that, captain?"

"I'm personally going to stuff him alive into the boiler of that locomotive, shovel in coal myself and put a match to it. I'm going to watch that silly ass evaporate in steam, right up through the stack. And do you know what else?"

"What?"

"I'm going to laugh, really laugh while that pain in the ass condenses on the ceiling. I mean it. I don't need this."

He was back at his office by six. Sergeant Arey, who was on the desk, told him he'd had a phone call from London. They'd said it was important.

"Who was it?" Hanrahan asked, expecting to hear Heather's name.

Arey went through slips of paper until he found the right one. He handed it to Hanrahan. The call was from Inspector Albert Burns of Scotland Yard. Hanrahan had worked with Burns on two previous cases, one of which took him to London to testify at the trial at the Old Bailey. He'd gotten a kick out of it, seeing men with deep voices in black robes and wearing wigs pursuing justice in a system his own had come from. "It's just like TV or a movie," he'd told his then wife.

"Thanks, Jim," Hanrahan told the sergeant. "Did he say what he wanted?"

"Nope, but you should call him whenever you got back, no matter what the time."

Hanrahan looked at his watch as he went to the office. Six o'clock in Washington meant eleven in London. He was about to put through a call when a typed list on his desk caught his eye. It had the names of people who'd been at the transvestite party in Georgetown. Such lists were sent to him routinely by Vice, although he seldom had use for them. He knew that another copy would have gone to the FBI, a practice established under J. Edgar Hoover...Hoover's legendary files on *everyone* in Washington were a fact, and it was those files that had given him such immense power. Hanrahan had always hated the practice but had been powerless to change it.

He tossed the list aside and dialed an MPD operator, who put through his call to London. Burns came on the line.

"I tried the office first, Bert," Hanrahan said, "figuring you wouldn't be there and would get your home number. I was wrong."

Burns laughed. "It'll be another late one, Mac, I'm afraid. We've had an interesting day."

"Glad to hear it."

"I thought it worth checking with you. We had a murder last night in Belgravia. That's a posh section of town, lots of money and high-tone types. This chap who was murdered is an Arab named Ashtat, Rashad Ashtat. I don't know very much about him except that he's evidently well known in art circles, was quite a collector."

"Ashtat? Doesn't ring a bell. I assume you're telling me because of the Tunney case."

"Exactly. To be honest with you, I probably wouldn't have linked it up except for another murder that came to light this afternoon, a chap named Peter Peckham."

"Tunney's friend ... I've heard about him."

"It stuck me as strange that two fellows in the same business would be murdered in the same week, particularly on the heels of the Tunney business you're dealing with."

"You're right, Bert. How'd they get it?"

"Ashtat was found in his home with a kitchen knife in his belly. Peckham was dragged out from under a bridge on the Thames. His skull had been smashed, although we'll have to wait for the forensic chaps to finish up."

"Look, Bert, I think there's something you might want to do before you end up with another body in the river." He told him about Heather.

"Want me to pick her up?"

"No, she's too feisty for that, but I sure would appreciate somebody keeping close tabs on her. She's staying at a hotel called the Chesterfield."

"In Mayfair. I'll get on it right away."

"Thanks. And keep me informed, will you? She's quite a lady."

"I certainly shall. How's the family?"

"Fine, Bert. Yours?"

"Tip-top. Well, back to work. I'll ring you up tomorrow when I've got more details under my belt."

Hanrahan hung up, picked up the phone again and told the operator to put through a call to Miss Heather McBean at the Chesterfield Hotel in London. A minute later he heard a desk clerk say that Miss McBean had checked out that morning. Hanrahan broke in on the conversation. "Connect me with Dr. Evelyn Killinworth." He waited as the phone in Killinworth's room rang at least a dozen times. He slammed down the receiver.

It took a while but he finally got a number for the McBean castle outside Edinburgh and put a call through.

No answer.

He was about to leave the office when he spotted the list from Vice, angrily scanned the names. Two jumped off the page at him—Ford Saunders and Norman Huffaker.

"I'll be damned," he said.

CHAPTER 22

HEATHER HAD GOTTEN UP THAT MORNING FEELING almost unaccountably rested and relaxed. She'd stayed in her room, fussing with her hair and makeup and reviewing papers that had a bearing on the conversion of the McBean castle from a private residence to a public museum. As she read them she was glad she'd decided to leave for Edinburgh that afternoon. There was more to be done there than she'd realized.

She went downstairs to the Buttery, where she ordered a full British breakfast—juice, eggs, porridge, toast and jam, kippers, bacon and sausage. "The lass eats like a lumberjack. She'll not *faa throu ane's claes*," her Uncle Calum used to say about her, meaning she'd not grow up thin.

An East Indian waiter delivered copies of the morning papers with her juice. She glanced at the front page of one of them, then turned inside. A small headline in the lower left-hand corner didn't at first stop her, but, like a double take, her attention quickly returned to it. The headline read: ARAB ART DEALER SLAIN. And the brief story:

Authorities have reported the slaying of a prominent Arab art dealer, Rashad Ashtat, at his home
at 7 Belgrave Place, Belgravia. The victim, who
was reputed to have dealt in contraband works
of art and historic artifacts, was found last night
in the living room of his Belgravia townhouse, a
large kitchen utility knife protruding from his ab-
domen.

She looked up from the paper and closed her eyes.
"Belgravia...but wasn't that where—?"

"Good morning, sleep well?"

Killinworth stood over her. He was dressed in a
vested royal blue silk suit, white shirt and yellow-and-
blue striped tie. A handkerchief that matched his tie
bloomed from his breast pocket.

"I startled you," he said as he sat down. "Sorry."

"No, no, you didn't...I was just...daydreaming."
She glanced down at the paper on her lap, then quickly
away.

"Ordered yet?"

"Yes."

"Good. I'm famished." He motioned for the waiter
to take his order. "Well," he said as he tucked a napkin
into the folds of his vest, "what does the day hold in
store for you, my dear?"

"What? Oh, some shopping...a few people to see..."

"I've an early appointment." He looked at his watch.
"Hmmm, I'd better eat up and be on my way. I'm
running late. Lunch? Will you be free? I thought the
Connaught would be nice."

"I don't think so, I...I have a tentative luncheon
date with someone from the B.M."

"Pity. Well, should you change your mind, which,
I'm told, is not uncommon with members of your fair

sex, I'll be at the Connaught at noon. I try to break the habit but can't."

"Habit?"

"The Connaught. One simply can't leave London without lunching there. Please try to break free, dear. You're leaving for Edinburgh this afternoon?"

"Yes, on the three-twenty shuttle." Why do you *talk* so much, she scolded herself.

"I do hope I can spring free and join you in Scotland for a day. I'd love to see the castle again."

"Yes, I..."

"Is something wrong, my dear?"

She shook her head. "No, nothing's wrong...yes, please try to come up."

"I certainly shall, my dear. But if not, I'll of course see you back in Washington."

"In Washington, yes...here's breakfast."

Killinworth ate quickly. He wished Heather a pleasant day, reminded her he'd be at the Connaught and left for his appointment. The moment he was gone she picked up the newspaper from her lap and finished reading about this Ashtat's murder.

Local authorities, in a preliminary statement, said that there was no sign of forced entry, and that the murder had been reported by a phone call to Scotland Yard from an anonymous male caller.

She walked aimlessly for most of the morning, browsing in small shops. There wasn't anything she really needed, except to get her mind off what had happened recently. She bought a basket of soaps in chamomile, wild thyme, rosemary, myrtle, sweet woodruff and bergamot, a packet of notepaper and envelopes, and two pairs of lace panties in a shocking wild rose color.

She lunched alone at the Red Lion on Waverton Street, only a few blocks from her hotel, returned, checked out of the Chesterfield and took a cab to Heathrow, where she boarded the 3:20 British Airways shuttle to Edinburgh.

At Edinburgh she picked up a rental car, tossed her luggage in the back and drove toward the city, stopping once on Princess Street to look at Edinburgh's oldest building, the Edinburgh Castle, that loomed over the city like a gigantic temple, a fairy-tale structure of ancient masonry that flowed up out of volcanic rock as though it grew from it, buildings and hardened lava one continuous mass. That castle, even more than the smaller one she'd been raised in, had special meaning for her. She sat at the curb, motor running, full of an overwhelming sense of history that made her feel insignificant, a feeling she welcomed at that moment. How many births and deaths had occurred within its thick, scarred walls and cold, dank rooms? The castle had survived since the seventh century, when it was first fortified by the Picts, and had been a continuing symbol for all Scots, stronger than those who'd built it, as permanent as its inhabitants were transient.

She closed her eyes and gritted her teeth as her thoughts inexorably went to Lewis and her birthday party at the Chesterfield. They'd toasted their engagement with champagne, glasses raised, rims clinking together, wishes around the table for a long and happy life. They'd made love that night in his apartment. "I'll love you until the day I die," he'd said...

She slammed the gearshift into first and continued down Princess Street, Edinburgh's main shopping thoroughfare, turned left on Frederick and right on George until she reached the George Hotel. She'd decided during the flight not to stay at the McBean castle. It was too forbidding, too isolated. She hated to admit it, but she was afraid to be alone. Especially after the Belgravia—she caught herself up short. Stop jumping to conclusions, she told herself. My God, to suspect Evelyn... he was hardly the only one who'd gone to Belgravia that day. Her nerves were beginning to go on her... pull yourself together, Heather McBean...

She walked past the desk and went directly to the office of Ian Sutherland, the hotel's sales manager. They'd met during the year after Calum's death, and had almost become romantically involved. Sutherland was forty, widowed, a former star rugby player on the Scottish national team and a lover of classical music; their dates usually took them to Friday performances of the Scottish National Orchestra at Usher Hall. He was stocky, had thick, black hair. Although the practice had faded, he still wore traditional Scottish outfits to formal occasions, a kilt in his mother's Macquarrie clan tartan; large squares of brilliant red broken by smaller patches of green, a green velvet jacket with horn buttons, a sporran, or purse, made of sealskin and worn around his waist, a red Balmoral bonnet bearing the Macquarrie crest and a razor-sharp sgian-dubh tucked into red knitted hose that reached the knee.

This day, however, he was in more conventional slacks, button-down shirt, tie and tweed jacket. He sprang up from his desk and hugged her.

"Hello, Ian," she said.

"I didn't know you were coming," he said, holding her at arms' length. "I'd heard that..."

"It's all right, Ian, you can mention it. Coming here was a last-minute decision."

"It doesn't matter. It's just good to see you. Tea? A drink?"

"I could use a whiskey."

He ordered two Knockando single-malt Scotch

whiskeys in the Clans Bar. They sat on a couch in front of a fireplace, and he offered a toast. "To seeing the fair Heather once again. I've missed you."

She lowered her eyes. She was glad the whiskey was strong. She needed it.

"How long will you be here?"

"A few days. The castle is still in the process of being turned over to the city, and I have a million things to check on."

"I was talking to someone about that the other day. I understand the city has finally agreed to accept the castle and maintain it."

"You know more than I do," she said. "Ian, I'd like to stay here instead of at the castle."

"Fine. We're fairly booked up but I can always find room for you. I know at least one suite is available."

"Anything, a closet, it doesn't matter."

He stared at her. "You look tired, Heather. It's been a rough road, hasn't it? I'll do anything I can. I hope you know that."

"I do know it, Ian."

"Tell you what. Let me get you squared away in the suite, give you a chance to unwind and then we'll have dinner. Unless, of course, you have other plans."

She finished her drink. "That would be just fine," she said.

A porter showed her to a suite in the older west wing. Large windows in the beige-and-brown living room looked out over rooftops to the Firth of Forth, a wide inlet from the North Sea. She went to the window and looked in the direction of Cramond, a village at the mouth of the River Almond that was, as far back as the second century A.D., an important Roman fort and supply base. She located it, then shifted a little to the right, where she saw an orange sun's rays bouncing off the roof of the McBean castle. She felt a sudden, overwhelming urge to go to it, reminded herself that morning would be time enough...

She joined Ian Sutherland in the Carver's Table, where she had another whiskey, a peaty Laphroaig this time. Sutherland recognized the mood she was in and didn't try to be part of it. They ate Aberdeen Angus beef from the buffet, and Ian had a bottle of wine delivered to the table. After dinner they sat in the lobby. He sipped a brandy, she had nothing, said almost nothing.

"Heather, you better go to bed," he said. "You're exhausted."

"Yes, I am ...you always were understanding."

"I tried, although I sometimes wonder whether things would have worked out between us if I'd been more understanding. I loved you, you know. I'm sorry, this is no time—"

She took his hand. "Don't apologize, please. I think I loved you too, Ian, but it was the wrong time, wrong place. Fate, maybe."

"And we must *dree ane's weird*."

"Yes, we all must endure our fate."

"Sleep well, dear Heather. Pleasant dreams. If I can do anything for you tomorrow, don't hesitate."

"I won't. Good night." She kissed his cheek, then went to her room, where after an hour of confused and tortuous thoughts she finally fell asleep.

She was up and on her way to the McBean castle by 7:30. Traffic was heavy coming into Randolph Crescent but thinned out on Queens Ferry Road. She bore right at Davidson's Mains and followed local roads until she reached Lauriston Castle, which had been willed to the City of Edinburgh by its last owners, William and Margaret Reid, with whom Calum McBean had been friendly.

She continued on to a break in a belt of yews, turned into it and followed a narrow dirt road for approximately a quarter of a mile, dense growths of rowans, hollies and rhododendrons lining her route. Directly ahead was the McBean Castle, small when compared to other fortress structures in Scotland but certainly large enough to establish its credentials as "a castle" rather than a house. The main tower, built in the sixteenth century, was four stories tall and sported two corbelled two-story turrets. Attached to the tower was the more recent portion of the complex. A scots pine, symbol of a Jacobite refuge for victims being pursued by redcoats, stood next to the turret door. A pair of chestnut trees flanked the door to the mansion. Pheasants and partridges fed on rolling lawns while peacocks preened among them, their brilliant tail feathers creating sudden bursts of color against the monochromatic green grass and gray stone of the buildings.

She pulled up in front of the turret, got out and walked around to the side. A flat expanse of lawn stretched toward the Firth of Forth, where tiny white sails and larger stacks of ocean-going vessels provided a mini-skyline. Heather had often played croquet on that lawn with her uncle and close family friends. "Stroke it firmly, lass," Calum would say, sometimes taking the mallet from her and demonstrating. Once, when she showed annoyance, he said, "Ye a lassie o pairts, Heather, but ye tyne the gate of if ye don't listen." At least he'd complimented her first before suggesting that she'd lose her knack for the game unless she listened to him.

She felt a lump in her throat as she remembered it. No matter how stern Calum McBean could be, she never doubted for a second that he loved her deeply, would have given up everything for her.

"Is it ye?" a female voice asked.

Agnes, their housekeeper of many years, was crossing the lawn.

"*Hello*, Agnes." They embraced. When they stepped apart, Heather was suddenly aware how old Agnes looked. She was in her late seventies but somehow had always seemed younger. Now there was no question of her age, and Heather wondered whether eighty wouldn't be more accurate.

"You surprise me, but then you always did that," Agnes said, grinning. "You'll be stayin' for a spell?"

Heather shook her head as they walked toward the house. "No. I can't stay long, I'm afraid, just a few days. I'll be in the city with friends."

Agnes stopped and frowned. "You'll not be stayin' here overnight, in your old room? The master would be disappointed."

"I can't, Agnes. I'd like to but—oh, look." She pointed to a clump of larch from which a pair of roe deer peered back at them.

"They're thick as meal," Agnes said.

The deer withdrew into the trees. Heather walked to the trees and looked down at a small marker over the grave of Calum's favorite dog, a Shetland sheepdog he'd named Ceit, Gaelic for Kate. The dog had lived to be seventeen, and when she died Calum buried her by the larch trees and inscribed the stone:

> *Ye were my Frien, Sweet Ceit,*
> *And I be keen o ye;*
> *Ye rin the gless on earth,*
> *But ye byde forever i me hert.*

He'd cried the day they buried Ceit, and that evening in the foyer he hung a painting a local artist had done of the dog.

"Hello, Ceit," Heather said to the watercolor of the sheltie as she and Agnes entered the house.

"A fine animal, that," Agnes said. "Broke your poor uncle's heart when she went. I'll make ye some tea."

"That sounds wonderful, Agnes. It's good to be home."

Agnes disappeared into the kitchen and Heather wandered into the library. It was weeks after Calum died before she could step foot into it. She stood now just inside the door and slowly looked about the room. The floors were covered with Persian rugs subdued enough not to detract from the rich display of art on the walls, including two large leather panels that had originated in Cordova in the mid-seventeenth century. The ceiling was a rococo display of cupids and heraldic beasts frolicking in high relief, and the fireplace carried through on the ceiling motif. The furniture was mostly Chippendale. Everywhere were works of art—Chinese porcelain, Mortlake tapestries, Ellicott clocks, pieces of Derbyshire flourspar known as Blue John given to Calum by William Reid from his extensive collection at Lauriston, original oils and watercolors, priceless firearms, Egyptian statuary and illuminated manuscripts.

Heather crossed the room to a display cabinet behind which were outstanding examples of Calum McBean's artifacts from past secret societies. One shelf was devoted to the Legion of Harsa, although only a few items remained from that collection. Once, the Harsa medal held center stage in that cabinet, but then Calum had donated it to the Smithsonian. Heather asked him about it once and was told that he wanted to distribute certain pieces to public places in every corner of the globe. Calum could make decisions like that on the spur of the moment. He was as impetuous as he was irascible, pondering the simplest decisions for months, making snap judgments on major issues within moments . . .

"Will you have your tea in here?" Agnes stood in the doorway, holding a silver tray.

"Yes, I will. Thank you, Agnes."

The housekeeper set the tray on the desk and asked if Heather needed anything else.

"No, but you could do me a favor. I'd just as soon not have many people know that I'm in Edinburgh." She wasn't in the mood to conduct a wake.

"As you say, Miss Heather. I'll not be here all day. I planned to leave sometime after the noon hour."

"That'll be fine. Will Clifton be here?" referring to a caretaker who lived in a cottage at the far end of the property close to the firth.

Agnes made a face. "I've not seen him for a fortnight, miss. Been on a bash lately."

Heather smiled. "He's been cockin' the wee finger, has he?" Clifton, she thought, gave credence to the saying, "The British drink for pleasure, for the Scots it's a profession."

"That he has, miss. I'll leave you now. Just ring if you need me."

"I will, Agnes, and thank you."

There was a pile of unopened mail on the desk, which she quickly went through. A file folder contained documents relating to the changeover of administration and maintenance from the McBean estate to the City of Edinburgh. One of the letters confirmed what Ian Sutherland had told her: the city had come to a final vote accepting the terms of the takeover. She slipped that letter into the file, leaned back and sipped her tea. Agnes had put a wheat scone, clotted cream and bramble jelly on the tray. Heather closed her eyes, and for a moment imagined Calum sitting in the chair, thin, sinewy and bent like a walking stick, gray hair stabbing the air from what seemed a hundred different directions, his face deeply lined with experience and wisdom, a man who'd looked into the sun for a very long time. She opened her eyes, whispered, "I miss you," got up, stoked the fire and looked out the windows to the shimmering firth on the horizon. Scotland's weather was up to its usual tricks. The morning's sunshine was now threatened by dark clouds rolling in from the east, where heavy rain could be seen as black mist over the water. A gust of wind rattled the hand-blown glass in the window, and seconds later the sky above opened, unleashing a torrent of rain.

Heather stayed at the window and watched the storm's rapid progress. It was over, at least for the McBean castle, in ten minutes, followed by a brilliant rainbow that slashed through the lightening sky and dove into the Firth of Forth.

Heather spent another half hour at the desk. She put in her purse a signed copy of a letter agreement that had been drawn between the estate and a leading antique dealer in the Edinburgh area, Ranald Robertson, who had been one of the few dealers Calum ever trusted. Knowing that, Heather had allowed Robertson to take on consignment selected pieces from the castle and to sell them to the public, with the lion's share of the proceeds returning to the McBean estate to help pay for taxes and renovations. There was a note from Robertson that he would be participating in a week-long antiques fair at the Assembly Halls on Princess Street and that his booth would feature items from the McBean collection.

"Is it all right if I'd be leaving now, Miss Heather?" Agnes asked from the doorway.

"Yes, of course. Are we still locking up in the same way?"

"Yes, mum. Everything is secured excepting for the main door."

"Good. I'll stay a while and be back in the morning. Will you be here?"

"I expect so. Miss McBean, might I mention something to you?"

"Of course, Agnes. Since when haven't you been able to?"

Agnes approached the desk. "I just wanted you to know, Miss Heather, that what you did for me after Master McBean died was generous to a fault. He'd provided nicely for me in the will. There was no need for you to make more of it."

"You deserve it, Agnes. Uncle Calum was very fond of you and deeply appreciated your loyalty. So do I." She squeezed the older woman's hand.

Agnes started to leave, stopped halfway to the door, turned and said in a grim voice, "And I'll go to my grave knowin' that he didn't use his own hand like they say he did."

"And so will I, Agnes, so will I. Maybe we'll get to the bottom of *that* before our graves call us."

"Better make it soon, Miss Heather. I've been feelin' a bit wabbit lately."

"So have I, Agnes. We both need a rest. I'll see you in the morning."

"Aye, you will." She shook her head. "They never believed me, the bobbies, that I heard two shots. They said I was hearin' things, like I was daft."

"I know, Agnes. Some day the truth will be out. Take care."

"You, too, miss."

Shortly after Agnes left, Heather decided to walk to Cramond village for lunch at the Cramond Inn. Her uncle seldom went out to eat or drink, preferring the comforts of the castle and, as he put it, "me own conversation." But he sometimes made an exception and went to the inn, where Robert Louis Stevenson had enjoyed many evenings downing whiskey and ale with bar friends...Calum would arrive in an ancient automobile, wearing a flowing black-and-gray tweed cape and a black tam-o'-shanter, brandishing his ebony walking stick like a bobby's nightstick, with, of course, Ceit at his heels. If he didn't like the people at the bar he'd go to a table in the dining room and drink alone until someone came in whose company he could tolerate, Ceit sitting passively beneath the table and accepting an occasional affectionate pat from her master. But such visits were rare, no more than once a month, and were virtually nonexistent toward the end.

Heather stopped at a kirk just up the road from the inn and strolled through its burial grounds, once the scene of a Roman garrison. She felt like she was in a limbo, a place where the senses were never allowed to be resolved, the mind prohibited from seeing far enough ahead to know the reasons for things, or the answers...

They greeted her warmly at the inn. She enjoyed a whiskey at the bar, then had a delicious local lunch in the dining room—prawns wrapped in smoked salmon, Dover sole, a small salad and coffee.

After lunch she took a walk along the River Almond. The tide was out and the river's muddy bottom stretched to the deeper waters of the firth. Hundreds of gulls screamed as they swooped low over the mud flats in search of food. She looked out over the firth and the boats bobbing in the water. The eastern horizon was black; another storm was on its way. Her hair rippled in an increasing breeze, and her face felt the sting of sea water whipped up from the firth and carried inland. Since Lewis's death she'd been fairly successful in controling her emotions, at least the outward show of them. But now, alone, in her native country, the beauty of it overwhelming and with the realization that she would never share it with the man she loved, she stopped fighting it. She leaned on a piling and let it out, not bothering to hide her heaving body from whomever might be watching, not caring whether a crowd gathered, feeling nothing but the awful loss, and the pain.

As she walked back toward the castle along the water's edge she felt a little better. Her Scottish heritage taught her to keep things inside, hidden, exclusive. It was wrong. She'd lost something important; it had been plucked from her like a gull snatching a mollusk from the sand. "Damn you," she said to whomever had killed Tunney. "*Damn* you for all of your days." Her words blew back in her face and she quickened her pace, eyes straight ahead, never looking up to the narrow road, where a dark green sedan moved slowly along, the driver matching his speed to the lone, small figure on the beach.

Five minutes before she reached the castle the day's third storm erupted. It was dark as night. The winds bent the chestnut trees low to the ground, and a bolt of lightning splashed intense white light over everything, followed by a booming clap of thunder. ("They're *booling* upstairs," Calum used to say.)

She drew a deep breath and ran toward the turret, holding her purse over her head. The rain soaked her as she fished for the key, found it and opened massive doors imported from Spain. Another flash of lightning, thunder reverberating off stone walls, objects dancing on the walls as the wind forced itself through crevices and turned the foyer into a wind tunnel.

The phone rang. What a time. Heather kicked off waterlogged shoes and wrung water from her hair onto the floor. She heard something fall in the kitchen, probably a pan from a wall rack. *"Hoot awa,"* she muttered, and ran in stocking feet toward the nearest phone, picked it up from its cradle, dropped it, put the wrong end to her ear, reversed it. "Hello . . . ?"

They'd hung up. "Damn," she said, slamming the receiver. She looked at her watch. She'd have to hurry to catch Robertson's booth at the Assembly Halls. She went to the bathroom, where she brushed out her damp hair and vigorously rubbed her legs and feet with a coarse towel. One thing she'd wanted to do before leaving was to gather up a collection of antique, hand-painted miniature soldiers to give to Roberston. Calum had enjoyed the collection but considered it an adolescent indulgence. She was quite sure he'd approve of her decision to sell off the collection.

She walked down a long, cluttered hallway leading to what was called the reception hall, another room dominated by Calum's collections. In addition to being a showcase for the miniature soldiers it housed an eclectic array of ancient armament, brickbats and broadswords, pepper boxes and perriers, scimitars and sgiandubhs, foils and gaffs. The room was almost pitch-black; thick purple drapes cut off what light was available from the outside.

She reached for a wall switch, found it, flipped it up. A chandelier flickered to life, followed by a violent explosion of thunder and the room went dark again. During the brief moment of illumination Heather had advanced halfway across the room. She skirted a table in the center and approached the cabinets that held the soldiers. A door leading to an adjacent study was open. She stopped in front of it and stiffened at what sounded like a groan from the next room. The wind, she decided. A sliver of intense light slashed through a small gap in the drapes as lightning again lit up the sky.

Heather glanced up at a row of ten-foot-tall Italian *glaives* lined up on the wall next to the doorway. They dated from the sixteenth century, the fashionable weaponry of the day—long curved blades projecting from elongated, studded wooden handles inlaid with gold, silver and mother-of-pearl and laced with bands of gold damascene. Again a sound from the next room. She peered into its dark recesses, saw nothing, took a step toward the cabinet. The *glaive* nearest the doorway pitched forward from its clamp, the blade diving toward her head. Indeed, if she hadn't taken that first step the outcome might well have been... well, the blade missed her by inches and clattered to the floor.

Heather's heart, she was sure, had stopped beating for a moment. She looked through the open doorway, saw nothing, leaned over and picked up the *glaive*. "That would have been nasty," she said once she was able to breathe again. She leaned the weapon against the wall, went to the windows and opened the drapes. The sky had cleared over the firth and another rainbow had appeared. She hoped it signaled the end of such natural terrors.

Heather put the soldiers in a box, left the castle and drove away... passing the green sedan that had followed her from the Cramond Inn but, of course, paying it no notice as it fell in behind her and maintained a consistent distance all the way to town.

The Assembly Halls were teeming with antique dealers. Ranald Robertson had taken a large space to the rear of the exhibit area. Heather couldn't help but smile as she approached his booth. Robertson, who was about fifty, had the perpetual look of a man bemused by life. Half-glasses sat on the tip of an aquiline nose, and his constantly elevated eyebrows nearly doubled the distance between eyes and glasses. He was as eccentric

as her uncle had been, only more social. He lived with
a dozen cats, a demented mother who sometimes believed she was handmaiden to Mary, Queen of Scots,
and a parakeet named Macbeth, who, Robertson
claimed, spoke Gaelic at odd hours.

He was in the midst of a transaction with a matronly
woman who couldn't decide between two icons from
the expendable portion of Calum's estate. Heather was
tempted to recommend one over the other but resisted.
The woman made her choice, paid Robertson and
walked away.

"Well," Robertson said over his glasses, "you look
splendid, Heather."

"Thank you. How are you, Ranald?"

"Tip-top, doing a brisk business. By the way, there
was a fellow looking for you this afternoon."

"Really? Who?"

"He didn't give his name. A big, fat fellow, well
dressed. An Englishman."

Evelyn Killinworth? But he would have come to the
castle... "What did he say?"

"Nothing much, just wondered whether I'd seen you.
He seemed to know who I was and that I was handling
your uncle's things. He didn't stay long, chatted about
some of the items, mentioned the murder of that Arab
in London."

"Oh?"

"Aye. He wondered whether I'd known him. The
Arab, I mean. I didn't, although I certainly knew about
him. A bad sort, dealing in anything stolen. I'm certain
there's a legion of people not spilling tears over his
demise." He peered into the box she carried. "For
me?"

"What? Oh, the soldiers from Calum's collection."
She handed the box to him.

"Just in time. I've someone stopping by who's in

the toy-soldier business. He wants everything I have. Well, how are things at the castle?"

"The city has approved the takeover."

"So I'd heard. I hope you're doing the right thing."

"What choice do I have? Unless the city runs and maintains it, taxes will eat up the estate and the castle will end up being bought by some Frenchman who'll turn it into an inn with fancy food, modern rooms and postcards in the lobby."

Robertson laughed. "Dreadful image you paint."

"Imagine the image Calum would have drawn."

"Spare me that. How long will you be in Edinburgh?"

"Not sure, Ranald, but no more than another two days."

"Pity. I'll try to get out to the castle before you leave."

"Yes, that would be good. I'm not staying..."

"Pardon?"

"Nothing. I'm not staying long. Please drop by."

"With a check. Death and taxes, as they say."

She walked slowly through the halls, stopping at tables but never really examining them. She could only think of what Robertson had said about a big fat Englishman inquiring about her. It had to be Evelyn. But why hadn't he called, or stopped at the castle? What about the Arab, Ashtat, at ... Belgravia, Belgravia, where—

"Heather, Heather."

She turned to see Robertson pushing through the crowds. "I almost forgot. The fellow who was looking for you asked about Collinsworth."

"Seth Collinsworth?"

"None other. He wanted to know his whereabouts."

"Name a prison."

He laughed. "I haven't heard anything of him for more than a year. You?".

She shook her head.

Seth Collinsworth was Scotland's most infamous art thief. He'd made international headlines ten years earlier by stealing a truckload of paintings from the Scottish National Portrait Gallery. He was arrested within twenty-four hours and served a six-year prison term, but everyone knew it was small payment for a life of crime. Collinsworth had been the Scottish conduit to London's art underworld. He'd lived the high life in Glasgow—a Rolls-Royce, town-house, trips to cities around the world, including extended stays in the capitals of the Middle East, a clutch of beautiful young women on his arm who didn't know that Matisse painted or Stravinsky composed, but who knew that Seth Collinsworth spent.

Seth Collinsworth...why would Evelyn want to find him? Unless...But that was too farfetched. Wasn't it...?

She left the Assembly Hall. Outside George Street was alive with men and women leaving their offices and heading for home now that the storm was over. The gloamin', Scotland's unique, slowly fading evening light, was casting its soft spell over the city. She felt good being here. She was home. If only Lewis were standing next to her, sharing the feeling that she felt...

Was Evelyn Killinworth here?

That was her uneasy thought as she looked to her right, saw that no traffic was coming and stepped from the curb.

"Look *out*," a woman called from behind.

Heather saw out of the corner of her eye a car coming down the street on the wrong side. She threw herself back, just in time as the car sped by, its right fender nearly grazing her thigh.

"You stupid ass," a man yelled, running into the street and shaking his fist at the driver. Heather looked up the street. The car had turned a corner and disappeared.

"You all right miss?" someone asked.

"Yes, I think so."

"Stupid American, you can bet on that," someone else said.

"Did you see him?" Heather asked.

A man shook his head. "Just another rich overfed American driving on the wrong side of the road."

"Didn't even stop," a woman said.

Heather, properly shaken, returned to the George and immediately put through a call to the Chesterfield Hotel in London. She asked for Dr. Killinworth. His room did not answer. "Is he still a guest?" She was assured that he was, that, in fact, he had been good enough to inform the desk in advance that he planned to check out two days later.

She left Edinburgh at noon the following day, flying to London and connecting with a British Airways flight to New York.

CHAPTER 23

"*How was the trip?*" Hanrahan asked after he'd gotten Heather a cup of coffee. She'd arrived at his MPD office early; her internal clock was still set to London time. Her McBean tartan pleated skirt, navy blue blouse and blazer were fresh looking. She looked tired and worn.

"Hectic, to say the least. But it's good I went . . . Have there been any developments here?"

"Nothing firm . . . what did you find out from your private detective?"

"Precious little, I'm afraid. And please don't say I told you so."

"That's not my style"—though he was tempted. "But what *did* he say?"

"Only that Lewis had seen Peter Peckham the week before he was killed, and that now Peter seems to be missing."

"Missing?" Hanrahan was surprised that she hadn't heard about Peckham's death, and wasn't anxious to be the one to break the news. She'd already had enough death in her young life.

"According to Mr. Paley, who by the way is a vile little man, Peter's friends haven't seen or heard from him for over a week. I tried his home several times and went to his shop. No luck."

Hanharan leaned back and focused on a crack in the pale yellow wall behind her. "How's the coffee?" he asked.

"Quite good, thanks."

"I've got some news for you, Heather, and I'm afraid it isn't good."

She'd started to return the cup to the desk's edge, stopped halfway there. "Go ahead," she said, not looking at him.

"Peter Peckham is dead."

The cup stayed poised midway between her lips and the desk top. "How do you know?" she finally asked in a low, flat voice.

"Scotland Yard." He started to give her the details, then stopped. Better take it slow.

"How did it happen?...was he murdered too?"

"Seems that way."

"Tell me."

He told her what he knew.

Her voice was stronger now. She put the cup on the desk and went to a window. It was dirty, and the heat and humidity outside seemed dirty too, as though it would stick to your skin if it touched you. She took several deep breaths, then raised her head.

Hanrahan got up and grabbed what had become a thick purple file folder bearing the label *Lewis Tunney: Case #641-T.* He came around the desk and slapped the file on it. Heather turned at the noise. "I'm all right," she said. "I guess one becomes toughened ...How did Peter Peckham die?"

"A blow to the head. Whoever did it dumped him under a bridge on the Thames...I'm sorry, but you asked."

She wrapped her arms about herself and slowly shook her head from side to side.

Hanrahan picked up the folder again and held it in the air. "See this? It's your fiancé's file. It's got his name and a department file classification on it. It's purple because somebody was selling purple file folders cheap. Another couple of months and victims will be filed in orange, or yellow, depending on the price. You know, I've been dealing with folders like this for most of my adult life. The only thing that ever changes are the colors. Somebody gets killed for the usual reasons, jealousy, greed, a short circuit in the brain, a mistake, fear, self-defense. It's like plots for stories. How many are there? Nothing much seems to change. At least that's the way I've always looked at it. But this one is different, not because the file's purple instead of white, but because I see it different. Feel different."

She started to say something but he shook his head.

"I was really worried about you while you were away. Now, Heather McBean, I'm here to tell you *that's* different for me. It means I've got an interest in this case that goes beyond the usual. I care, damn it, about what's in this folder. That's different. I accept that many cases never get solved. The folders and everything in them goes into a dead file, and the only time anybody cares or remembers is when a cop gets drunk and asks whether I remember when so-and-so got it. Sometimes I do, sometimes I don't. But that's not true with purple folder Number 641-T. Okay? I'm going to remember this case because I'm going to get to the bottom of it. I'm also going to try to make damn sure that nobody else gets hurt, especially you."

"I appreciate that, but I—"

"You're lucky you aren't in this folder, you know that? You keep sticking your neck out and making it easy. Do you know how they chop a guy's head off in Arab countries for stealing or killing someone? They tie his hands behind his back, get him down in the sand on his knees and poke him in the back with a stick. His body reacts, his neck extends and the guy with the sword does his job. With you, nobody needs a stick. *Your* head's stuck out all the time."

She returned to her chair, crossed her legs and played with the strap on her purse.

"You know what, I'll level with you. I don't like feeling this way about a case. I like it better the other way, just looking at it as another file folder. I sure as hell don't need to be worrying about you, and I've already told you that. I've got enough troubles of my own without picking up extra ones. End of speech."

She was quiet for several moments, then looked up uneasily at him. "I've been trying to find some answers myself. I appreciate everything you've said, but can I also remind you that *I'm* the one whose fiancé was killed." She slung her purse over her shoulder and started for the door.

"Where are you going?"

"I'm not sure."

"Sit down."

"Why? What's your next move, to arrest me, put me in solitary confinement and keep a twenty-four-hour guard over me until you've found Lewis's murderer, or until your purple folder goes to its final resting place in dead storage."

"That's not a bad idea." He allowed a sour grin.

"I don't see the humor in it, captain—"

"And I keep trying, although it isn't easy. Sit down and I'll tell you what I've come to. Maybe if I do you'll understand a little better why I'm so worried about you."

She sat in the chair.

"Let's start with this." He pulled a sheet of paper from the folder and handed it to her. Typed across the top in capital letters was EVELYN KILLINWORTH.

She had just started to read when Joe Pearl opened the door.

"Not now, Joe."

"Only take a minute, Mac," he said, motioning Hanrahan to accompany him to the bullpen, where he gave Hanrahan a list of Evelyn Killinworth's travels over the previous five years.

"And?"

"Lots of unexplained chunks of time, as we knew. Not that it's unusual for a professor to have lots of time off to travel."

"Get to it, Joe."

Pearl glanced through the glass at Heather, who seemed deep in her reading. "There've been six separate trips to the Middle East over the past five years— Jidda, Beirut, Morocco, a couple of others."

"What'd he do in all those places?"

"Ask him, Mac. Whatever, he always stayed at the best hotels, that's for sure. Anyway, you wanted it and we got it for you. What's going on with her?"

"I'm not sure. Well, thanks, Joe. Keep on it."

"Mac."

"What?"

"You ought to take that suit back and have it re-altered. It bunches in the back, up around the neck."

Hanrahan looked down at his suit. It was new; he hadn't worn it before, had picked it up only two days ago from Cavalier at F and Ninth, where he bought all his clothes off the rack. "I think it fits fine," he said.

"Just thought I'd mention it. I like the color, though. Slate blue."

Hanrahan returned to his office, took off his jacket and hung it on a rack. He ran his thumbs around the waistband of the pants, caught a fast look at his reflection in the door's glass and sat behind the desk.

"Why did you give me this?" Heather asked, handing him back the paper on Killinworth.

"You read it?"

"Yes. I knew all these things about him. It's really nothing more than a short biography."

"Nothing strikes you as strange?"

"What do you mean?"

"Where does he get all his money?"

"All his money? I didn't think Evelyn was a rich man."

"He lives like one. What about it? No questions about him, no doubts?" He sensed that she'd suddenly become uncomfortable. "Haven't even thought about it?"

"Well...not exactly."

"You don't sound too sure. When Dr. Tunney was murdered, Killinworth was here in Washington. He was here when you were attacked, and when your hotel room was broken into. Now, he's in London when someone else is murdered."

"He wasn't there when Peter was killed. You said he'd been dead a week before they found him." Wasn't she overdoing this defending him. After what had happened to her...?

"I'm not talking about Peter Peckham, I'm talking about an Arab art dealer named Rashad Ashtat. Ever hear of him?"

"Well, I read about him in London."

"Then you know he was killed while you *and* Killinworth were in London?"

"Yes..."

"What was your reaction?"

"I didn't know the man—"

"I didn't ask you that. Well, did Dr. Tunney know him?"

"I don't know."

"How about Peckham? Did he know this Ashtat?"

"I don't know that either."

"Killinworth...did he ever mention an art dealer named Rashad Ashtat?"

"No..."

"He's spent a lot of time in the Middle East...Look, I'm just trying to put some things together. That's my job."

"I understand that."

"Good. You said that the private detective confirmed that Dr. Tunney had spent time with Peter Peckham before coming to Washington. Do you have any idea what they talked about?"

"No...I don't."

Hanrahan picked up the purple folder, bent it and its contents back and forth. "Like I said, this one's *not* ending up in a dead file. Anything else to add to it?"

"Captain Hanrahan, I know you feel I don't always tell you everything I should, but I—"

"Now that you mention it, I'll say you're right. For instance, I heard you almost got yourself run over in Edinburgh."

"How did you know *that*?"

"It's not important, but where I come from that might be considered a pretty close call."

"It was, but people on the scene said it was just a stupid hit-and-run *American* who couldn't remember the right side of the road to drive on...by the way, did you have me followed?"

"That would annoy you, wouldn't it? Even if the reason was that I was worried about you."

"I do seem to be a problem for you, don't I? In fact,

I mostly seem to be apologizing to you. I'll be going now."

She went to the door and took hold of the knob. Hanrahan sat back, folded his hands across his chest and looked at her. She turned slowly.

"Forget something?"

"Do you also know that I dropped Dr. Killinworth off in Belgravia, on the corner where I believe Mr. Ashtat lived, the night of his murder?"

Hanrahan kept a straight face, didn't indicate whether it was news to him or not. "Did he tell you he was going there to see Ashtat?"

"No."

"Did he tell you after he came back what he'd done in Belgravia?"

"No, except that it was boring and frustrating. And there are a lot of people in Belgravia one could be seeing."

"True enough."

"I've told you this in confidence, captain. I assume you'll honor that confidence. I'm sure you wouldn't want to hang a man on the basis of a coincidence."

"Wrong on the first count, right on the second."

"I'm half-relieved. What will you do with what I've told you? If it has no relevance—"

"That's not for me or you to decide. For example, I think Scotland Yard should know, don't you? They're on the scene, after all. I have a friend at the Yard. I don't know what color file folders they're using over there these days, but he hates to see one go into a dead file as much as I do. I'm going to tell him what you've told me. If he wants to follow up with Dr. Killinworth, that'll be his decision."

"I'm feeling a bit wabbit," she said, sitting in the chair.

"Wabbit?"

"Not well."

"Can I get you something? Water?"

"No, thank you, I'll be all right. I really must go."

"Sure . . . Miss McBean, Heather, I'd like to see more of you." Before she could say anything he quickly put it in a professional context. "I'm not an enemy, I'm on your side, for God's sake. We want the same thing, to find out who killed Lewis Tunney."

"I know. I know . . . well, here I go again, apologizing . . ." This time she managed a half-smile.

"Please don't . . . by the way, are you still staying at Killinworth's house?"

"Yes. Do you think he might murder me in my sleep? Oh dear, there I go again."

He sighed. "Yes, there you go. Well, keep in touch."

Not in your sleep, he thought, at least not in his house . . .

The moment she was gone Hanrahan put through a call to Scotland Yard in London. When Bert Burns came on the line, Hanrahan told him. "Bert, I think we both just got lucky."

CHAPTER 24

LIEUTENANT JOE PEARL SAT IN THE GARDEN CAFE OF the National Gallery of Art. It was noon. A large circular fountain in the middle of the room spewed jets of water into the air, its streams cascading into the center. A brown-and-burgundy marble wall surrounded the fountain; lush green plants sat on the wall. The tabletops were white-and-gray marble, the bases dark green wrought iron. A large skylight above the fountain directed light down to where the water joined, giving it a shimmering, ethereal quality. The flow of water created a constant, soothing whisper.

Joe Pearl leaned an elbow on the wall and looked through the spray at a table directly across the fountain, where Evelyn Killinworth and Janis Dewey sat. Killinworth, in a tan safari suit and a pale pink open shirt, had just been served, for him, a shockingly prosaic ham sandwich. Dewey, wearing a loose kelly-green dress, had just ordered a shrimp salad. Pearl, wishing they'd met in a restaurant offering heartier food, had ordered roast beef on pumpernickel.

He had tried to get out of Hanrahan's assignment to follow Killinworth for the day . . . after all, he hadn't pulled surveillance duty in years and always found it

219

boring. Still, he couldn't talk Hanrahan out of assigning him as Killinworth's tail. "It'll keep you honest, Joe, get you back to basics," Hanrahan had said, "Might even take your mind off my lousy-fitting suits."

The day had started with Pearl driving a safe distance behind Killinworth to Chloe Prentwhistle's house. A red Citation and a gray de Ville were in the driveway. Killinworth was greeted at the door by a man Pearl knew to be Walter Jones. Killinworth didn't stay long, twenty-six minutes, precisely, according to Pearl's watch and log.

He followed the large professor from Prentwhistle's house to a Mobil station where Killinworth made a brief call from a booth while a young man with long blond hair filled his car with premium unleaded. From there Killinworth had driven directly to the National Gallery, made a call from a lobby phone booth and then had taken a table next to the fountain. Janis Dewey joined him ten minutes later. Two things struck Pearl about her. First, she was beautiful; he'd always been partial to redheads, especially those with long red hair.

He also noted that she seemed flustered. She'd obviously not met Killinworth before, and once she sat down she had the appearance of someone wishing she were somewhere else.

Pearl could not hear their conversation, momentarily considered changing tables and decided against it. He had the rest of the day to go and didn't want to draw attention to himself.

After they had eaten, Janis Dewey stood and extended her hand. Killinworth got to his feet and took it. For a moment Pearl thought he was going to kiss her hand; he didn't.

Pearl then got behind Killinworth in the cashier's line, positioning himself so that he would be seen only in profile if Killinworth turned. He needn't have bothered. Killinworth walked straight out of the museum, got into his car and drove to the Georgetown University library, where he spent four hours. Pearl was losing out to boredom and sleepiness in the parking lot when Killinworth reappeared and drove to F. Scott's in Georgetown, where the afterwork crowd was now gathering. Pearl gave Killinworth a three-minute head start through the doors before following him inside.

Business was brisk at the black-and-chrome bar. Killinworth had found space at the bar and was talking with a young man dressed in a glen plaid suit, button-down shirt and brown silk tie. Pearl approached the bar as nonchalantly as possible, slipped in behind Killinworth and ordered a glass of white wine. Killinworth couldn't see him, which was good, but his bulk also made it impossible for Pearl to see the other man and to hear more than snippets of their conversation.

Killinworth was saying, "...she's a nice girl ...dreadful food, for little old ladies with tiny stomachs...yes, I saw Chloe and Walter this morning...of course they did..."

The young man said, "I still find this..." Pearl wasn't sure but he thought he said, "ludicrous."

"Think what you will, Mr. Kazakis," Killinworth said, "but it is more a matter of—"

"Joe. Hey, Joe." Pearl felt a slap on his back, turned to see a former MPD colleague, Johnny Carter, who had been quietly eased off the force for shaking down an after-hours social club owner who turned out to be the son-in-law of a leading politician.

Carter was drunk. The woman hanging on his arm was a walking Revlon investment. Black hair sprouted out beneath a blond wig, and a black dress was cut to the navel, exposing flat breasts. "Hey, Joe, what's a *cop* doin' in a place like this? Lookin' for action?"

Pearl smiled tightly at Carter, nodded to the woman.

"Have a nice night, Johnny," he said, and turned his back on them, hoping Killinworth hadn't heard the exchange. Killinworth, still deep in conversation with Kazakis, seemed not to have noticed.

Carter now poked Pearl in the back, "Hey, Joe, so what's going down?"

Pearl turned. His smile had vanished.

Carter said, "Say hello to Brooke, Joe, Brooke Brown."

"Please to meet you." And to Carter: "Please get lost, Johnny."

Carter seemed not sure how to react. He squeezed Brooke's arm, narrowed his boozy eyes at Pearl. "How's things at MPD?" he asked loudly. Pearl understood he was doing it deliberately. "Hey, Don, give my *cop* friend here a drink on me."

Killinworth now turned and looked at Pearl.

Pearl tossed money on the bar and walked toward the door.

Carter followed him outside. "Hey, Joe, what'd I do, blow a collar?"

Pearl abruptly laughed and slapped him on the shoulder, "No, Johnny, just killing time...hey, how about a big favor?"

"What?"

"I need wheels for an hour. You planning to stay here that long?"

Carter shrugged. "Yeah. Seems the broad wants to eat."

"Is that really her name, Brooke?"

"Who knows, who cares? What do you need a car for?"

"Believe it or not somebody made mine. Just an hour. Nothing's sacred."

"All right, sure, Joe. Glad to." Carter reached into

his pocket, pulled out a set of keys. "It's that maroon LTD over there." He pointed across the street.

"Oh...yeah. Thanks."

Pearl took the keys and Carter started back toward F. Scott's. "Hey, Johnny," Pearl suddenly called out. He went up to Carter, slapped his head and laughed. "Don't know what's wrong with me, Johnny. I don't need a car until later. Got my assignment mixed up. I'll check one out from the motor pool."

"You sure?"

"Yeah, I'm sure, but listen, thanks anyway." He handed Carter back the keys.

"Any time, Joe. Hey, you're sure you're not sore at what happened in there? Just havin' some fun."

"Million laughs, Johnny. Drop in some day. Lunch is on me."

"Yeah, I will." He turned conspiritorial. "Hey, Joe, Brooke here's got a friend who..."

"Good for her, Johnny. Well, enjoy, see you..."

Pearl waited for Killinworth, followed him home, lingered a half hour, then went to his own apartment, where he called Mac Hanrahan at home.

"Find out anything?" Hanrahan asked.

"No, Mac. I'll give you a full report in the morning."

"Okay."

"I'm not pulling that duty tomorrow, am I?"

"No."

"Good. Then I won't call in sick."

CHAPTER 25

TWO EIGHT-YEAR-OLD KIDS WERE DOING A BRISK BUSI-
ness in fireworks around the corner from MPD headquarters. Hanrahan stopped on his way to work and
examined their merchandise. "It's illegal to sell this
stuff," he said.

One of the kids told him to get lost.

"Watch your language," Hanrahan said as he walked
away. He hoped his nephews wouldn't have firecrackers at the Fourth of July family picnic, which was two
days away. He'd ended up the heavy last year when
he took them away.

Sergeant Arey was on desk duty. "Mornin', captain," he said as Hanrahan pushed through the glass
doors.

"Arey. What's new?"

"Not much. Can I ask you something? What's the
chances of getting off on the Fourth? They've got me
down for nine-to-four."

Hanrahan looked at him. "You know I never get
involved in duty rosters outside homicide."

"Yeah, I know, but I figured maybe you'd put in
the word. I like being home on the Fourth."

Hanrahan was tempted to switch with him. It would

be worth it to get out of the picnic. Ever since his divorce he dreaded the annual event, found his relatives boring and nosey and, in some cases, even smug and cruel. Kathy would be there this year. One of his kids called and told him so.

"Just thought I'd try, captain," Arey said.

"No harm in trying, Arey."

He hung up his jacket, got coffee from the bullpen and settled behind his desk with the morning paper. There was an editorial critical of the MPD's handling of the Tunney murder. What especially rankled him was:

> The best Capt. Mac Hanrahan and his staff have been able to accomplish is to arrest a Hispanic dishwasher named Montenez, whose common-law wife delivered, on a silver platter to MPD, the missing Legion of Harsa. MPD has hounded Montenez, caused him to lose his job. For shame, MPD, for allowing a sordid murder in a revered institution to linger into the national holiday, the Fourth of July. For shame.

By the time Joe Pearl walked into Hanrahan's office a half hour later Hanrahan was, as Kathy used to say, a cross between Attila the Hun and Henry VIII.

"Hey, Mac, have dinner with your mother last night?" Pearl said it with a smile.

"No, Joe, and one more wise-ass comment from you will put you back checking parking meters."

"Sorry. Well, here's the rundown on my day with Killinworth."

"Don't bother. He called a few minutes ago. What did you do, Joe, hand him your business card?"

"What?"

"He demanded to know if he was being followed."

"Mac, I'm sorry about that...it was on account of that fool Johnny Carter—"

"And you slashed his tires."

"What?"

"Carter called too, says you cut two of his tires."

"That's ridiculous. You know Carter. He's a psychopathic liar—"

"I told him as much. Considering the way you've handled this assignment, though...well, I got some other calls too, Joe. Commissioner Johnson, for example."

"Oh?"

"Oh yeah. He wants us to be sure than nothing unfortunate happens between now and the Fourth. The vice-president is concerned that the celebration not...how did he put it?...not 'sully the American spirit of the Fourth'...*sully*, Joe. Your kind of talk. No matter what, no sullying. Got it?"

"Yeah, I—"

"Did you read the funny papers this morning?"

"No."

"'For shame,' they said. Our record on the Tunney case was the object of their affections."

"What else? I mean what else turned you into Attila the Hun this morning?"

"Never mind...tell me about Killinworth."

Pearl read his notes to Hanrahan. When he was through he said. "What's with Janis Dewey, Mac?"

"Meaning?"

"What's her connection with the Tunney murder?"

Hanrahan ran his hand over his beard. "I don't know. Did you pick up on what she and Killinworth were talking about?"

"No. I kept a low profile."

"Real low, Joe. According to Killinworth you wore a sandwich board announcing your profession."

"It wasn't *that* bad."

"Bad enough. You say Janis Dewey seemed flustered?"

"That's the way I read it. She looked like Killinworth hit her with something fairly heavy."

"Any idea what it was?"

"I couldn't hear."

"But you know he had a ham sandwich, and she had a shrimp salad."

"I could *see* that."

Hanrahan shook his head, picked up the phone. "Get me Alfred Throckly at the National Museum of American History." He looked at Pearl. "Call Janis Dewey. Get her over here this afternoon. Make it three o'clock, and growl at her on the phone. You should be able to handle that, Joe."

When Throckly came on the line Hanrahan said, "Mr. Throckly, Mac Hanrahan from MPD. Hold on a minute." He pulled a computer print-out from the Tunney file. "Mr.Throckly, I have a question for you."

"Yes?"

"I tried to reach you a few days ago. Your secretary said you were away."

"That's right."

"Where did you go?"

"I don't think I'm under obligation to answer that—"

"Want me to put you under obligation?"

"That sounds like a threat."

"There's no need for threats, Mr. Throckly. I called your office, your secretary said you were away. I asked where you'd gone. She told me England. I thought to myself how nice that sounded, getting away to jolly old England for a few days."

"I thought the same thing, captain—"

"Yeah, sure. How did you get there, Mr. Throckly?

I checked passenger manifests between New York–Washington and London. I missed your name."

"I don't quite follow—"

"I had reasons for checking those manifests, Mr. Throckly. Some nasty things going on in London recently. I wanted to see who was there that I knew when they were happening."

"And you found that I *wasn't* there. What good fortune." He laughed.

"Not necessarily, Mr. Throckly. Where *were* you?"

It took Throckly a beat or two to say, "Can I depend on your discretion?"

"You can't *depend* on anything with me, Mr. Throckly, but then again, I've never been known as a great conversationalist."

"I'm glad to hear that. Well...actually, I told people I was going to Europe so that I could find a few days' peace and quiet. I needed to get away. The fact is, I never went further than Georgetown."

"Where did you go there?"

"To a friend's home...I read a book, slept, ate and, as they say, recharged batteries that were running low."

"Who was this friend?"

"Does it matter?"

"I don't know. You tell me and I'll have a better idea."

"If I tell you the name of my host, will it somehow get him involved in your Tunney investigation?"

"I don't know, Mr. Throckly. But it would help *your* story."

"I don't appreciate the implications of that, captain. But, all right, I was at the home of an old friend, a Mr. Norman Huffaker."

Hanrahan was tempted to mention the arrest sheet from Vice on Ford Saunders and this same "old friend," Huffaker, but decided not to. "Well, sorry you didn't get to Europe, glad you found some rest. Thanks for your time and your cooperation..."

Hanrahan's switch to noncommital pleasantness seemed to make Throckly uneasy.

"Is there more to this than you told me?"

"Why do you ask?"

"I don't know, I just have this feeling that—"

"Mr. Throckly, I spend most of my working days and nights asking questions and getting answers that have nothing whatsoever to do with anything." True enough, but he was pleased to see Throckly's failure to be reassured.

"All right...if I can be of any help, please don't hesitate to call."

"Count on it, Mr. Throckly."

Hanrahan went over the passenger manifests again. His staff had done a thorough job. The name of every transatlantic passenger between Washington–New York and London were on the sheets. It had been a shot, one he had to take. He'd hoped to see a name from the Tunney investigation that could be linked to the Ashtat murder, but that hadn't happened. The absence of Throckly's name, however, had caught his attention...

"Mr. Huffaker?" Hanrahan said when his call was answered.

"Yes."

"This is Captain Mac Hanrahan, Washington MPD." Silence. "Mr. Huffaker?"

"Please, leave me alone."

"Sorry, but I need to talk to you."

"Good God, what have we come to?"

"What?"

"A man is entitled to live his private life *in* private,

not be harassed because of his sexual preferences. It's not only unconscionable, it's unconstitutional."

Hanrahan wanted to be patient and was tempted to take on the issue Huffaker had just raised, but this wasn't the time to indulge himself in philosophical debate. "Mr. Huffaker, I want to question you about the Lewis Tunney case."

"Oh, my God, you can't be serious."

"What time would be convenient for you?"

"I don't know, I ... not here, for God's sake. I don't need any more police cars with sirens and flashing lights in my driveway. I'll come to you."

"Fine. An hour?"

"God, no, I'm not even up yet. This afternoon. Could I come by at two?"

"Sure. You know where we are."

"I think so. Your name was ... ?"

"Hanrahan, Mac Hanrahan."

Hanrahan hung up wishing he had a tap on Huffaker's phone. The nasty conversations with Throckly and Ford would be interesting.

Joe Pearl called. "Janis Dewey will be here at three. She's upset, Mac. I thought she was going to cry."

"I'm counting on it."

Commissioner Johnson called and asked whether Hanrahan was free for lunch. "No," Hanrahan said. He quickly left his office and drove to Connecticut Avenue, N.W., went down a flight of steps that looked like they led to a subway station, pushed through a door and was in Jo and Mo's, a favorite steak house. One of the owners kidded him about the editorial, about his tie and the extra pounds he'd put on since he'd last been there.

"Drink?" a waiter asked after telling him the latest and worst Polish joke.

"Gin on the rocks."

He sipped his drink, chewed on a thick piece of dark pumpernickel, doodled on a lined yellow legal pad. He checked his watch a half hour later, waved a waiter to the table and ordered a rare sirloin, fried onions and another drink. He never stopped writing, making numbered lists with lettered subcategories, drawing arrows to connect words and names, chewing his cheek as he worked, looking up only to check on who'd come through the door.

His steak arrived. He sliced into the meat, took a bite and glanced up at new arrivals. Leading a party of four was Commissioner Johnson, who spotted Hanrahan immediately, excused himself from his luncheon companions and came to the table.

"Commissioner," Hanrahan said.

"Eating alone, Mac?"

"Yeah. My date stood me up."

"Tough. Real tough." Johnson sat down. "What's with this Killinworth character?"

Hanrahan put a portion of steak in his mouth, holding up a finger as he chewed.

"Looks good," Johnson said.

"Best in the city." Hanrahan added half an onion ring to what was in his mouth and savored the combination. "Killinworth is a fat, pompous pain in the ass, Cal. Along with that, he pretty much heads my list of suspects in the Tunney case."

"He wasn't even at the party."

"Maybe he pulled the strings. All I know is that there's too much about him that keeps me awake nights. He gets my ten-Tums rating."

Johnson shot his cuffs. "He's lodged a complaint."

"Yeah, I know. He called this morning."

"He told me he had. He claims you didn't give him any satisfaction."

"That's his version. What was I supposed to do,

offer an out-of-court settlement because he's offended at being tailed?"

"Who'd you put on it?"

"Joe Pearl."

"Evidently Pearl wasn't very subtle."

"You might say that." Hanrahan attacked his steak again.

"Mac."

"What?"

"Lay off. I've already told you that."

Hanrahan swallowed. "Lay off what? Killinworth? The others on the list? I'm supposed to be investigating a murder at the Smithsonian. What I hear is lay off. That's a no-win deal."

"Maybe so, Mac, but I'm telling you again, slow down. Let the Fourth slide by and make everybody happy."

"Does it make *you* happy, Cal?"

"Happiness isn't written into my job description."

"Who's on your back this time, besides Killinworth?"

"Would you believe the vice-president of the United States? It seems your fat pompous ass complained to him, too."

"You're joking." Hanrahan told a waiter that he didn't want dessert. "Killinworth calls the vice-president because he's sore at being followed by MPD?"

"Seems so."

"And Oxenhauer listened to him? What is this? What does the V.P. do up there in the White House, take complaints and give refunds on duplicate Christmas gifts?"

Johnson looked across the room to where his party had been seated. He put his hand on Hanrahan's arm. "Don't let me down, Mac. There's more at stake here than a single case." He got up and joined the others.

Hanrahan paid his check, defended himself against a mock right cross from one of the owners and stepped out into the intense midday heat and humidity, wishing he were back in the dark, quiet cool of Jo and Mo's. If he hadn't had appointments back at MPD, if Johnson weren't there he might have scooted back inside, called in sick and spent the rest of the day drinking gin and exchanging tall tales at the bar. But that would have to wait, probably until his retirement. He popped a Tums into his mouth, started the engine and thought about Kathy, the kids and the upcoming Fourth of July picnic. It seemed his life had somehow come unstuck so fast he never even had a chance to watch it happen. Or maybe he wasn't paying enough attention...

Norman Huffaker was waiting for him. He was considerably older than Hanrahan had anticipated, with a fleshy, florid face and watery blue eyes. He parted his gray-and-red hair from just above the left ear to maximize its covering power. Pudgy hands were freckled with liver spots, and he wore four rings, one on each pinky and on each ring finger, the largest of which was the initial "N" in diamonds. He had a small rear end and a large belly; the seat of his jeans bagged, and the buttons of a red-and-white cowboy shirt strained against his stomach. His boots were tooled and highly polished.

"Sit down, Mr. Huffaker," Hanrahan said, after taking in the vision before him.

Huffaker moved across the room with exaggerated care, one shoulder leading the other. Hanrahan noted how small his feet were.

"Well, I'm here," Huffaker said, crossing one leg over the other and lighting a cigarette. "I don't want to be but I answered the summons."

"The summons?"

"I was summoned. I obey the law. I believe in the law. I may disagree with it but I obey it."

"I wish more people felt that way."

"No fencing, captain. Obviously your call has upset me. I've never been arrested in my life, never stolen anything, pay what few parking fines I've received and treat my neighbors with respect. Of course I've been harassed, as recently as a few days ago, but no charges were filed. You can check."

"I did. Vice isn't my department."

"Vice. What a characterization for human behavior."

Hanrahan said, "I don't care how you live your private life, Mr. Huffaker, any more than I'd want you to care about how I live mine. Understand that and we can get to the reason for having you here today."

"*Summoned* me. Why am I here?"

"Well, for some reason, Mr. Huffaker, just about every time I take a step forward in the Tunney investigation, Norman Huffaker pops up."

"Are you suggesting that *I'm* a suspect in that grizzly affair?"

"No, but you sure know a lot of people connected with it in one way or another."

"Ford Saunders."

"Uh, huh."

"Because we're friends who share certain interests."

"Dressing up like women?"

"Yes, although I'm not about to explain that. You wouldn't understand."

"I don't care about that, Mr. Huffaker."

"You have a strange way of not caring about it, captain."

"The raid? I had nothing to do with that. I told you, another department. Look, Mr. Huffaker, we'll be here all afternoon if we keep talking about things that don't interest me."

Huffaker sat in silence, lit and drew on a cigarette, chewed his lip, crossed and recrossed his legs. Turning away from Hanrahan, he said, "I've already been questioned about Ford Saunders's visit to me the night of Tunney's murder. I told the truth. He wasn't feeling well, left the party early and stayed at my home. That's all there is to it." He turned and faced Hanrahan. "Now, as a result of your police department not having anything better to do than force their way into a private party and harass decent people, I end up being interrogated. You know, of course, that Ford was at my party the night of the raid."

"Yes, I do. You two are pretty close?"

"Should I resent that question?"

"Depends on how you look at it. If I ask whether you and Ford Saunders are lovers, I don't ask it sarcastically. If you are, that interests me purely in terms of the Tunney case. That's it. I'd ask the same thing of a heterosexual. When people are intimate, it can mean they'll do certain things for each other, including bending the truth to protect one another."

"I told the truth."

"I haven't said you didn't, Mr. Huffaker. I am asking whether you and Ford Saunders are close."

"We have a relationship."

"Okay . . . what about Alfred Throckly."

"Why do you ask about him?"

"He didn't tell you that he told me he stayed with you recently?"

"No."

"Mr. Huffaker, you're losing your credibility."

"Why would—?"

"Hold on a minute." He picked up the phone.

"Who are you calling?"

"Alfred Throckley."

"Please don't...all right, yes, he stayed with me. We've been friends for years. He needed to get away for a few days. He was on the verge of a breakdown. I suggested he tell everyone he was in Europe and stay at my place, where no one would bother him."

"And he took your advice."

"It was good advice."

"I'm sure it was. Believe it or not, I'm not crazy about asking this next question, Mr. Huffaker, but I feel I have to. Do you and Throckly have a relationship?"

"Do you mean—?"

"I think we both know what I mean. No need for word games."

"In the past."

"How far?"

"In the distant past. We're just good friends now. We share a love of music and art and—"

"Why wasn't he at the party?"

"Which party?"

"The one at your house that was raided. For making too much noise."

"He wasn't invited."

Hanrahan looked closely at him, decided to back off. He'd gotten all he was going to get, he decided.

"I won't keep you much longer...who else are you friendly with at the Institute?"

"No one."

"Walter Jones, Chloe Prentwhistle?"

"I've met them."

"Through Ford Saunders and Alfred Throckly?"

"I don't know, over the years, that sort of thing. Some mutual interests. Anything wrong with that?"

"Mr. Huffaker...you're what we call a constant in

our business, somebody who links up with a lot of other pieces."

"It doesn't sound very attractive, the way you put it."

"I suppose not, but there it is." Hanrahan stood and offered his hand. "I appreciate your cooperation. I know it wasn't easy."

Huffaker shook Hanrahan's hand. "I think I almost believe you."

Ten minutes later Joe Pearl came in, saying, "She's here, Mac."

"Janis Dewey?"

"Yeah. Your place or mine?"

Hanrahan smiled. "Your place. You good cop, me the heavy."

"Go easy, Mac. She seems really upset."

Walking down the hall to Pearl's office Pearl said, "I hope she had nothing to do with the Tunney murder."

"Why?"

"I like her. Any crime in that? Even for a super professional like myself?"

Hanrahan stopped. "You know what, Joe? Sometimes I wonder about you."

"Why?"

"You're bucking for membership in the good-guy club. Could be dangerous . . . by the way, *did* you slash Johnny Carter's tires?"

"Yes."

"Why?"

"Because he deliberately got between me and Killinworth. Because he's a creep. Because I was sore at you and frustrated and, God knows, I got out of line. I know, I know, I'm lucky a cop didn't come along."

Pearl hadn't overstated Janis Dewey's anxiety. The

tall redhead fidgeted with anything within reach. She had a slight tic in her left eye. Hanrahan felt sorry for her too, but not enough to hold back. He ignored her greeting when Pearl introduced them, tossed his jacket on a table, propped his foot on it. "Okay, Miss Dewey, let's get down to it. What's the connection between you, Evelyn Killinworth and the late Lewis Tunney?"

She stiffened, looked up at Joe Pearl, who started to say something and was waved off by Hanrahan. "My patience is running out. Answer my question, Miss Dewey."

"Connection between... I don't understand. There's no connection between me and what happened to Lewis Tunney."

"Killinworth?"

"The professor? I don't even know him. I mean, I've met him once and—"

Hanrahan pulled out a notebook, pretended to read from it. "Lunch, cafeteria, National Gallery of Art, West Wing..." He was reciting from memory what Pearl had reported. "Shrimp salad for you, ham sandwich for him... what'd you talk about?"

"Nothing. He called me at my office, introduced himself and said he wanted to ask me questions. I told him I couldn't but he insisted, so I met him in the museum cafe."

"If you didn't want to meet him, what did he say that changed your mind?"

"He said he knew some people I knew and—"

"Walter Jones?"

"Yes, and... why are you asking me these things? You must have had a microphone or something at the table. Why ask me if you already know everything?"

Hanrahan had been guessing, mixing speculation with the little Pearl's surveillance had turned up. It was working, though. If she thought she'd been taped during lunch with Killinworth, she was unlikely to lie.

"Miss Dewey, you're in fairly serious trouble. I'd like you to stop being belligerent and cooperate. For example, if I ask about some stolen art in, say, the Middle East,"—a shot in the semidark—"you'll be helping us both by telling what you know—" He realized his voice was rising, and didn't like it. Joe slashes tires, I berate ladies. What next?

Pearl stepped between them. "Mac," he said quietly, "could I have a minute alone with Miss Dewey?"

Hanrahan understood. "Just one minute, Mac, okay?"

Hanrahan made something of a show of angrily snatching his jacket from the table. "I have some calls to make from my office . . . and Miss Dewey, remember, you're not under arrest, haven't been charged with anything. You're here voluntarily. We appreciate that. So just answer our questions and you can leave. I'll be back."

He went to his office and dialed Pearl's number. "Joe, lean on the Middle East thing. She and Killinworth sure as hell must have talked about it . . ."

Next Hanrahan called Heather McBean. No answer. He checked his watch; he'd give Pearl and Dewey another ten minutes. He had just started to read a report on a homicide that had occurred the previous night during a floating crap game when a young detective opened the door. "Captain, he did it this time."

"Who?"

"The Smithsonian bomber. The kook set one off on the third floor of the American History Museum. There are injuries."

Hanrahan let loose a string of obscenities as he followed the detective to the basement garage, where they got in Hanrahan's car and sped to the scene of the bombing. It wasn't until they were pushing their way through crowds that had gathered outside the museum that he realized he'd forgotten Joe Pearl and Janis Dewey. "Call Joe's office and tell him what happened," he told the detective. "Tell him to get what he can from Janis Dewey and let her go home."

The bomb had been planted in the *Philadelphia*, a single-masted, square-rigged gunboat that had been launched on Lake Champlain in August, 1776, as part of a ragtag flotilla under the command of Benedict Arnold. The cumbersome fifty-four-foot-long oak vessel and its crew of forty-four had been sunk by the British off Valcour Island in October, 1776. It was raised in 1935 and donated to the Smithsonian.

The bomb, which was not very powerful, had blown off the ship's upper bow. The injuries to bystanders were not serious, according to a patrolman. Paramedics from a nearby hospital and from MPD had gathered the injured in a corner of the exhibit hall. The patrolman gave Hanrahan a note written taped to a stanchion:

> *Do you believe me now? Do you finally understand that the time has come for actions to speak louder than my words? This is only the beginning. I will leave my explosive message every other day until the Congress of the United States agrees to sit down and seriously discuss returning the Smithsonian Institution to its rightful owner.*

Hanrahan went to where the victims of the blast sat on a bench. Medics blocked him from seeing the injured. He paused to talk to a museum security officer, then moved closer until he could look over the medics' shoulders.

And saw Heather McBean sitting in the midst of the

injured. Her right leg and foot were bandaged. A spreading pink stain colored the instep. She saw Hanrahan, closed her eyes, pressed her lips together, opened her eyes and said, *"Hoot awa."*

"God damn," was what Hanrahan said.

CHAPTER 26

THEY SAT IN HER LIVING ROOM AT KILLINWORTH'S house. It was dusk; a gray light tinged with orange came through the windows. Hanrahan had taken off his jacket and loosened his tie. Heather was on the couch, her injured foot resting on a purple throw pillow.

"Sure I can't get you anything?" Hanrahan asked.

"No, nothing, thank you."

"Tea?"

She shook her head. She was depressed, not surprisingly. Hanrahan had tried to break through, no luck. She had scarcely responded to anything he had said during the ride from the museum to the house, and his attempts at the apartment had worked no better.

Once again she'd been in the wrong place at the wrong time, in the middle of the Smithsonian craziness that was just about to drive *him* crazy. Having the Tunney killing still unsolved was bad enough, but now the bomber had gone from threatening note-writer to acting out. Had the bomb been bigger...he pushed that thought from his mind and looked at Heather, who seemed on the edge of sleep. Good.

"If you'd like to nap, I'll clear out."

She said softly, "I don't mind your being here."

"Well, I can't stay long . . . would you like Sergeant Shippee to stay with you—?"

"No. I'll be fine."

"Heather, do you know where Dr. Killinworth is . . . ?"

"No. He's been very busy and hasn't been here much."

"Any idea what's keeping him busy?"

"No."

Hanrahan allowed a moment to pass, then: "Has he ever mentioned the bomber?"

"What? Oh, well, just a word or two about stories in the press . . . I really didn't think Evelyn is the Smithsonian bomber, captain."

"You read my mind," Hanrahan said. And she did, but only partly. He might not be the bomber . . . but he might have hired someone to play the part to divert attention from the Tunney killing—or confuse it . . . He decided to back off, she really had had quite a day. "I guess," he said, "you know our Fourth of July celebration is coming up. You might sort of enjoy it. We make a big deal out of it—picnics, fireworks, music, the works. I was just thinking, maybe you'd like to join me and my family for our picnic . . ."

"That's very kind of you, captain, but I really couldn't. I think I'd rather be by myself, sort of take stock, get myself pulled together a bit."

"Sure . . . right, I understand. You've been through more than enough. But if you get lonesome and want to change your mind—"

"I can stay with Chloe Prentwhistle if I get lonely, I stayed there last night. She's quite a hostess."

"You did?"

"Yes. It was a lovely evening. She put together a last-minute little do for me, just a few people. We had cocktails and dinner and sat about and talked. I felt much better for it, at least until this happened." She pointed to her foot.

Hanrahan put on his jacket. "Well, afraid I have to go. Duty calls, and so on. How's the foot?"

"Not bad. Thank you for bringing me home. I felt very special. The others didn't get such V.I.P. treatment."

"You've got connections . . . well, be sure to call if . . . if you need anything."

At MPD Joe Pearl had left a note about Janis Dewey. She'd told him Killinworth had wanted to know about the Gainsborough collection that was under her curatorship. Pearl said he'd pressed, but hadn't come up with anything else. His impression was that she had more to tell but was afraid.

Reading Joe's note, Hanrahan cursed the bomber's timing. He was convinced that if he'd put a little more pressure on Janis Dewey she would have told more. He'd have to try again with her soon.

As he drove home he realized he was glad in a way that Heather hadn't accepted his halfhearted invitation to the picnic. He would have felt awkward. Kathy would assume she was his girl friend; he could do without that.

At home he took a Welsh rarebit from the freezer, threw some bacon on his Jenn-Air grill and popped two halves of an English muffin in the toaster-oven. He poured a drink, turned on the TV and watched a report about the bombing.

"*One of the injured was Heather McBean, who'd been engaged to marry Dr. Lewis Tunney. You will recall that Dr. Tunney was murdered with Thomas*

Jefferson's sword at the Museum of American History, a murder that has gone unsolved..."

The phone rang. It was Heather. "I don't know how they found me here but I've been getting calls from the newspapers and TV people."

"Don't answer the phone."

"I always answer the phone. I'm too curious not to."

"Well, then I'm afraid there's nothing I can do ...except invite you over for a little Welsh rarebit."

"I'm tempted, captain. I really am, but, well... I'm also exhausted. Can I, as they say, take a rain check?"

"You can, and I'm going to hold you to it. Good night. And for God's sake don't talk to any strangers, or *anyone*, for that matter."

"I'm too tired to argue, captain. I promise."

Heather replaced the phone in its cradle and pressed her head into the couch pillows. Her foot throbbed, and so did her head. The phone rang and rang and rang. She didn't answer. She was quite proud of herself. She hobbled over to it and took it off the hook.

Premature Fourth of July celebrants set off cherry bombs on the street. Heather started, then sank back into the cushions. She considered calling Chloe Prentwhistle, but the effort to get up and make the call was too much. Everything had started to ache. She closed her eyes and eventually dozed off, only to be awakened by a knocking at the door. She sat up and shook her head. "Who is it?" she called out.

"Evelyn."

"Oh, I must have drifted off. Just a minute." She sat on the edge of the couch and held her head in her hands, got to her feet and winced as pain from her injured foot sped up her leg to her head. She hobbled to the door, stopping midway to steady herself on a chair and put the phone back in its cradle.

She undid the latch and stepped back. The door swung open and Killinworth stood in the backlight of a small hall lamp. He filled the open doorway. When he didn't speak, Heather said, "Is something wrong?"

"I don't know what to say, Heather. I'm very disappointed in you." He entered the room and looked down at her bandaged foot. "I heard about the accident." He crossed the room, looked out the window, then drew flowered drapes across it. Heather turned on another lamp and sat on the couch. "Why are you disappointed in me?" she asked, having a good idea what the answer would be.

"Scotland Yard has contacted me concerning the death of an Arab in London."

"Ashtat . . . ?"

"You remember the name."

"Well yes . . . it's not exactly a common name." She was feeling resentful of what seemed like an interrogation. And perhaps a little guilty too.

He went to the kitchen, poured himself a glass of single-malt Scotch whiskey from a bottle he'd given her when she had moved in, took a full swig and returned to the living room.

"Evelyn," Heather said, "I can understand why you're upset, but you must understand the position I was in—"

"I only understand, Heather, that your friend, the good Captain Hanrahan, told an Inspector Burns at the Yard that I was in Belgravia the night of the Arab's demise. Obviously, he received that information from you."

"Yes, he did, but under the circumstances—"

"You have a unique way of treating friends, Heather."

"Evelyn, I—"

"I came forward in your hour of tragedy and befriended you, took you in, comforted you. My reward has been, how shall I put it? I am hurt, my dear. To use an understatement, of which, I realize, I am rarely guilty."

Heather started to explain again but Killinworth was not having any of it. Instead he delivered a filibuster about friendship and its demands, about trust and honor and chivalry. When he was finished with his speech, and his Scotch, Heather said, "I'm *sorry*, Evelyn, but, well, I was led to believe that Captain Hanrahan already knew about our sharing a cab to Belgravia that night, and I was, I think, understandably upset by—"

"He tricked you."

"Perhaps."

"And you still trust him."

"He's investigating Lewis's death, he's a—"

"Remember the people who investigated Calum's death?"

"Evelyn, I can't distrust everyone. I need to believe in *someone*."

"Have I ever given you cause for disbelief?"

"All right, Evelyn...let's have it out...when I read about this Ashtat being murdered in Belgravia, I did wonder. I admit it. Can't you understand that?"

"I am appalled."

"I'm sorry—"

"It's a bit late for *that*. It adds, I assure you, a terrible complication in my life at this moment. I'm not sure what I'll do—"

"Why not just answer their questions truthfully? You didn't have anything to do with that Arab's murder..." She almost added, *"Did you?"*

He looked at her as though he had heard her unspoken words. "Heather, I must be away for a day or two."

"Because of this—?"

"Because of *business*. I expect to be back by the Fourth of July. Until I return, I suggest you remain here, admit no one. Do you understand?"

At least he and Hanrahan had that view of her future in common..."I don't like being cooped up."

"Heather, I insist that you follow my instructions—"

"I will do what I feel is best for me, Evelyn. I've been ordered about and allowed myself to act like a victim for rather too long now. Please go. I'll be *fine*. Do have a pleasant trip."

He was obviously angry as he left the room, which didn't displease Heather at all. Damn all of them, she thought as she latched the door behind him. It's *my* fiancé who's dead, my foot that has daggers in it. A half hour later she heard him slam his downstairs door. She looked out the window and briefly watched him waddle up the street, a small overnight bag in his hand...

Evelyn Killinworth's progress was observed by another, who sat in a car. The moment Killinworth turned the corner, the car door opened and the driver stepped out...

Heather put on her raincoat, slung her purse over her shoulder and left her apartment. Her foot still ached badly, but she needed to be out in the air where she could think, walk as far as her foot would allow, perhaps stop in for something to eat in a local restaurant.

She came down the stairs and opened the front door.

The driver of the car, who had slowly been approaching the house, stopped and turned away.

Heather breathed in the pungent, warm evening air and walked in the opposite direction.

She returned two hours later, soaked her foot and

went to bed, the sound of the pending Fourth of July celebration crackling outside her windows, the room's darkness occasionally illuminated by a burst in the sky from a skyrocket or a Vesuvius Fountain.

CHAPTER 27

THE BRISK BREEZE THAT RUFFLED THE REPORTER'S hair had blown out the previous day's oppressive heat and humidity and carried in with it a dry and sunny Fourth of July.

"I am standing on the west lawn of the Capitol, where tonight Mstislav Rostropovich will conduct the National Symphony Orchestra in a musical salute to the Fourth...In front of me, at the other end of the Mall, is the Lincoln Memorial's Rainbow Pool, the site of this year's fireworks display that is being called the most ambitious ever..." She glanced down at her notes. *"Preceding all the nighttime activity will be the Annual Independence Day Parade down Constitution Avenue, from Seventh to Seventeenth Streets...The Jhoon Rhee Martial Ballet will kick off five hours of musical entertainment at the Washington Monument, beginning at two-thirty...there will be jazz and bluegrass and, of course, the continuing Folk Life Festival on the Mall..."* A particularly stiff gust of wind caused her to hold on to her hair. *"Well, it's all part of this year's gala Fourth of July festivities, which according to the National Park Service will draw more than three hundred thousand onlookers...Now, back to you, Ed."*

Ed Filler, Washington's most popular morning TV host, said, *"Thanks, Elaine, for that live report...More in a moment."*

A jeans commercial filled the screen with female posteriors. Heather yawned. She had had a fitful night's sleep. Her dreams had been bizarre, menacing people with grotesque faces chasing her through fields of thistle into twisted forests where long black tree limbs groped for her. The worst was the dream she'd awakened from. It had seemed endless. She was attached by her waist to a long tether that suspended her in infinite space, spinning endlessly, the air cold and painfully dry, the light a monotonous bright glow without source. She had awakened shivering. The sun was already up, and the cool breeze rippled white curtains in the bedroom.

She had decided before going to bed that she would face this day differently, would immerse herself in this uniquely American holiday. No problems, at least for twenty-four hours. The TV report about the day's activities reinforced her thought. She showered and dressed in light tan, close-fitting slacks, a salmon-colored blouse and walking shoes. She didn't have much choice about the shoes. Her foot felt better, but still pained under sustained pressure.

She breakfasted on English muffins, which she never saw in England, and coffee, checked herself in the mirror, decided to carry a lightweight white cardigan with her and left the apartment. She reached the foot of the stairs and glanced at Killinworth's door. It was ajar.

She wasn't sure what to do. Had he come back and was now sleeping? She didn't want to disturb him, didn't even want to see him.

But she couldn't ignore the door. She pushed it open and peered into the living room. Her first thought was of looking into her room at the Madison the night it had been ransacked. Furniture was tipped over, drawers emptied, drapes torn from their fixtures. She listened, heard nothing except her heart that was perfoming a frantic paradiddle, stepped into the apartment and went to the bedroom, where the same wild sight greeted her.

"Tatty," she called anxiously. She went to the kitchen where a paper plate of cat food had been kicked over. Tatty the cat wasn't there. She opened the bathroom door. Tatty purred, caressed her leg. Heather picked the cat up and nuzzled her, trying to calm herself.

She returned to the kitchen, still carrying the cat, took a box of dry cat food from a cupboard. She left Killinworth's apartment, carefully closing the door behind her, and went upstairs, where she poured a saucer of milk. She found a paper plate, put it on the floor next to the saucer and opened the flap on the box of food. She bent down and shook the box over the plate. A few pieces of dry meal fell from the opening. She shook harder. Something was blocking the opening, and she noticed that the top of the box had been slit open, then taped shut with transparent tape.

Heather carefully peeled the tape from the box, opened the top and looked inside. A chamois bag the color of burnt ocher filled the cavity above the foot. She removed the bag, filled the plate with food, then sat down on the living room couch.

She held the bag on her lap as though it might be radioactive and traced the outline of a heavy object through the leather. Slowly, deliberately she undid the drawstring and widened the bag's mouth. She reached inside. Her fingertips touched metal, glass, a band of silk. She closed her fingers on the object and slowly slid it from its nesting place.

"My God," she said quietly. "It can't be, but it is. *The Harsa*."

She'd seen it in the museum. Seen pictures...She picked up the phone and started to dial MPD's number, stopped on the third digit and hung up. Hanrahan wouldn't be there. She found his home number he'd given her, dialed it. No answer. He'd left for the picnic.

She paced the room, the Harsa in her hand. Were there two Legion of Harsa medals? There must be...one in the museum...And Evelyn had the other one? How did he get it? Who searched his apartment? Did Lewis know there were two? Was it that knowledge that caused his murder? God...what should she do? She returned the medal to the sack, put it in her purse, picked up the cat and put him in Killinworth's apartment. She left the house and walked as fast as she could, paying no attention to the direction, hoping that her mind would somehow clear.

She reached Georgetown Hospital, caught her breath and tried to take her weight off the injured foot for a few moments, then continued down Thirty-Seventh Street, past Georgetown University, to the Key Bridge and the Potomac. The breeze felt cool on her face; she'd started to perspire. She looked across the river and saw American flags flying, their red, white and blue fields slapping against a cloudless, azure sky. She reached into her purse and touched the chamois sack, thought of Evelyn Killinworth. "My God," she said out loud, "what has he done?"

Evelyn Killinworth stood at the check-in gate for British Airways' Supersonic Concorde flight to Washington, D.C. With him was a British Airways' service representative whose name tag read G. Coleman.

"I still maintain your policy is a disgrace to everything that is British," Killinworth grumbled.

"I understand how you feel, sir, but you must try to understand our dilemma. The fare across the Atlantic on the Concorde is two thousand dollars. If you insist on having two seats we must charge twice the fare."

"Young man," Killinworth bellowed. "I happen to be a large man, and your seats on this infernal machine were designed for midgets. If you had thought ahead sufficiently to provide armrests that are removable as in other aircraft, it would not be necessary to have the bloody thing removed with hammers and pliers whenever a man of my dimensions is forced into flying on this aeronautical beast."

Agent Coleman sighed and shook his head. "I understand, sir, and I wish there were something else I could do—"

"Last boarding call for British Airways' Supersonic Concorde service to Washington, D.C."

"Perhaps if you weren't in such a rush, sir, you could fly to Washington on one of our jumbo jets," said Coleman. "The Concorde is built primarily for speed—"

"If I had more time, young man, I certainly would never have considered flying in an aluminum tube in the first instance. I spent most of the flight over here standing in the aisle watching that obscene digital machmeter tell me how fast I was flying. It was not fast enough by half, I assure you."

"I'm afraid you'll have to board immediately, Dr. Killinsworth. Your seat—" his smile was subtle—"your seats are ready." A mechanic stood near the jetway entrance, an armrest in his hands.

"Yes," Killinworth said. "Good *day*, Mr. Coleman."

"Good day, Dr. Killinworth. Do have a pleasant trip."

* * *

Heather stood in front of a bandstand on the Mall, where a gospel group was performing, thirty men and women in purple robes raising their voices above the din of the Folk Life Festival. She was caught up in the infectious music, and it was not until the group sounded its final note that she realized she had lost track of time. She had, of course, wanted such an escape. Reality was overwhelming. She looked at her watch. Almost eleven. The walk from the Key Bridge to the Mall was not part of her conscious memory, nor were subsequent activities at the festival. She had tried Hanrahan's house again without success, and had called MPD and left a message with Sergeant Arey, who promised to relay it to Hanrahan when and if he called in. "We've tried to beeper him on another matter but he didn't answer," Arey told her.

"They're just kids having fun, Mac," Kathy told Hanrahan after he'd confiscated an assortment of torpedoes, Roman candles and mandarin crackers from two of his nephews.

"That's right," he said, "kids with ten fingers and two eyes each. Better they should stay that way."

Kathy smiled and touched his arm. "I know, I know, you're right. You're responsible and I'm not. But I'll tell you one thing, Mac Hanrahan."

"What's that?"

"I'm more responsible than I was before. I've done a lot of growing up..."

"I'm glad, Kathy. Can we leave it at that...?" His mother waved for him to join her at the barbeque pit.

"But what do you feel, Mac?" Kathy asked. "I meant what I said at dinner. We should get back together, chalk up whatever happened before as a case of time and place that's passed. It's all so damned insignificant compared to the bigger picture, two people who love each other and who've shared a lot in common—"

"Excuse me," Hanrahan said, wishing he could outlaw family picnics when the word "family" was a name not a fact. "I walked out this morning without my beeper, I have to call in." He went to a public booth at the perimeter of the park and called MPD. Sergeant Arey answered. "Hello, captain. Happy Independence Day."

"Yeah, you, too, Arey."

"I tried to beeper you a while ago. You didn't respond."

"I walked out without...any calls for me?"

"Only one you need to know about. A woman said the guy who lives next door to her is the Smithsonian bomber."

"Yeah? What's her name?"

"She wouldn't say, but she promised to call back this afternoon."

A frisbee narrowly missed Hanrahan's head as it careened into the booth. He swore and tossed it to a group of kids. "Arey, get her name when she calls back."

"I'll try. She said the guy next door is always talking about the Smithsonian, says he says he's related to the limey who donated it."

"Get her name."

"I'll sure try, captain. If she calls back, I'll beeper you."

"Good. I'll call in again."

Hanrahan's son approached him. He was tall and tan. A full head of black hair curled down to his neck, his black beard glistened with sweat. He'd been playing softball and wore cut-off jeans and sneakers. "Hey, Dad, what's with Mom?"

"What do you mean?"

"She seems upset."

"Ask her."

A cousin told Hanrahan she'd heard that he and Kathy were about to get back together. A nephew who'd lost his firecrackers wanted them back. Hanrahan played a game of bocci and ate a hamburger with onions and ketchup. Occasionally he looked over at Kathy, who was playing volleyball. She wore tight jeans and a bright green T-shirt. She looked good. Familiar. Forget it.

"Is Miss Prentwhistle there?" Heather asked. She had stopped in the Museum of Natural History to use the bathroom and the phone.

"No, she's not. Who's calling?"

"Heather McBean."

"Oh, hello, Miss McBean. This is Ford Saunders."

"When do you expect her back?"

"I'm not sure, probably this afternoon. Can I take a message for her? I'm house-sitting as it were."

Heather paused. For some reason once she'd decided to call Chloe it never occurred to her that she might not reach her. "It's very important that I speak with her. Can you give me any idea when to call back?"

"I wish I could. Can she reach you?"

"No. I'll try again."

"Fine...what is it you want to talk to her about? Maybe I can help."

"No. I'll call this afternoon."

Evelyn Killinworth looked at his watch, glanced at the mach-meter (m 2.00, 1,340 miles per hour, cruising altitude 55,000 feet); then turned a page in a note pad. He had been writing since the flight left London, his only interruption a small boy who noticed that Killinworth took up two seats and giggled. Killinworth

snapped, "Why don't you go *outside* and play." He
rather liked the startled look on the boy's face.

He continued making notes during a lunch of sev-
ruga caviar, délice de turbot Marignane, a Belgian endive and radicchio salad and gâteau Japonaise for
dessert, all accompanied by Laurent-Perrier Grand
Siécle Champagne. Before putting the notebook away
and taking a short nap he found a small address book
in his jacket and flipped through it until coming to a
series of numbers for Vice-President William Oxenhauer. One of them had "Private" penned next to it.
Killinworth wrote the number in his pad, put everything away, rearranged himself in his dual seats and
closed his eyes. "Four thousand dollars," he mumbled
as he closed his eyes. "A bloody expensive lunch and
nap."

Heather tried Chloe again at one, Saunders answered. "Sorry," he said, "she's still not back, Miss
McBean. I did hear from her, though."

"Oh? When did she say she'd be back?"

"That's the problem. She'd planned not to return
until tomorrow, but she said she'd change her plans if
it's as important as you say—"

"It is important. It's urgent. I've found something
that . . . I really must talk to her."

"She told me she can be back in town by seven.
Can she meet you then?"

"Seven? I'd hoped . . . well, yes, seven will do. Thank
you."

"Where are you now?" Saunders asked.

"At the Mall."

He laughed. "How can you stand all those people?"

"I'm sort of enjoying it. It is crowded, though."

"Shall I tell Chloe that you'll be here at seven?"

"Her house? No, I think not . . . I hate being a pest

but I'd like to meet her here." Her foot had begun to throb.

"In that madness?"

"Please, it's important to me. Her office then?"

"She told me she'd meet you anywhere except her office. That's the last place she wants to be on a holiday."

"I can understand that but—"

"I have an idea, Miss McBean. The courtyard between the East and West buildings of the National Gallery will probably be relatively empty at seven. Can Chloe meet you there?"

With visions of being attacked in the courtyard racing through her mind, she took a deep breath, said yes, hoped for the best, would not be surprised at the worst...

"It's nice to spend a day with family again," Kathy told Hanrahan as they sat on a picnic bench in the park. "Even your mother has been nice to me. I think she's hated me ever since we split. It's really too bad...she and I had a nice relationship while we were married....Mac, we can have it all again, I know we can if—"

He looked around to be sure no one was near, grabbed her by her bare arms and said, "Let's get something straight, Kathy. I've missed you since it happened. It's been a long time, but even now I sometimes reach for you in the middle of the night. I married you because, among other things, you were the most beautiful woman I'd ever seen. When you made the decision to leave with what's-his-face you said something basic about us. You told me that what seemed to be good and sometimes terrific was built on sand. I know you look at it as just an *experience*, and I'm supposed to be sophisticated or worldly enough to accept it that way. Sort of the old double standard in reverse. Sorry, but I'm too damn old-fashioned. A square cop." He let go of her. "I wish you the best Kathy, I always have, but I won't go through that crap again. Not ever. So please stop talking about getting back together. I don't need it, I don't want it, period."

"You're making a mistake, Mac. Throwing out the baby with the bath water. Dirty bath water, I admit, but—"

"Excuse me, Kathy, I have to call in again." He realized he was losing his temper and didn't want to play it out with her. To be frank, he'd had an urge to belt her ever since the day she announced she was taking off with her lover. But the picnic wasn't the time. Get out of the area, he told himself, before you make a damn fool of yourself.

The phone booth was a considerable walk from where the family had set up camp. He stopped on the way to watch a softball game, get his anger under control. He continued on to the booth, waited impatiently for a young girl cracking gum to conclude a marathon conversation with a boy-friend, then dialed MPD. "Arey, Hanrahan. What's up?"

"Jesus, glad you called, captain. Lieutenant Pearl's looking for you."

"Pearl? He's off today."

"We called him. The Smithsonian bomber turned himself in—let me get the lieutenant for you."

Pearl came on the line. "Joe, is Arey serious about the Smithson nut?"

"Looks like it, Mac. He picked a great day, huh?"

"A great day for publicity."

"Mac, I think he's legit. I mean I think *he* thinks he's legit. He's also crazy as a loon."

"Where is he?"

"In the holding pen."

"I'm on my way."

Hanrahan told his mother that he had to leave. He kissed her on the cheek. Kathy stood ten yards away. Hanrahan nodded to her, walked quickly to his car. His son chased after him and caught him up just as he was opening the door.

"Something broke downtown," Hanrahan said. "I've got to get to the office."

"Pop," his son said, "don't be too hard on Mom. She's trying."

God, was that the real victim of this mess. The boy, missing his father, protecting his mother? The MPD was a welcome escape.

"Yes, ma'am," Sergeant Arey told Heather when she called in again. "Captain Hanrahan is on his way back right now. I'll tell him you called."

"Please tell him something important has happened...about the Harsa medal."

"The what?"

"The Harsa medal. Please tell him that I'm meeting with Miss Prentwhistle at seven."

"Meeting with Miss Prentwhistle at seven."

"Yes. We're—"

"Please deposit ten cents or your call will be interrupted."

"I don't have...hello, *hello?*"

The line went dead.

"We're about to begin our approach to Dulles International Airport," the Concorde captain announced. "It's been a pleasure having you on board today, and on behalf of the flight deck I'd like to wish you a pleasant stay in America's capital city, Washington,

D.C. And to all, including those of the mother country, happy Independence Day."

Heather, with a thousand other people, sat in bleachers and watched a rodeo display. Next she visited a mock Apache village and enjoyed a demonstration of traditional Indian dances. Children from the audience were invited to join in. One little blond boy cried and ran for the protection of his father's arms. A young girl got carried away and spun around so vigorously that she lost her footing and sprawled on the makeshift stage. The crowd loved it.

It was four o'clock. A front that had been forecast moved in, and the clear blue sky was now obscured by low, cottony clouds. There was still a breeze, but the air was heavy and humid; rain was imminent.

Heather ambled away from the Apache village—and was bumped by two drunks in cowboy outfits. Her purse was knocked to the ground. The men offered slurred apologies, continued walking. Heather, aware of what her purse contained, scooped it from the ground and held it close to her as she made her way through the crowd in the direction of the Washington Monument, stopping at a food concession to get the change of a dollar bill. She looked up with hundreds of others at a whining sound. Directly above was what had become a common sight over Washington, the British Airways' supersonic Concorde, its movable nose tilted down so that the cockpit crew could see during the landing at Dulles Airport.

The Concorde captain's final words to his passengers were, "If you look down and to your left you'll see quite a crowd of people celebrating the Fourth of July. Sorry we're not a few hours later when you could see the fireworks. They're quite impressive from up here. Cheery-O."

Killinworth looked out the small window next to him. The ground was barely visible beneath the sea of people about the Mall. He checked his watch. "Not fast enough, not for four thousand dollars," he muttered.

"Fill me in, Joe," Hanrahan said. He'd arrived at his office minutes before, and Pearl was waiting for him.

Pearl shook his head. "A certifiable ding-a-ling, Mac. Wait'll you meet him. I figured him to be young but he's not. Middle-aged. A nervous wreck, twitches a lot and never finishes a sentence. A piece of work, as they say."

"Why'd he turn himself in?"

"He says he never wanted to hurt anyone, and when he read about people getting cut from the bomb he decided to come in and take his punishment. From what I gather he wouldn't have bothered if the injured had been men. Women, that's a different story. He has a definite psychosexual personality."

"He does?"

"No doubt about it."

"Why are you sure he's the bomber?"

"You'll know it when you talk to him. He knows too much to be faking it. He's the one. I'd stake my career on it."

"Your *career*. No kidding. Well, bring him up here. I want a steno. You read him his rights?"

"Sure, and he called a lawyer. I think he has a little money."

Pearl no sooner left the office than Commissioner Johnson called. "Mac, what's with the bomber?"

"Pearl called you?"

"Of course he did. I left a standing order that if anything developed over the holiday in the Tunney case I was to be notified immediately."

"I was going to call after I had a chance to talk to him."

"Do you think he's the one?"

"I don't know, I haven't seen him yet. Joe's convinced he is."

"Well, I can be reached here all day. We're having a little family get-together, a barbeque. One thing before I get off, Mac. Don't let the press get hold of this until morning, and not until I've had a chance to think it out. We'll hold a press conference and make sure it gets reported the way it should."

The alleged Smithsonian bomber was led into Hanrahan's office by Pearl and two uniformed officers. His hands were cuffed in front of him. Hanrahan judged him to be in his late forties. He wore thick glasses, behind which a pair of small, green eyes were in constant motion. He wore a shiny blue suit, a green tie and tan shoes with perforations. He was slight, about a hundred and forty pounds. Hanrahan pegged his height at five-six or seven. What struck him most, however, was his head, which tended to come to a point. He had fine blond hair, corn silk cascading down from a pyramid.

"Hello," Hanrahan began.

"I want my attorney. I'll say nothing more without my attorney."

"Sure. I take it, he's on his way. Sit down." He told an officer to take off the handcuffs. A stenographer arrived and complained about working on a holiday. "Time and a half," she was told.

Everyone sat silently until the bomber's attorney arrived. He was tall and distinguished looking, cut from a D.C. attorney's mold. "Hello, Harold," he said. "Are they treating you all right?"

"Yes, they've been very nice to me."

"That's good." To Hanrahan the attorney said, "I'm Dell Tierney, captain, attorney for Harold's family."

"What family is that, Mr. Tierney?"

Tierney glanced at Harold, then said, "Could I speak with you privately, captain?"

They went into the bullpen. Tierney shoved his hands in his rear pants pockets and shook his head. "His name is Harold Benz, captain. He lives with an aged aunt in Rockville. His father, Morgan Benz, made a lot of money in real estate out west. Morgan Benz claimed to be descended from the duke of Northumberland, Sir Hugh Smithson. Whether that's true or not is unclear. It's also unimportant. The point is that Harold *believes* that his father was linked to that family. With normal people that might not be a problem, but Harold has some difficulty with reality. He's a disturbed young man, I'm afraid. He's also brilliant."

"Anybody who goes around setting off bombs is disturbed, Mr. Tierney."

"Yes, of course. I take it he's confessed."

"No, but he turned himself in. We wouldn't take a confession without an attorney to represent him." Hanrahan sounded calmer than he felt.

Tierney nodded. "Naturally I'll advise Harold to say nothing."

"Naturally."

"Even if he did confess it wouldn't stand up, not with his history of institutional confinement."

"Remains to be seen. What are you suggesting, Mr. Tierney, that we let him go?"

"I can think that's reasonable—"

"He might have killed people. As it turned out he

injured a few. If he's as disturbed as you say, he ought to be back in an institution."

Tierney sat on the edge of a desk. "Captain Hanrahan, I agree with you. If I promise to see that he's confined and receives treatment, would you allow him to leave with me? In my custody?"

"I can't do that and you know it. Let me ask you something, Mr. Tierney. Is he disturbed enough to have run a sword through Dr. Lewis Tunney?"

"No, of course not."

"Well, I'm still going to have to book him. I'd like his statement."

"I won't allow that. I don't practice criminal law. I'm basically a real estate and tax attorney. I've been handling Harold's aunt's investments for years. But I can't allow him to incriminate himself. There's enough money to hire the best counsel, which we'll do."

"Fine. Thanks for filling me in."

"My pleasure, captain."

An hour later, and despite Tierney's objections, Harold Benz gave a complete if rambling statement to Hanrahan. He was filled with remorse, he said, that people had been hurt, especially women.

Hanrahan's final question was, "Harold, did you kill Dr. Lewis Tunney?"

He seemed confused by the question. He frowned. "Kill someone? Me? I'd never do that."

"Okay, Harold." Hanrahan said.

Harold was led away by the uniformed patrolmen.

"Buy you a beer, Mac," Pearl said when they were gone.

They went around the corner to a bar popular with cops. Sergeant Arey had gotten off duty and was there with a couple of buddies.

"Well, captain," Arey said. "Was he the one?"

"Looks like it."

"Did you get my message from the McBean woman—?"

"What? No, no I didn't."

"Yeah, she called a few times. I left the message on your desk."

"I'll be back," Hanrahan told Pearl.

He returned to his office and found Arey's message shuffled in a pile of papers. *"Miss McBean called. Is meeting a Miss Prentwhistle at seven. Something to do with a Harsa medal."* Hanrahan tried Heather's apartment. No answer. The same when he phoned Chloe Prentwhistle's house.

He called Cal Johnson and filled him in on Harold Benz. Johnson was pleased. "Good job, Mac."

"I didn't do anything. He walked in and gave himself up."

"Well, we'll prepare a statement in the morning for the press. Can you be in early?"

"How about eight?"

"Make it seven."

Hanrahan returned to the bar and downed a beer. "Where are you headed, Joe?"

Pearl shrugged. "I was just hanging out at the apartment when they called. I suppose I'll go home and finish *War and Peace*. Going in for the light stuff these days."

"Yeah. Funny. How about staying around the office?"

"For what?"

"In case I *need* you. I've got to take off...the Tunney case. I'd like you on hand in case Heather McBean calls in—"

Joe started to protest, cut it short. It had been a long cold month of Sundays since Mac had shown even a passing interest in a female of the species.

"Okay, Mac. You got it." He smiled.

"Don't be a jerk, Joe." And he told Pearl about the

message from Heather. "It's got to be damned important for them to be meeting at seven o'clock on the Fourth of July. I don't much like it."

"Probably nothing, Mac. They're pretty strange folk, that whole museum crowd."

"I'd still feel better trying to hook up with them. The fact that Heather McBean called means she's worried too. I'll get back to you."

He got in his car and headed for the Mall. Traffic was heavy as tourists tried to get close to the site of holiday festivities. He cursed and slapped a flashing red light with a magnetic base on the roof, activated it and sounded his siren. Cars slowly made room as he snaked his way to the Constitution Avenue entrance to the Museum of American History. He went to the administrative offices, found them deserted except for a security guard. He showed his badge and asked if anyone was working. The guard shrugged. "Just me up here, captain. They're never around on holidays."

"Has Miss Prentwhistle been in?"

"No, sir. Her assistant, Mr. Saunders, was up here for a while but he's gone."

Hanrahan left the museum by the Mall entrance. He stood on the steps and looked out over three hundred thousand heads. The aroma of barbeque and chili was thick enough to feel. "Where would someone be meeting at seven o'clock on the Fourth of July?" he muttered. "Heather McBean, where the hell *are* you?"

Evelyn Killinworth walked through his front door, saw the disarray in his living room, went to the kitchen and opened a cabinet. The box of cat food was gone. He hurried upstairs and used his key to enter Heather's apartment. The box was in her kitchen, the top open, the chamois sack gone. "Damn that girl," he said aloud as he returned to his apartment. He dialed MPD, where

Sergeant Arey was on duty. "Sergeant," Killinworth boomed, "Dr. Evelyn Killinworth here. Is Captain Hanrahan there?"

"No sir. Was he expecting your call?"

"No. Actually, I was looking for Miss McBean. Captain Hanrahan wanted me to contact her concerning the Tunney case."

"Yeah, well, she called in looking for the captain."

"Did she say where she was?"

"No. She's meeting up with a Miss Prentwhistle at seven. She said—I'll tell Captain Hanrahan you called."

"Thank you."

He called a local cab company and ten minutes later was squeezing himself with difficulty into the back seat of a compact sedan. "The Mall," he said.

"No way," the driver said. "That's like New Year's Eve in Times Square."

"I don't care if it's like VE Day in Trafalgar Square, you twit. Take me there."

Heather arrived fifteen minutes early at the courtyard between the National Gallery's East and West buildings. Saunders had been right. It was all but empty. The afternoon's threatening weather had blown through without depositing a raindrop. The air was again fresh and comparatively bracing for a July day in Washington.

A young man sat in a corner strumming repetitive chords on a guitar. His girl friend, a frail young blond who needed sun to look healthy, sat at his feet and listened. Or was it absorbed? Whatever, Heather was glad they were there. She sat on a sculptured stone bench and felt the Harsa through her leather purse. She began to relax. Chloe would be here soon. For all her shifts in mood, Chloe was a strong woman. Between them they would somehow make sense of this...

She looked at her watch. Seven straight up. She walked to a phone booth and rummaged about in her purse for the change she'd taken care to get earlier. She inserted a dime in the slot and started to dial MPD's number when a hand reached into the booth and depressed the switch hook. Startled, Heather quickly turned her head.

"Hi," Ford Saunders said. He was dressed in white jeans, a blue Popeye T-shirt and brown deck shoes. His bizarre getup diverted her from her initial scare.

"You...you startled me," Heather said.

"Sorry about that. Also that I'm late. I assume you were calling to see where Chloe was."

"Yes, I was...where is she?"

"She's been detained. She asked me to come ahead."

"But I wanted to talk to her."

"Relax, Miss McBean. Chloe told me to find out what you had to say that was so important. Not to keep you waiting."

"I...I'd like to see her. She *is* coming?"

"Yes. Let's sit down and talk."

"Where is she?"

"As I told you, she's on her way." He took hold of her upper arm, holding it too tightly.

"You never told her about the meeting, did you?"

His answer was to press harder. And then: "What did you find, Miss McBean?"

"Let *go* of me."

"When you give it to me. You know what I'm talking about."

"No, I don't I—" But by now she was afraid she did.

"The *Harsa*, damn it. Give me—"

What Heather gave him was what she had given the London masher. She brought her knee up into his groin. Saunders doubled over, his face contorted. The guitar player looked up briefly, went back to playing chords for his worshipful companion.

Heather ran toward the Mall. She looked back, saw Saunders still clutching his groin. The mass of people loomed as a refuge, and she plunged into it. She felt sharp stabs in her injured foot as she moved through the throngs, adroitly skirting some clusters of sightseers, pushing her way through others. Ahead she saw the Arts and Industries Building and the Castle. Crowd noise was all around her, yet penetrating through it were the constant, tinkling sounds of the Mall's permanent carousel playing, "Wonderful, Wonderful Copenhagen." A green-and-white "Spirit of '76 Tours" bus offered refuge but pulled away too soon.

She was surrounded by people, not one of them a friend.

She reached the carousel, stopped and looked back. If Saunders had come after her, he'd apparently been swallowed up by the crowd. She drew a sharp breath, checked that she still had her purse and its prize, then started west toward the Washington Monument. Hanrahan's suggestion that she go up to its top while visiting Washington came into her head. What a thing to think of now, she told herself as she pressed on, constantly checking behind her...

The National Symphony Orchestra started playing "The Stars and Stripes Forever," and three hundred thousand voices cheered as one.

She had almost gotten to Fourteenth Street. She looked to her right. The Museum of American History stood silhouetted against a sky streaked with orange-and-white clouds. The music was louder; people around her sang, mostly out of tune. She closed her eyes against a pain in her head that rivaled the one in her foot. She took a deep breath and cut across the Mall to the museum. The steps were filled with people using their elevation to better observe the festivities. Uniformed security guards had abandoned their interior posts and now occupied the top step.

Heather snaked her way through them and stopped at the doors. A series of cannon volleys, part of the orchestra's program, shook the air. She looked back at the mass of people; more cannon fire, cheers, hats tossed into the air.

She pushed through the doors, and was assaulted by silence. The museum was dark except for low-wattage perimeter lights. She blinked against the abrupt change, and then her eyes focused on the outline of the Foucault pendulum shaft as it slowly, relentlessly moved back and forth against dim light coming through windows facing out on Constitution Avenue. It was strangely hypnotic, seductive...

She went to it, laid her purse on the railing and looked down. Oh, God.... Lewis had fallen from here, the sword in his back...She slowly lowered her gaze as though she were following his body, all the way to its landing with a sickening thud on the floor below her. And, involuntarily, she let out a cry of misery and terror that pierced the stillness as the sword of Jefferson had pierced her lover's back—

"Heather...?"

CHAPTER 28

SHE TURNED AROUND. CHLOE PRENTWHISTLE CAME out from the shadows.

"Oh, thank God, it's you."

"Yes, Heather, it's me, I'm glad you finally got here. And that you're safe."

Heather slumped back against the railing. Chloe stopped a few feet from her. "I'm very glad to see you, Heather. What kept you?"

"Kept me? Oh, I see...he told you to meet me there, then told me the National Gallery and met me himself—"

"He? You mean—"

"Mr. *Saunders*. He must have been the one who ransacked Evelyn's rooms. He couldn't find it and when I called you, well...he must have guessed I had it and..."

"And what, Heather? What did he guess you had? Don't hold back now, Heather. I'm your friend, I've proved it. I don't blame you for being suspicious, even of me. My God, what you've been through...Heather? Is it the Harsa...?"

"Yes...how did you know?"

"Good lord, girl...I've been looking for it for a very

long time now. It's difficult to explain, Heather. Come with me to my office where no one will bother us. I'll explain there." She held out her hand. "I'll take it now, dear."

Heather opened her purse, clutched the chamois bag.

"I know it's been a nightmare, Heather, but it's over now."

Heather pulled the bag halfway from her purse, paused. "I'm very confused about something, Chloe. I have the Harsa, but there's a Harsa on display. Two Harsas? Why?"

Chloe nodded vigorously. "Yes, there are two Legion of Harsa medals, Heather. One is real, the other is an expert reproduction. I'm afraid there has been a terrible scandal inside the Smithsonian, and the Harsa is at the core of it. Not because it's *especially* valuable, but because it surfaced at the wrong, or right time, depending on which side you're on—"

"Which *side*? Which side should I be on, Chloe? Was Lewis on the wrong side? Is that why he was killed?"

"Oh God, I'm afraid so. He found out about the scandal from Peter Peckham and came to Washington to expose it. Those behind it couldn't allow that to happen..."

"But what could be so terrible that someone would kill a person to keep it secret?"

"Yes...I agree, but there are people who will do anything to preserve their reputation, however ill deserved. They knew Lewis and I were close to exposing them and their schemes. It would all have been resolved much earlier but I had to wait until the Fourth for it to become public. Even now, I'm afraid, it will badly reflect on the Smithsonian, but perhaps the impact won't be quite as traumatic...The Harsa you have there in your purse is the key. I'm so terribly sorry you had to go through what you have, Heather, but at least we must take advantage of it, if only to see that Lewis's awful death wasn't for nothing. That would be unpardonable."

"I don't know, Chloe..." Heather allowed the sack to drop to the bottom of her purse, turned and leaned on the railing. Chloe did not move. She did not speak. Heather watched the giant pendulum move back and forth across the compass rose, silent, perpetual, its brass bob sparkling as it caught rays of incidental light. "Which Harsa do I have, Chloe?"

"The real one."

"The one on display is a...a—?"

"A replica. Yes. We had to create the impression that it was real so that the public wouldn't be aware of the investigation."

"What about that man in London? The Arab? Who killed *him*? And who killed Peter Peckham?"

"Heather, please, let's go to my office. I'll make some tea and we can go over everything in detail. Answer all your questions. You're certainly entitled to know..."

Heather stayed as she was. She heard the faint strains of music and crowd noise from outside. She was breathing normally now, and the air conditioning had evaporated her perspiration, leaving her skin cold, clammy.

"Come on," Chloe said kindly.

Heather turned. She badly wanted to believe, to trust in this seemingly warm and understanding woman. She went back to her purse, took the sack from it but did not yet hand it over.

Chloe smiled reassuringly.

"Don't, Heather," a male voice said. Both women looked in its direction and saw the huge outline of

Evelyn Killinworth as he stepped out from behind a glass display case. "I'm surprised at you, Heather, and very disappointed," he said.

"With *me*?" Heather said.

"Yes, indeed, Dr. Killinworth. How dare you, considering *your* role in this—" Chloe said.

"What are you doing here?" Heather said, holding tight to the chamois sack.

"I am here, young woman, among other things, to attempt to help you distinguish friend from foe, something it seems you have difficulty with on your own—"

"You had this," Heather said sharply, raising the sack with the Harsa. *"I found it in your apartment."*

"Of course you did, and I would have expected you to have waited to talk to *me* about it. Instead you ran off in quite the wrong direction, to very much the wrong person—"

"*Stop* it, damn you, Evelyn, I still hate having to face it . . . you were my friend, or seemed to be. My uncle swore by you. But you fooled us all, and for too long . . . you went to Belgravia and killed that Arab and took the Harsa from him. I think I knew it even then . . . at least the killing part . . . but I refused to accept it—"

"Tell her, Chloe," Killinworth finally broke in.

"Tell her *what*, Dr. Killinworth, that she is looking at the man responsible for her fiancé's death—?"

"Nonsense . . . Heather, you know that I was not even here the night of Lewis's murder."

"But those who have been involved with you for all the years you've plundered the Smithsonian were here to do your dirty work," said Chloe. "He's been behind it for years, Heather, stealing pieces from the back rooms and selling them on the black market—"

"Is that what happened to the Harsa my uncle donated?"

Killinworth said nothing.

"Exactly. He waited until your uncle was *presumed* dead, then removed the Harsa from the back room with the help of friends who worked here. The medal was offered for sale through the Arab, Ashtat. But unfortunately for Dr. Killinworth your uncle was not dead. He returned, knowing that his Harsa, which he'd given the Smithsonian, had gone on the market. Which is why Ashtat killed your uncle."

"And made it appear to be suicide?"

"Precisely, my dear. Well, am I correct so far, Dr. Killinworth?"

"Continue, Chloe. I find it fascinating."

"I certainly shall, doctor. But I doubt you will continue to find it so fascinating... You see, Heather, when Peter Peckham learned what had happened to the Harsa, he confided in his good friend, your Lewis. That was terribly unfortunate for him. Both Peter and Lewis had to be... what shall we say, Dr. Killinworth, eliminated? Silenced? Otherwise your whole highly lucrative career in crime would be revealed."

Heather stood rigid. She fought to keep her rage from erupting. "I *trusted* you," she said to Killinworth. "And Saunders is your man, accomplice... he does what you tell him. Such as trying to get the Harsa from me. *Such as killing Lewis—*"

"Exactly right, Heather," Chloe said. Her voice took on a threatening edge. "Dr. Killinworth, Heather and I are walking away from here now. I suggest you not try to stop us. I've just come from my office, where I dictated a full account of my investigation. You will only make things worse for yourself if you harm us in any way—"

Killinworth did not move, but said to Heather, "Much of what this incredible woman has said is true, Heather. She knows a great deal. But that is only because *she* has masterminded this whole sorry business...I know it is difficult for you to believe this, but you must. If you go with her and give her the Harsa you will jeopardize months of important investigative work, not to mention your life—"

Heather shook her head. "No, damn it, you're lying, you've lied all along—"

"It's no use, Dr. Killinworth, these clever lies and accusations. The only way Heather will be in danger is if she believes you...It's all right now, Heather, give me the Harsa and we'll turn it over together to Captain Hanrahan—"

The sound of fireworks crashed in on them, the flash of the airborne explosions causing the windows to become momentary strobe lights.

The sound of footsteps coming from the Mall entrance made them turn around...and see Ford Saunders running toward them.

Chloe's previous composure seemed to leave her. She looked from Killinworth to Saunders. Her mouth tightened.

"You bitch," Saunders stopped some ten feet from them, fighting to catch his breath and pointing at Chloe. "Damn you—"

"Be *quiet*." Her look was murderous.

"So smart, so proper, and yet when it comes down to it, just a pair of thieves falling out...Enough of this, Heather," Killinworth said. "Give me the Harsa and we'll see that these people never again play their terrible games—"

"*No.*"

Killinworth shook his head and turned his attention to Saunders. "What do you plan to do now, Mr. Saunders? What control she's managed to exert over you all these years...was Lewis Tunney the first person she had you kill? Were there others—?"

"Tell them what happened, Chloe, *tell* them," Sanders said. "Yes...I'd dress up like a woman for you and steal her purse and search through rooms for that damn medal, but you know I'd never *kill* anybody for you or anybody else—"

Chloe lost more of her composure. "You disgust me," she said. "So incredibly brazen...trying to switch your guilt..." To Heather she said, "They'd been in league all along, Heather. My own assistant and *Professor* Killinworth. When I found out about it I was devastated. I'd been good to him, was even fond of him. I've defended, protected him in his perverse needs...now this. I told you how he lied to me about where to meet you—"

"*You* are the liar...oh God, *she* killed Tunney, all I did was get rid of the medal that night—"

Saunders was cut short by Chloe reaching into the folds of her caftan and bringing out a Swiss .357 Hammerli "Virginian" revolver.

"More killings to keep people quiet, Miss Prentwhistle?" Killinworth asked. "Tunney, and Ashtat and Peckham in London. Nobody to do your dirty work there, I reckon." Killinworth couldn't be sure of those last accusations, but it made sense, he felt.

More so when Chloe ignored him and said to Heather. "I won't ask again, Heather. You and I are both in terrible danger. We *must* act now. Come with me, we'll call the police and it will be over—"

"Over my dead body—" Saunders began.

"*Damn* you." Chloe raised the revolver, pointed it at him. He raised his hands as she pulled the trigger. The bullet struck him in the chest. He collapsed inward and pitched forward, his head thudding against the floor.

"The Harsa," Chloe said. "Give it to me now, Heather."

Killinworth quickly stepped between. "Give the gun to me Chloe. This is, as you say, over. You are only making it worse—"

This time, Chloe's aim was lower. Killinworth's eyes opened wide. His mouth formed a word that was never said or heard. He clutched his stomach, as though trying to close flesh torn apart by the bullet, then fell forward, hands still gripping his stomach, his large body hitting the floor with a thud. Somehow, as though refusing to be humiliated by his position, he managed to roll over onto his back.

Heather bolted and moved quickly into the shadows of the Harsa-Cincinnati exhibition, went behind a towering statue of George Washington and looked around it at the pendulum railing where Evelyn Killinworth writhed in pain a few feet from Ford Saunders's motionless body.

Behind them was Chloe Prentwhistle.

Chloe turned and looked in the direction Heather had gone. "Heather? It's all right now. No need to be afraid. Heather . . . ?"

Heather looked for the next place to hide. She watched Chloe walk away from the bodies and slowly approach the exhibition area, gun still in her hand.

Heather held her breath as Chloe reached the exhibit entrance and stopped. "Heather," she called, "don't be foolish. Can't you see the truth *now*? Killinworth was right about one thing . . . You don't seem able to tell who your friends really are . . . Listen to me, Heather . . . Lewis was killed for the medal you have right now. He would want us to work together. Let's not let his death be even more tragic than it is. He *cared* about the Harsa and what it meant, Heather. You know I do. Come . . ."

Heather quietly slipped off her shoes. Her injured foot throbbed. She reached about in the darkness and touched a display case, moved around it and went deeper into the vast black cavern. She glanced back, did not see Chloe, gasped as she bumped into a heavy cannon. She held her breath.

"Heather? I realize you're confused, but you must trust me."

The voice was shockingly close—to her left, which put Chloe on a line that made them equally distant from the exhibit entrance.

"Damn it, Heather"—Chloe's voice had more of an edge now—"this has been difficult for me too—"

Heather ran toward the vague light of the rotunda and the pendulum circle. A loud noise came from behind as Chloe apparently collided with something and called out for Heather to stop.

Heather reached the railing, gripped it with both hands. The Mall entrance was too far away, Chloe's path from the exhibit area would cut it off.

"Heather—"

She looked down at the voice, a male voice. It came from the edge of the pendulum pit, and belonged to Mac Hanrahan. He'd gotten her message.

"Heather—" This time the voice was once again Chloe's. She had planted herself ten feet away and held the revolver in both hands, the barrel pointed directly at Heather.

The pendulum had now swung to where Heather stood. No time to think, calculate the odds. She lunged for it, gripped it with both hands and was pulled over the rail as it started its return trajectory. A shot, the bullet just missing its mark. She slid her hands down to the brass bob, fell from it and sprawled across the compass rose.

Hanrahan called up through the opening in the ceiling, told Chloe to put down the gun, that there were other police surrounding the museum.

Joe Pearl, who had arrived moments earlier, joined Hanrahan. Hanrahan extended his hand to Heather and helped her over the railing.

"Dr. Killinworth's up there...he's been shot..."

Hanrahan told an officer to call for an ambulance. Then: "What about you? Are you—?"

"I'm all right. Now..."

They went to the second level, where Pearl and another detective had Chloe. The lady was not done yet..."Thank God you're here," she said to Hanrahan, her voice cool as it has been that afternoon in her apartment. "It's over, Lewis Tunney's murderers, no matter what they say, are *there*." She pointed to Saunders and Killinworth. "I'll explain everything..."

Hanrahan knelt beside Killinworth, whose face was twisted in pain. Blood stained the floor beside him. "Take it easy," Hanrahan said, feeling anger at his helplessness, as he always did in such circumstance, "there's an ambulance on the way."

Killinworth looked at Heather. "Do you understand now—?" his words cut off by violent coughing.

"Never mind that now, what's important is for you to get help—"

"Heather, listen to me...You must know that your uncle did not commit suicide. I met with Scotland Yard, found out the truth...Ashtat, the Arab, killed him...Chloe Prentwhistle, others at the Smithsonian have been stealing pieces from storage for years. They wait for a donor like Calum to die, then sell the piece in the black market, usually the Middle East. Ashtat had been their prime middleman for years. They gave him the Harsa when Calum was presumed dead. He tried to sell it but Calum got wind of it, came back and confronted Ashtat. Ashtat went to the castle and killed him. The Edinburgh police never bothered to compare the bullet that killed Calum with the gun they found in his hand. The revolver was registered to him, was in his hand, his finger on the trigger and matched the caliber of the bullet that killed him. Sloppy, lazy work by the Edinburgh bobbies. Not unusual, they look for the easy way out too often..." Heather glanced at Hanrahan, told Killinworth to rest, but he wouldn't.

"Ashtat killed Calum with *his* revolver, which was the same model and caliber as Calum's. He probably fired a round from Calum's gun, then put it in his hand."

"Agnes swore she heard two shots. She was right," Heather said.

"I convinced the Yard to make the ballistic comparison..." Killinworth was gasping for breath now. "The bullet that killed Calum came from a revolver found in Ashtat's house." Killinworth heaved with coughing. Blood ran from the corner of his mouth. Heather looked away so he would not see her crying.

A groan came from Ford Saunders. Hanrahan moved to him. "I didn't kill..." Saunders's voice was strained, hoarse. "She told me to but I wouldn't ...neither would Walter..."

"Her husband?"

"Yes...Look, I admit I did most everything else she wanted, she threatened to expose me, called me a pervert—" An explosion of air came from deep inside, causing his chest to heave, blood to erupt from his wound. He looked up at Hanrahan, then went into a series of death spasms.

CHAPTER 29

JULY 6. TWO DAYS AFTER THE CELEBRATION OF THE nation's birthday. After the death of Ford Saunders. After the arrest of Chloe Prentwhistle.

Hanrahan sat in his office with Commissioner Johnson, who had picked up a new Alan Flusser double-breasted blue-and-white cord suit the day before and was not anxious to sit on Hanrahan's furniture. "Just as soon stand, Mac," he said each time Hanrahan offered him a chair . . . "The professor will make it?"

"Killinworth? Yeah, he's past the crisis stage. I'm going over to see him later this morning."

"Where do we stand?"

"Prentwhistle still claims she's innocent as a lamb, accuses Saunders. We've booked her for Saunders's murder, and we'll keep digging into Tunney. We picked up a passport at her house that was cleared through British Customs the night of Ashtat's murder." He handed Johnson the passport that read: *Linda Clare Salzbank.* "We know she's the one who's been running the ring at the Smithsonian for years. Janis Dewey at the National Gallery isn't what you'd call hard-nosed. She spilled all about it, confirms what Killinworth said. Prentwhistle's husband, this Walter Jones, recruited young curators into the Smithsonian, people he had something on or knew were easy marks. Once he had them in place he taught them the ropes. When a donor of a piece to the Smithsonian died, they waited a while, then took the piece and fenced it through people like this Ashtat in London."

"Sounds like Jones was really behind it—"

"No, like my mother said, look for the woman. Jones, it seems, has been uneasy for years about the deal but his wife wouldn't let go of it. Apparently she liked the excitement—she is quite a woman, in a rotten sort of way—and liked the extra loot to keep her and Jones in a life-style her salary couldn't provide."

Johnson shook his head, almost sat on the edge of Hanrahan's desk but caught himself in time. "What took the people at the Smithsonian so long to catch on?"

Hanrahan propped his feet on the desk. "They made it easy, Cal. Apparently they've been trying to get a computer inventory system going for years but it's slow. In the meantime they've got pieces worth thousands stashed in shoe boxes in back rooms. Hell, nobody knows where half the stuff is."

"What about the gem cutter...Kazakis?"

"He's like Janis Dewey, small-time. Dishonest enough to steal a little to put gas in his Corvette and keep the apartment in videotapes of first-run films. He's got talent, though. I look at the real Harsa next to his and can't tell the difference. Obviously plenty of others couldn't either. He should have stuck to setting engagement rings."

"You have a confession from Jones?"

"Yeah. He said he got started by being called in by Prentwhistle as an independent appraiser. Nobody knew they were married and his was the last word. Nobody suspected collusion. He'd declare a piece relatively worthless after a donor died, which meant it was never even considered for public display. They'd let some time pass and out it went under their coats. All very neat until the Harsa came along."

"And Vice-President Oxenhauer wanted it exhibited."

"Right, but I'm not too partial to him right now. Okay, he wanted his own investigation, wanted to keep scandal away from the Smithsonian, but I still think he should have let us in on it."

"Mac, I don't say you're wrong, but from his point of view he was doing the best for the Smithsonian, avoiding scandal as long as possible, at least until after the Fourth—"

Hanrahan stood and got his jacket from the clothes tree. He noticed that a button was hanging by a thread. So was his temper. "Are we finished?"

"For this morning. I've scheduled a press conference at three. That'll give the TV people time to get back for their six o'clock broadcasts. I've prepared a statement for you." He gave Hanrahan a sheet of paper that he fished from his inside pocket. Hanrahan glanced at it, tossed it on the desk.

"You can make changes if you want, Mac, but I'd like to see us stick to the script. Let's face it, solving this case is a big—"

"Solving it?"

"We're the Metropolitan Police Department, the agency of record. A crime was committed, a crime has been solved. We did it. The public deserves to believe that."

"I won't be there."

"Suit yourself. If you are, read that statement. If you're not, do me a favor and don't give interviews."

Hanrahan hung around the office until it was time to leave for Doctor's Hospital, where he was to meet Heather and visit Killinworth. He was heading for the door when Kathy called.

"Kathy, I'm running—"

"I just wanted to congratulate you on the Tunney case. You must be relieved it's over."

No answer.

"Mac?"

"What?"

"Buy me dinner?"

"I'm pretty busy. Maybe."

"Are you tied up?"

"I may be."

"Another woman?"

"Good-by Kathy. I'll call."

Heather was in Killinworth's room when Hanrahan arrived. The professor was sitting up in bed. An IV was attached to his arm. He was very pale. Otherwise he was very much himself. Including the part that rankled Hanrahan.

"Hello, captain," he said with surprising vigor. He held out his hand, which obviously caused him pain. Hanrahan shook it and pulled up a chair next to Heather.

"Evelyn was just telling me about Peter's death," she said.

"Peckham? I'd like to hear."

"Well, my dear captain, after Ashtat killed Heather's uncle, he was still in possession of the Harsa. The rule had always been that a stolen piece was never to be sold in the region from which it originated, in this case the British Isles. But Ashtat became greedy. He offered it for sale in London, and Peckham bought it."

"I thought Peckham was a legitimate dealer."

Killinworth shrugged. "Even the most legitimate of

people have their weaknesses, as I'm sure you've discovered in your work, captain. Also, remember that Peckham did not know the piece was stolen, but he did know Ashtat's reputation, no question of that. He asked his friend...Lewis Tunney...to verify the piece. Lewis's reaction was not what Peckham had anticipated. He told Peckham he was going to Washington and expose to the world what seemed to be a theft of the Harsa. Which left Peckham in a difficult position. He, in turn, called Ashtat and told him what had happened with Tunney. Ashtat called Chloe Prentwhistle in Washington, which made her decide to kill Tunney. Or have him killed. I rather think the former."

Heather turned away, and Killinworth reached for her, touched her arm. "Dear, I know how difficult this is for you, but in the long run it will be better to know the truth, not need to guess..." To Hanrahan he said, "Chloe Prentwhistle must have called Ashtat and told him to get rid of Peckham, who now knew too much, which he did. Earlier I thought she might have done that as well as taken care of Ashtat—when I heard of your discovery of the fake passport she used to London—but of course she could not have. Peckham was dead before she arrived, courtesy of Ashtat."

"But Ashtat now had the real Harsa," Heather said. "I mean, if he killed Peckham he must have taken it back from his place."

"Yes," Killinworth said. "And when Vice-President Oxenhauer insisted upon an exhibit of the Harsa, Chloe had Mr. Kazakis create a replica, and a rather good one I might add. That probably would have been the end of it if Lewis had not threatened to expose matters. I would guess Chloe tried to find out from Lewis at the museum what he had told others, perhaps not. In any case, she couldn't be sure, couldn't take chances. She'd already gone too far, was responsible for two deaths. So as far as she knew, even with Lewis Tunney dead, there was still the chance that the bogus medal might be examined. That was when she decided to stage a fake robbery of the replica on exhibition in conjunction with Tunney's murder."

Hanrahan was finding Killinworth as annoyingly all-knowing as ever, but of course had to hear him out. "A fair amount of this is speculation on your part, isn't it. Dr. Killinworth?"

"Not so much as you might think, captain, I must admit that I was operating at a distinct advantage over you. Much of what was going on within the Smithsonian was known to me because of Vice-President Oxenhauer. When he called me in to conduct a private investigation, he had already placed many pieces into the puzzle. I was able to add the rest. Miss Dewey at the National Gallery was most helpful, albeit reluctantly. I noticed a small Gainsborough in Ashtat's house that I knew had been donated to the Smithsonian. I confronted her about it and she responded with a great deal of information. A misguided girl. Too bad."

"And Throckly?" Hanrahan said.

"His only crime was weakness. He knew what was going on around him but never imagined it could involve murder. I believe the vice-president and Mr. Costain are even now arranging his departure from the Smithsonian."

Heather suddenly asked, "Why were you looking up Seth Collinsworth in Edinburgh? Ranald Robertson told me you were."

"Charming rogue, Collinsworth. He knows more about art crime in the British Isles than any ten men. He owed me a favor or two; I collected. Just information, some rumor, but useful in piecing things together."

Heather nodded. "But what about the dishwasher

finding the fake medal in the garbage. Who put it there, and why?"

Killinworth shifted his position in bed, grimacing at the pain. "As I said, once Dr. Tunney was dead they had to get rid of the medal before it could be examined. They couldn't very well put it any place in the museum, so Ford Saunders carried it outside and deposited it in the trash, no doubt assuming that it would end up at or near the bottom of a garbage heap and never be seen again."

"Why are you so sure it was Saunders?" Heather asked.

Hanrahan was glad to answer *something*. "He was the only guest unaccounted for at the end of the evening. Given what we know about his talent for dressing up as a woman, I think he dressed up as one and hid in the First Ladies' exhibition until the coast was clear, then left the museum and deep-sixed the Harsa in the garbage."

Killinworth laughed, which caused such pain that his eyes teared. "Dressed up in ladies' clothing and posed as a mannequin? That's . . . well, captain, that's certainly creative, but it does strain the imagination—"

Lucky for him, Hanrahan thought, that he was a patient. He smiled tightly, said: "There was an extra mannequin in the exhibit the night I inspected it after Dr. Tunney's murder. I'm sure of it."

Killinworth continued to fight against his pained laughter. "I won't argue with you, captain," he managed to say. "God, it hurts."

Tough, Hanrahan thought.

"I think we should let him sleep," Heather said. She leaned over and kissed his cheek.

Hanrahan stood up, forced himself to say, "I appreciate your help, doctor. Get some rest. Maybe we'll catch up again some day."

"I'm sure we will."

"By the way, any special reason why the vice-president picked you to conduct a private investigation?"

"We're old friends. He trusts me. And I've been doing this sort of thing within the art world for years. I've never been involved with anything this . . . extreme before, of course. It's been rather exciting, I confess. Well, thank you for visiting the wounded.

Hanrahan and Heather silently rode the elevator to the ground floor and went outside. "In case you're wondering about being almost run over in Edinburgh, I now come clean and admit that I did have you followed by Scotland Yard. But the way I figure it, whoever was driving that car was nothing more than a crazy bad driver. Not my man."

"Yes . . . you know, when it happened I actually thought that it was Evelyn. Someone said the driver was overfed and with everything else that had been happening, well, I guess paranoia took over."

"You know what they say, just because you're paranoid doesn't mean they aren't following you . . . Anyway, how about dinner?"

She looked at him, half-smiled. "I'd like to, captain. But somehow it doesn't seem the right time, or place . . . I'm going back to Edinburgh tomorrow morning and—oh, I almost forgot. I've been carrying this around with me ever since I got back from Scotland. It's for you." She took a can from a plastic British Museum shopping bag and gave it to Hanrahan. He read the label—*Haggis*. "I know how much you like cooking—how good you are—and I thought you'd enjoy the Scottish national dish."

"I've heard of it. What's in it?"

"I'm delighted you asked. The heart, lights and liver of a sheep cooked with finely-chopped suet, toasted oatmeal and seasonings, all stuffed into the sheep's paunch and boiled. I prefer it with chappit tatties and bashed neeps, but it's quite acceptable by itself." She said it all with a straight face.

Hanrahan winced. "Thanks, thanks a lot, but I wouldn't think of trying it without you."

"Then you must come to Scotland. Soon. I'll whip up a batch for you."

"Watch out, I just may take you up on that."

"I'm counting on it captain. And meanwhile—" she kissed him on the lips—"take care of yourself. Whatever else, I think I've found a new friend."

"Count on it, Miss McBean."

He watched as she went down the steps to a line of cabs, and was still watching moments after she'd gotten into one of them, and it pulled into Washington's traffic and was lost from view.

Back in his office, he suffered Joe Pearl's inevitable comment on his loose button. He read over the statement prepared for him by Commissioner Johnson, decided he wouldn't show up at the press conference to read it.

He thought about his promise to call Kathy about dinner. He was free, but somehow he didn't think it would be a good idea.

He called and did his best to tell her that.

And then he went home, decided he wasn't really hungry, and poured himself a Scotch neat.

What else?

ABOUT THE AUTHOR

Margaret Truman is the author of three acclaimed Washington murder mysteries: MURDER IN THE SUPREME COURT, MURDER ON CAPITOL HILL and MURDER IN THE WHITE HOUSE. Born in Independence, Missouri, she now makes her home in New York City.